Executioner's Enthrallment

Ares Infidels MC # 2

By Ciara St. James

Ciara St. James LLC

Copyright

Dedication

This book is dedicated to my partner in crime, my sometimes only sanity in the wilderness of being an author, and the only one who I know is crazy enough to join me in such an endeavor. The one and only Cee Bowerman- my collaborating author for the Ares Infidels MC's main allied club, the Time Served MC.

Thank you for saying yes when I asked if you wanted to do a joint series and then working with me so hard to create the Tenillo world- businesses, streets, characters and everything in between. Hard to believe our first talk about doing this was just seven months ago! I couldn't do it without you, lady!

Also, I can't forget my other sanity helpers, who are there to read as I write, bounce ideas off of, cry and scream with and specially to laugh with. For saying you'll bring the shovel if I call. My Crazy Coven- Jen, Paula, Cee, Brea and our prospect- Sis. Love you crazy women! XO

Blurb & Note

Executioner's years as a U.S. Marine have made him a hard, dangerous man no one wants to mess with. He uses that to carry out his job as enforcer for his club, the Ares' Infidels.

While working with his brothers and an ally club, he visits a local business and has his world turned upside down. They've met before, but he had lost hope of ever finding her again.

She's tried to forget him and what he made her feel. He's incensed when he finds out the extortionists who targeted her family, made darker threats toward her. He's determined she'll be his and he'll do whatever it takes to make that happen and to keep her and her family safe.

Skye's life hasn't been the best or easiest even before her dad left the family high and dry years ago. They battle daily to keep their little family afloat. A chance meeting with him is the last thing she expected or wanted. He needs to realize she's not looking for a relationship.

She's had hard lessons that taught her happily ever after isn't in the cards for her. She keeps pushing him away while he keeps pushing closer. However, Executioner isn't going to lose this fight. Even when she puts distance between them to protect her heart.

Something has to give, and it does. Her past comes to light. Her present takes a crazy turn. And her future is looking like it might be the best thing to ever happen to her. If she can let go of her fear and pain, she'll forever be Executioner's Enthrallment.

NOTE: This book contains steamy sexual encounters, violence, foul language, and may have triggers for some as it does mention abuse that the characters have been faced with. However, there is always a happily ever after and no cheating.

AIMC Members

Members:

Kye Korbyn (Sin)- President
Connor Terrell (Saint)- VP
Slate Ashton (Executioner)- Enforcer
Deckard Hale (Phantom)- Secretary/ Hacker
Chase Bracco (Talon)- Treasurer
Asher Kendrick (Rampage)- Road Captain
Cole Landis (Pitbull)
Liam Dickerson (Wrecker)
Wyatt Carling (Torpedo)
Brayden Wilde (Boomer)
Drake Marshall (Cuffs)

Prospects:

Dash Nolan
Blake Price
Trace Boudreaux
Brennan O'Shea

Ciara St James Books

Dublin Falls Archangel's Warriors MC
1- Terror's Temptress
2- Savage's Princess
3- Steel & Hammer's Hellcat
4- Menace's Siren
5- Ranger's Enchantress
6- Ghost's Beauty
7- Viper's Vixen
8- Devil Dog's Precious
9- Blaze's Spitfire
10- Smoke's Tigress
11- Hawk's Huntress
12- Storm's Flame- coming July 19, 2021

Ares Infidels MC- A Tenillo Guardians Series
1- Sin's Enticement
2- Executioner's Enthrallment

Hunters Creek Archangel's Warriors MC
1- Bull's Duchess
2- Rebel's Firecracker-coming August 19, 2021

Executioner: Prologue- 2 ½ Years Ago

I ducked and tried to make myself smaller, which was laughable when you were six foot six and built like a damn truck! I crab crawled over to my buddy, Trace Boudreaux, or Omen, as we called him. He was huddled down behind a partially destroyed stone wall with his rifle at the ready. You could hear the rat-a-tat of automatic gunfire. The bullets were whizzing by all around us. We were in deep shit. I just prayed we weren't up shit creek without a paddle.

I wanted to tell Omen I was tired of him being right. He had the uncanniest ability to know shit was going to happen or get fucked up beyond all recognition— FUBAR—before it did. Just like this mess we were in right now. He claimed it was part of his Cajun heritage. Something about his family was a bunch of seers. That was how he earned his name, Omen, in the Corps. We'd met in boot camp and been buddies ever since. We'd both gotten the idea to go through Marine Force Recon training together. What in the hell had we been thinking?

However, that wasn't what I wanted to talk to him about now. Before we left with our squad for this mission, he'd told me that his gut was telling him this was going to be bloody, and we might not all make it back. Some of the others, who hadn't been with our squad as long, had scoffed. But me and the other four who had been with him for a long time took it to heart. He'd rarely been wrong, and my gut was in a knot before he said anything. I wasn't as good as Omen at predicting, but I got it right a lot of the time too.

We'd tried to tell the upper command there was

something off with the intelligence we'd been given. An informant, who no one would tell us who it was, had brought news to the command that there was a small group of insurgents in the town of Sangin, as if there weren't insurgents all through the Helmand Province of Afghanistan every damn day. God, we'd been eating sand and dirt while chasing their asses for the last nine months.

Based on this tip, the nine of us were sent out to bring in the three insurgents, who were thought to be mid-level commanders in the Taliban's ragtag group. Not that those ragtag fanatics didn't inflict a deadly amount of damage, pain, and death. They were the main reason the U.S. Marines had been brought to the province to begin with. Some days I wondered what I had been thinking to go into the Marines and especially Marine Force Recon.

"Fuck, Omen, why did our guts have to be right on this one? Three insurgents my ass, more like at least a dozen, maybe more. Whoever gave us the tip was either wrong, or this was a setup."

"*Mon ami*, I think this was a setup, and our illustrious commanders were too damn eager to show they caught some Taliban members that they didn't do their home-work. Gawd, I'm so tired of this shit," he said in his slow Cajun drawl. He spoke well, but certain words came out more French than proper English because he was Cajun.

"You know, if we live through this, I can't wait to tell the Corps goodbye. You know I put in my papers, and if everything goes right, I'll be back in the States by Christmas and on terminal leave. As soon as I am, Texas, here I fucking come."

"So, you're really going to join that motorcycle club

that guy, Sin, from the SEAL team is forming?"

"I am. I like Sin and a few of the others who're joining him. They think like we do, and they have seen enough shit to want to live a different life. Mom and the girls are in England. I can live anywhere. You have another what, three years left? Damn, you shouldn't have re-enlisted, Omen. You could have gotten out soon and joined us."

"I know. I had a weak moment and thought it was better than trying to go back and be a civilian. I was a damn idiot. Let's get our asses out of this disaster and if I live through the next three years, I might just have to see what that MC is all about." I gave him a fist bump in agreement. I'd love it if he'd join the club.

As we crawled, slithered, and inched our way to the building where the gunfire was coming from, I sent up a prayer to whoever was listening. *Please let us all survive this and for both of us to make it home. I want to see what life has in store for me outside of the Corps.*

Executioner: Prologue-14 Months ago

I couldn't believe what we'd accomplished in the past year since I'd gotten out of the Corps and joined Sin and my Ares Infidels' brothers. The club was finally looking like a real MC. We'd enclosed the land that Sin had inherited from his family. We'd gotten a clubhouse built, and we were now working on getting the last of the businesses up and running. Then it would be time to build other things on the compound, like houses.

For me, it wasn't all that different from the reservation my mom and dad would take us to stay at in the summer. It was protected from the rest of the world. The compound felt the same way. My dad was part of the Navajo tribe in Arizona. He was half Navajo, which made me and my sisters a quarter. We'd go and spend time with his family and learn about our heritage. I'd enjoyed those times, even if the conditions weren't always as nice as you'd like.

But they did have a tradition of staying together, forming a large brotherhood, and fighting for each other. That and the talk of the Navajo Code Talkers from World War II had sparked my desire to go into the service. Now, that same sense of brotherhood, family, and camaraderie that I'd found and loved in the Corps and on the reservation was here in the club. We'd taken the good things from our time in the military and tailored it to our wishes when forming this club.

I looked around at the Harley dealership, Tenillo Cycles. After some discussion, it was decided that I'd oversee the day-to-day running of the dealership. My brothers had mentioned something about no one messing with the bikes or staff with me around. I had to laugh. Being the enforcer for the club had its perks. Scaring the shit out of wannabe tough guys was one of them. Nothing pissed me off more than to have some guy come in throwing around his weight and trying to intimidate or hurt people. That was one sure way to get my ugly side to come out.

I wouldn't have to do all the work. The ins and outs of keeping the books would be handled by others, but I would oversee that the business was performing how it should. And who wouldn't love to look at Harleys all day long? I loved my bike and never got enough of looking at others. Nothing felt like a Harley roaring between your legs as you were riding down the road.

Sara, Sin's mom, would be helping out at the front desk to wait on customers along with some other staff we'd hired. In the back, we would do basic servicing and changing out of parts if requested. If a customer wanted something more extensive, we'd refer them to our garage in town, Infidels Custom Motors. Saint ran that one and they mainly worked on bikes and cars. There were customizations available if you were willing to pay the price. Those included custom paint jobs. Taking one final look around, I nodded and headed to my office. It was time to get down to business. Another wonderful day in Tenillo was waiting for me. Life couldn't get any better.

Executioner: Prologue 1 Month Ago

My footsteps echoed as I walked down the hall of the Naval Hospital. I hated to be in any hospital. They always seemed to be so stark white, and the antiseptic smell burned my nose. I ran my thumb along the jagged scar that ran along my left jawline. I'd spent some time in a Naval Hospital when I got this little beauty. I'd vowed to never step foot in one again, but here I was, doing just that.

I knocked on the door before entering the room. Lying in the bed, hooked up to various lines and machines, was my buddy Omen. A week ago, he'd been flown in from the hospital in Germany after he was injured in Afghanistan. I hadn't known he was here in Texas, let alone in Fort Worth until he called me yesterday.

He'd been back over in the hellhole, and this time he hadn't gotten away scot-free. He'd been shot twice, once in the right thigh and once in the upper right chest. It had done a nice amount of damage, enough that there was talk about whether he'd have to medically retire or not. They couldn't have a Recon Marine who had limitations. Time would tell if he'd get out sooner or not. I hoped he did. If they gave him a medical retirement, then he'd get a military pension and medical disability from the VA, plus medical care for life. He had less than a year to go anyway before this enlistment was up.

That was one of the reasons I was here. Not only did I want to check and make sure he was alright and didn't need anything, but I wanted to talk to him again about joining the Infidels when he got out. He gave me a weary look. I could see the strain that he'd been under written all over his face. He looked older than the last time I saw him, which was almost a year ago.

I went up to his bed and grabbed the hand he was holding up. I gave it a tight squeeze. I hated to see anyone in a hospital bed, but it was worse when it was someone you cared about. He was my brother, just like the Infidels were. I wanted so badly to have them all united in one place where I could keep an eye on them.

"Damn, I swear you got uglier since the last time I saw you." I tried to tease a grin out of him. The sides of his mouth quirked up a little, but he didn't give me his usual shit-eating grin.

"We can't all be walking gods like you. How's life treating you, Executioner?"

"Better than it is you. Dammit, why didn't you call me sooner? I'd have been here a week ago if I'd known," I chastised him.

"I wasn't feeling up to any visitors. After all the flying from Afghanistan to Germany and then here, I wanted to rest. I'm going to be laid up for a while. You'll have time to visit me."

"What do the doctors say?"

"That I'll be in here probably at least another week, then I'll need to undergo rehab. After that's done, we'll know if I stay until my enlistment is up or if they will retire me."

"Do you want to make it to the end? You're less than a year away from retirement with your twenty. Most would say you're insane to throw it away. I think it's not worth it to stay, but that's me."

"You know, I really don't care about the retirement

thing. I'm tired, Ex. Tired of the dirt, the fighting against people we can't conquer. We take out ten and another ten pop up to take their place. It's a never-ending tide. I'm barely ever on American soil. It's easy to forget what you're fighting for when you so rarely see it. But enough about me, how're you? You look good."

I sat down in the chair beside the bed. "I'm doing well. The club is up and running like I told you last time. The dealership is booming. We've met another club in town. We're helping them with some stuff. It's been really good."

"That sounds great. I'm happy it's going so well. I appreciate you coming to see me. I want to hear all about it. And I bet I know what you're going to talk about as well."

I chuckled. "You know it. You need to get your ass better, out of the Corps and then get it to Tenillo. I'm telling you. You'd love it there. The guys are wonderful, and the compound is kick-ass. As soon as you're able to ride in a car, I'm coming to take you for a visit."

He didn't argue. We settled into a long chat session. We had a lot to catch up on, and I wanted to make sure he had what he needed before I headed back to Tenillo. It was late when the nurses came to tell me visiting hours were over. As I looked at him, I could see he was still down. I decided to stay the night and then head back tomorrow. That way I'd be able to see him again in the morning. Yeah, that was the plan. I'd let Sin know. Before I left, I told Omen I'd see him in the morning. He smiled this time.

Executioner: Chapter 1

Me, Boomer, and Captain from Time Served MC strolled down the street to the next business on the list. I'd promised Sin and Lyric I'd talk to this owner myself. It was the flower shop, Blossoms. It was run by the mother and sister of one of Lyric's students. One that she wanted to talk to about the strange things going on at Alamos High School. Hell, she'd been drugged by someone with fucking crystal meth in her coffee at school! It was time we found out what was really happening there and shut it down, just like we were working to shut down the extortion we'd found was happening all over Tenillo. That was the secondary reason for us to be here.

Not long ago, Boss, the new chief of police and president of the Time Served MC, had told us about the extortion that was happening. He and his club had so many fires going, they needed more feet on the ground. We'd been happy to volunteer. That had been the beginning of our treks to various businesses all over town. We were finding out who had been approached to pay "protection money", by who, and which of them were paying it. That had to stop. We were determined to make sure that it did.

A bell tinkled as I opened the door. The scent of flowers hit me in the face as we entered. I found the smell soothing. Bright explosions of colors were all over the place. I ignored those and went straight to the counter. Standing behind it was a woman; I'd say was in her mid to late forties. She was tiny, barely over five feet.

Her strawberry blond hair was down to her shoulders. She looked up and smiled tentatively as she said hello. She was a very attractive older woman, and something about her instantly started to nag at the back of my brain. It was like I knew her, but I knew we'd never met. "Hello. How may I help you, gentlemen?" she asked softly. I could tell she was a little unnerved by seeing three large men dressed in leather in her shop. While she smiled at us, I could see the wariness in her eyes. She made sure to keep the counter between her and us, smart woman.

"Hello, I'm looking for Jackie Fulton. Is she here?" I asked her. I was almost positive she was Jackie. Her eyes widening, confirmed I was right before she answered.

"I'm Jackie Fulton. What can I do for you?"

"Is there somewhere we can talk privately?" I saw her eyes dart around the shop, and she swallowed.

"Ma'am, please don't be afraid. We're not here to hurt you. Believe it or not, I think we can help you, but we'd prefer not to talk about it out here," I tried to reassure her.

She looked at me intently for almost a minute before she nodded. She looked to the left and softly yelled, "Tyson, come over here and watch the counter. If someone needs something and you can't do it, come find me. Your sister should be back soon."

A young boy, in his early teens, came sauntering over. He gave us an uneasy look. This must be the youngest son, Lyric mentioned. "Okay, Mom. Should I call Skye?" he asked her, with a shift of his eyes toward us. She shook her head.

"No, she's due back soon, like I said. If she comes back while I'm talking to these gentlemen, send her back to the office." He gave her a chin lift and watched us as we followed her to the back of the shop. I could tell by the set of her shoulders she was still nervous and wondering if it was safe to be alone in a room with the three of us. I didn't know what else to say to reassure her.

Inside the office, she gestured to a small table with four chairs around it. It was a typical office with a desk, this table and chairs, and two file cabinets. A computer sat on the desk. She took a seat behind the desk. "Well, we're in private, like you wanted. Do you mind telling me what this is about?"

"Sure. First let me introduce us. Sorry, we should have done that first. I'm Executioner and this is my club brother, Boomer. We're with the Ares Infidels MC. This is Captain, he's with another club, the Time Served MC. We really don't mean you any harm. We're here actually on behalf of the chief of police."

She gave me an incredulous look. "Your names are Executioner, Boomer, and Captain, and you're working with the police chief?"

I laughed. "I know, it sounds so wrong, but I promise we are. Those are our road names. I'm not sure how much you know about Boss, he's the new chief. He's actually the president of Captain's club. He's busy at work trying to clean things up around Tenillo," I explained. I couldn't give her details, but hopefully this would reassure her a little.

"The chief of police who was an ex-felon that somehow got his conviction expunged? I have to say, I was stunned that the town elected someone like that."

"Ma'am, I'm not going to lie and say Boss wasn't convicted and did time for it, but he was a cop before that happened, and he does have the best interests of the town in his heart. All of us live here and want it to be a safe and happy place to live," Captain told her.

"And the Infidels are all prior military members. We formed our club and settled here to have peaceful lives," I added.

"I'm glad to hear that. Not what I expected to hear, to be honest. But how can I help you?"

"We've been made aware that there's been some men going around to various businesses in town. They've approached owners about paying money to ensure something bad doesn't happen to their businesses. It's extortion plain and simple. We're trying to determine who they've approached, who they haven't talked to yet, and who's paying them."

She sat back in her chair. I could see the unease on her face. I wasn't sure if it was because she'd been approached already or if it was the thought of someone doing it to her. She chewed on her bottom lip. Again, the sense that I knew her from somewhere washed over me. Where had I seen her? Why was my mind pushing at me to find out how we'd met? Deep down, something was telling me it was important that I find out.

She fidgeted with a pen on the desk. Her eyes were looking all around the room. I was about to try to reassure her again when the door flew open and in came a younger woman. "Mom, what in the hell is going on? Tyson said you were in here with three big men," she half-yelled. Her voice made my heart speed up. As she swung around to face us, I got a full look at her. It was like a slap in the face. My breath actually caught.

There stood the woman I'd been thinking about constantly for the last month! The one I couldn't get off my mind. The one who I had no idea where to find her or even what her name was. There stood the woman who'd enthralled me after one night. I wanted to reach out and touch her to make sure she was real. It clicked why Jackie Fulton had reminded me of someone I knew. She looked a lot like her daughter. Or I guess it was because her daughter looked like her mom.

Her eyes grew round as she saw us. I knew the moment she realized who I was. She gasped, and I swear she got a little pale. She took a step back as if she was going to run. I quickly strolled over to her and shut the door. She edged away from me and toward her mom, who had risen from her chair. The beast inside didn't like that. I didn't want her to be afraid of me. I'd never do anything to harm her. She was the safest person in the world. Jackie rushed over to her and wrapped an arm around her waist.

"Skye, these gentlemen were just telling me why they're here. It's because they're helping the new police chief. This is Executioner and Boomer. They're with the Ares Infidels and this is Captain, he's with Time Served. Those are motorcycle clubs here in town, honey. Gentlemen, this is my daughter, Skye," she hurried to explain.

"Why would the chief of police need to use motorcycle clubs to help him? Mom, this is fucked up. They're here for some other reason," she said in a tone of disbelief. She was avoiding my eyes.

"Skye! Watch your language. Don't say those words! Sit down and let's hear them out," her mom scolded her, then led her to the table where we'd been sitting. She pushed her down in one of the chairs and she sat on the edge of her desk. I made sure I took the chair closest to Skye. She gave me a narrow-eyed look. Hmm, seems like she wasn't thrilled to see me. We'd see about that. Now that I knew who she was and where to find her, there was no way I was letting her out of my sight again.

I needed to deal with our original business then I could deal with her. "Hello, Skye. As we were just telling your mom, we are helping Boss, the new police chief, with an investigation. He's become aware that some business owners around town have been approached about paying some men money. They say it's to protect people in these uncertain times against something happening to their businesses. It's outright extortion. We need to know who they've talked to, who they haven't, and who's paying them," I quickly explained. When I was done, I saw the same unease come over her as it had her mom. Shit! They'd been approached. I just knew it.

She looked at her mom. There was some silent communication between them, then I saw Jackie nod. It was Skye who started to talk, not her mom, which kind of surprised me. She twisted her hands together and looked toward Boomer. She was avoiding looking at me again. I found I didn't like her looking at him. I wanted to demand she only look and talk to me, which was a little over the top, even for me.

"Boss, as you call him, is right. There have been some of us who have gotten visitors. They came in asking about what kind of security we had for the shop. When we wouldn't talk to them, they left. I thought that was the end of it until they came back a couple of weeks later. They presented themselves then as some kind of society that wanted to protect Tenillo businesses. They said we needed to become part of that society for our protection and livelihoods. We told them we weren't sure that was something we wanted to do. They left after saying they'd be back in a couple of days." She stopped to take a deep breath before she continued.

"When they did, we told them no. They didn't stop harassing us until finally we knew if we didn't pay, something terrible would happen." She shifted her eyes to look at her mom. I knew there had to be more to the story. I'd have to get her to tell me what it was. She continued after a brief pause. "Anyway, we later found out that they'd approached others in town. Some have paid, others are scared and plan to, while others are adamant, they won't do it."

"How long ago did you start paying them? Do you know the names of the men or anything about where we might be able to find them?"

"It's been almost six months. They didn't give us names. We have no idea where they live or hang out. One of them shows up to get the money on the first of the month," Jackie replied.

"How much do they have you paying every month?" Boomer asked.

"Five hundred dollars, though they were in here last week saying the price was going to go up," Skye ground out. I could tell she was pissed. "We can barely pay that. So, if you're here to ask us for money too, you're shit out of luck," she snapped.

I leaned toward her, so she had to look at me. "Baby girl, we're not here to take your money. We're here to stop the ones who are already taking it. Jackie would you, your sons and Skye be willing to come to a gathering of business owners at our compound? It's not far out of town. We're hosting it this coming Saturday. Several other business owners are coming. We want the opportunity to talk to you and show that we're here to help."

Both of them gave us unbelieving looks. I knew that we had to get them to come, not only because of the extortion or Lyric's need to talk to Tanner, but because I had to have Skye in my space. I could tell they were about to say no.

Captain jumped in, "Do either of you know Harvey Korbyn at Harvey's Garage. How about Hal at Hal and Sons Hardware or Maddie at Maddie's Diner?"

"Of course, we know them, why?" Skye asked with a bite to her tone. It made me want to lay my mouth on hers.

"Because Harvey is an uncle to the president of the Infidels, Sin. He, Hal, and Maddie are some of the business owners coming to the party. You can talk to them. They'll vouch for us. But we really do want you to come. Sin's lady, Lyric Marsh, teaches your son, Tanner, Mrs. Fulton." He dropped those facts on them.

"Please, you can call me Jackie. I had no idea Ms. Marsh was seeing him. I know of Sin because of his mom, Sara," she said thoughtfully. I wasn't surprised she knew Sara. It seemed like almost everyone in Tenillo knew her. I could see she was coming around to the idea, but Skye still had a stubborn look on her face. "We'll talk to them. If they tell us the same thing you did, then we'll be there," Jackie finally said.

"Mom, no, we're not going," Skye hissed.

"Can I speak to your daughter for a moment?" I asked quietly.

Jackie looked at me in surprise, along with Boomer and Captain. Skye looked like she wanted to run. *Not this time, sweetheart.*

"I-I guess so," Jackie stuttered. Skye was frantically shaking her head at her mother. Jackie stood up slowly.

I gave Boomer and Captain a chin lift. They both got up and went to the door. They opened it and ushered Jackie out. Skye tried to go for the door as well, but I got there first. I closed it and looked down at her. She was staring at me with a defiant look on her face.

"Now, why don't we start over. I'm Slade Ashton, but everyone calls me Executioner. You can call me Slade when we're alone and Executioner or Ex when we're with others. Nice to know your name this time, Skye." As she opened her mouth to blast me, I jerked her into my arms and sealed my mouth to hers. Finally, she was back in my arms!

Skye:

I felt like I was having an out-of-body experience. It had started as soon as I entered the office. When I saw who was in there, I felt like I could have fainted. Oh my God, it was him! The man who'd been disturbing my sleep and haunting me every hour of the day and night for the last month! The one I had thought I'd never see again. A part of me wanted to run like hell, but another part wanted to wrap myself up in his strong arms. I remember what it felt like to be in them. To have him touching me, kissing me, and then taking me somewhere I'd never been before. God, why was this happening to me?

His mouth was making love to mine. There was no other word for it. His lips were pressed over and over to mine. His tongue was teasing my tongue and his teeth were nipping and pulling on my bottom lip. I could feel my nipples getting hard and my panties damp. I had to stop this before things got out of control! Gathering all my strength, I broke away from him. He didn't let go of me, but he did let me get a tiny bit of space between our faces.

"Stop. You have no right to do this to me," I snapped at him. His eyes grew dark, and his arms tightened a fraction more.

"I have every right to do this. You gave me that right a month ago when I was buried so deep inside of you, neither of us knew where the other began or stopped. Or don't you remember? I'll be happy to show you again," he growled.

"That night didn't give you any kind of right, Executioner. It was nothing," I argued. I had to get him to see that we wouldn't be repeating that night, no matter how much I wanted to. Not if I wanted to keep my soul and sanity intact. I couldn't let him know the real me.

He responded by twirling me around and putting my back to the wall. He pressed into me and whispered, "Like hell it was nothing. You let me inside of you, Skye. You let me taste you. My hands and mouth were on every inch of this body. That's a claim. Then you walked away."

"You have to be joking. What, every woman you fuck, you claim? You must have a damn harem! I have no interest in being one of hundreds in it. Let go of me, before I unman you," I hissed. The idea of him claiming women had me seeing red. I knew I was just one of many, but it still stung. As much as I was lying to him about it meaning nothing, I knew the truth. It had meant everything to me.

"I don't have a harem. And no, I don't claim every woman that I fuck. But baby girl, what we did wasn't fucking, and you know it wasn't. Why did you leave without a word? Hell, you didn't even tell me your damn name!"

"You didn't ask what it was either. You wanted to get off. I needed the same. We fucked and that's it. Why would we need to know each other's names? I don't know why we're discussing this? You said you're here to stop the extortion. Fine. But there's nothing for us to discuss about that night. Forget it ever happened."

He stared at me intently for several moments. I was about to scream when he lowered his head and softly kissed me. He teased my lips and then drew away. His

fingers traced down my cheek. "Oh, baby girl, you have
no idea what I think or want, but you will. I'll let you
think about it. But know this, Skye, I'll follow you if you
try to run. I know who you are, and I can and will find
you. I'll see you on Saturday. Don't think about not coming, or I'll come haul your ass there."

As I gaped at his audacity, he moved away and
went to the door. Right before he opened it, he looked
back at me. "I promise you one thing, Skye. I'll be buried
in that body again and again, and you'll be screaming
my name this time. See you later, baby." He walked out
and shut the door. I sank to the floor and covered my
face with my hands. What in the hell was I going to do?

26

Skye: Chapter 2

My heart was about to beat out of my chest. How in the hell had this happened? How had the guy I'd hooked up with for one night a month ago, walked through the door of our shop? What was I going to do? As I panicked, I couldn't help but recall that night.

I'd been in Fort Worth. One of the people I did books for on the side had needed me to come to their office there. As things went, they ended up not being able to see me that day and I decided to stay overnight and then come home after meeting with them the next morning. In a moment of insanity, I'd gone to a nearby bar to have a drink and relax before calling my friend, Ang, to see if I could stay with her. I knew she'd say yes. There wasn't much time for relaxing back home.

I wish I could blame it on alcohol, but I'd only had the one drink when he came through the door. I had immediately started to drool. He was a mountain of a man, standing well over six feet tall. His midnight-black hair hung straight down past his shoulders. His skin was a gorgeous tan color. I knew he had some heritage mixed in there. Maybe some Native American would be my guess.

When he sat down at the bar, I could see a jagged scar on his jaw. It did nothing to take away from his looks. I thought it only enhanced them. I couldn't see his eyes because he had on sunglasses even though it was nighttime and he was indoors. He'd captured every woman's attention in there. He filled out his clothes like a muscular dream.

After getting my fill of him, I worked not to look at him. He was one of those guys who had the ladies falling all over him. He'd be finding one to go home with for sure tonight. I wasn't anywhere close to his league, but a girl could dream. And dreaming seemed to be all I could do these days.

I got lost in my thoughts about what to do to get my family out of the mess we were in. It was becoming almost impossible for us to continue. I was so lost in my depressing thoughts, that it took me a moment to realize someone was standing next to my table. I looked up and there he stood. The god from the bar. I just looked at him.

"Hello, sweetheart. Mind if I join you?" he asked. I couldn't say a word. I only could nod. He sat down. "What brings you here?"

I don't really recall what I said. I know we chatted about nothing specific for maybe a half hour. Then he pulled off his sunglasses. His eyes were the most amazing amber color. "Wanna get out of here?" I have no idea to this day why I said yes. Next thing I knew, I was on the back of a motorcycle, and we were pulling into a hotel. I'd almost chickened out, but something wouldn't let me.

It had been so long since I'd had sex—not since my freshman year in college. And to be honest, that had been less than something to write home about. I got my excitement these days from reading steamy romances. They only made it harder. I wanted a man who would take control and show me what it was really about when it came to sex. Just once, I wanted to experience that. Something told me this was my chance.

Once we were inside, it didn't take long for him to have me naked on the bed. I was a little hesitant to let him see me naked. I wasn't ugly or anything, but I wasn't a wafer-thin woman either. I had boobs and hips. There was no other way to put it. My mom said it was an hourglass shape like hers, and in the forties, we'd have been pinup

28

girls. I had laughed when she told me that. I had started to develop early and was teased to death in school. My waist was smaller, but I had nothing like washboard abs, though lately I've lost weight.

He didn't seem to mind. He'd groaned and then was kissing me all over. When he had spread my thighs and latched onto my pussy, I had almost gone through the roof. His tongue and lips were unbelievable. The man knew what he was doing. Surprisingly, he wasn't a selfish lover. He didn't just jump to the main event, get off, and then leave me hanging. He'd made sure I came over and over before he finally had his turn.

The feeling of him stretching me had been something else. He was a big guy, and the equipment matched his size. When I'd first seen his cock, I almost chickened out. However, when he entered me, he'd taken his time, though it still felt like he was stretching me to my max. When he'd gotten settled, he'd proceeded to drive me over the edge. When he came, I was speechless from the orgasms he'd wrung out of me.

I figured he'd roll off and tell me goodbye. That wasn't the case. He'd hugged me close, and we dozed off. I woke up two times that night to him kissing, touching, and pleasuring me. By morning, I was sore and totally sated. I'd woken up right at dawn. I turned to look at him. He was sound asleep. Something soft had moved inside of me. I gently pushed his hair out of his face. If only this could be more than one night came the unbidden thought.

The thought of never seeing him again hurt, but I knew nothing would come of us. I didn't want to go through an awkward goodbye. Nothing made a girl feel like shit, like being kicked out after being fucked, and I had never done something like this. One-night stands were not my thing, ever. I'd quickly and silently got dressed and raced out the door. Outside, I'd walked to the corner and called for a ride to take me back to get my car at the bar. As I rode away, I looked back one more time at the best night of my life.

The past month I'd thought of him constantly. I wondered who he was. What was his name? Where was he? What was he doing? At one point, I'd almost died thinking what if he was married? I tried hard to forget about him, but he wouldn't go away. My sleep had been crap. I knew my mom had seen the changes and was wondering what was up. I couldn't tell her I'd slept with a stranger and was now obsessed with him! Then to walk into the office and find my walking obsession there had almost made me run.

He didn't seem pissed to see me. In fact, he looked and acted glad if that kiss was anything to go by. But no way was I going to have a repeat. I wasn't in for an affair or hookup, or whatever you wanted to call it, though he acted like it was a given we would. My one night of forbidden wildness was over. I had to keep my head on my shoulders. My family was relying on me.

This was an unforeseen turn of events, but I'd have to find a way around it. I knew that Mom would insist we go to this party. She'd been racking her brain like me to find a way out of paying the money. If these Infidels and Time Served guys along with the new chief of police could help, she'd jump on it. And while I secretly wished they could help. I wasn't getting my hopes up.

I'd just have to avoid him as much as possible. Executioner, or Slade Ashton, wasn't going to be a problem. I'd just tell him if he tried anything again that it wasn't happening. He had plenty of women he could hook up with. The thought made me ill. He'd just been stunned to see me and probably had his male pride hurt that I left while he was asleep. Guys wanted to be the one to do that. I bet I was the first to ever do that to him!

Slowly, I got up off the floor. I needed to pull it together before Mom saw me and asked what was up. Shaking myself, I took a deep breath and went for the door. It opened before I could get there. Mom came rushing back in. She closed the door and turned to me. Her eyebrows were raised. She had that mom look that I'd better spill. It had worked on me as a kid, now, not as much.

"Skye Fulton, tell me why the hell that man wanted to speak to my daughter alone? And why did he leave with a smile on his face, and you looked like you saw a ghost when you saw him?"

"Mom, he just wanted to try and convince me we should come on Saturday. I guess he thought he could convince me if he spoke to me alone. I have no idea what you mean by seeing a ghost," I fibbed. I was lying to save my life. She stood there looking at me with her eyes narrowed and her lips pursed. I schooled my face to show nothing but innocence.

"I know it's more than that. But for now, I'll let you have your secrets. But make no mistake, we're going to do this thing. If Maddie, Hal, and Harvey are, then I know they can't be a bunch of outlaws, thieves, and murderers. Besides, Sin is Sara Korbyn's son and Harvey's nephew. No way he can be like that. Not with family like that." My mom liked to think people were inherently good. Hell, she'd done it for years with my dad.

"Okay, we'll go. But just don't get your hopes up, please. I'd like to think they could help us with this, but really, what can they do? Now, I need to get back to work. The delivery to the hospital was made. I need to work on the books and then I have others to do tonight. Do you need me to help out front first?"

She walked over and hugged me. "Skye, you're doing too much, honey. You're running yourself into the ground. Working at the front counter, doing the books, stocking, deliveries, then you go home and do people's books until the early hours of the night. You're burning yourself out. You need to slow down."

"Mom, you know I can't. You work just as hard. Tanner needs a new pair of tennis shoes. He's grown out of the ones he has, and Tyson needs some money for a school project. Besides, the next payment is due tomorrow. I need to get some cash coming in so we can pay next month," I reminded her.

"Honey, I don't think we'll have to do that."

"They're not going to be able to help, Mom! Don't get your hopes up," I pleaded with her. She shook her head.

"I think you're wrong. Those men are ones who are used to making things go their way. They get what they want. And if they want to shut down this extortion crap, then I think they will make it happen. Just keep that in mind, sweetheart."

"Why?"

"You know why. Now, enough talk, let's get this day over with. I have chili in the slow cooker for tonight." We ate a lot of things like soup, chili and such. Things that could be stretched to last more than a day, which was hard with two growing boys in the house. My stomach growled. I was starving. I hadn't eaten since dinner last night.

I stamped down on thoughts of Executioner and got to work. I won't lie and say I didn't think of him for the rest of the afternoon or that night. But I tried. Especially when I laid down in bed. But the images and memories sucked me into them. I tossed and turned, trying to get some sleep while thinking about him.

⟨II⟩ ⟨II⟩ ⟨II⟩ ⟨II⟩

Executioner:

The ride back to the compound was done in a haze. I couldn't shake off the fact that I'd found her! I'd found the mystery woman who'd been tying me in knots for a month. When Boomer and I got back, we went to the clubhouse to report in. I knew the guys were wondering what had me preoccupied, but they didn't pry. I didn't want to share with anyone yet what Skye was to me. However, make no mistake, she was something to me.

What it was, I wasn't sure yet, though I had an inkling. That night in Fort Worth had changed my damn life. After spending hours with Omen, I'd gotten a room and then headed to a nearby bar to get a drink before retiring for the night. I had no thoughts of hooking up with some woman. First, because I could hook up back at the clubhouse. Second, it was losing some of its appeal if I were honest.

When I entered the bar, I didn't fail to notice I got a lot of looks. It was inevitable when you were as big as me. For some reason, women thought I was good looking. Honestly, I didn't see it. I mean I wasn't an ogre, but I was no movie star either. I kept myself fit. It was ingrained after all those years in the Marines.

As I sat down at the bar and ordered, I glanced around. That's when I saw her sitting alone at a table in the back. She wasn't paying any attention to me, which was one of the things that caught my attention. The real one was just her. She literally was beautiful. She was short, though I had no idea how much with her sitting, but that wasn't unusual with my height. Her skin was creamy and pale.

From what I could see of her face, she was gorgeous. She had long, thick-looking strawberry blond hair that was hanging almost to the middle of her back. It had some gentle wave to it. She was dressed casually in jeans, heels, and a bright blue top. As I watched her in the bar mirror, I saw the looks she was getting from the other men. They had seen her as well. Something rose in me that demanded I get her before they did. I picked up my drink and walked over to her. She was staring off into space when I got there, then she looked up at me.

The impact of her full face and eyes made me almost weak in the knees. Her face was one of those perfect ovals, where the chin was slightly pointed. It was a delicate face. Her eyes were wide and a gray-green color. It was a color I couldn't recall seeing in anyone else's eyes. Her lips were this perfect bow with both being full. Those lips begged to be kissed. She had on very little makeup. In all honesty, she didn't need any.

"Hello, sweetheart. Mind if I join you?" I asked. Her eyes were showing her shock. She didn't say a word. She only nodded and I sat down. "What brings you here?" I asked her. She didn't strike me as the barfly type. It was dangerous for a woman to go to a bar alone, period, but one who looked like her would be even more in danger. I wanted to shake her for doing it.

Those possessive feelings didn't abate. As we talked about inane things, it grew. After what seemed like forever, but was only maybe a half hour, I'd asked her, "Want to get out of here with me?" I didn't know if she'd say yes. She also didn't strike me as a one-night stand kind of woman either, but I was praying she'd say yes. The hunger to touch her, to kiss those lips and feel her body was overwhelming me. I knew it would be unlike anything I'd ever experienced in my life.

To my surprise, she said yes softly. I took her hand as she stood. I was right she was short, maybe only five foot four or five. She came up to my chest and tucked under my shoulder perfectly. I also got a better look at her figure. She wasn't a stick like so many men seemed to want these days. She was curvy all over. Her arms were toned but not cut. Her breasts were impressive in her top, though no cleavage was showing. It all tapered into a smaller waist and then generous hips. The kind you could really latch onto as you fucked her.

Images of doing that flashed through my mind. I was already half hard. I couldn't wait to get her back to my room and naked. As we walked out, I saw the looks we were getting—pissed looks from the men and women. I smirked at them. When she got on my bike and wrapped her arms around me, I had to contain the groan that wanted to come out of me. God, she felt like she belonged there.

My hotel wasn't far. When we got there and inside, I started to kiss her. I couldn't wait. Her lips were soft and so tempting. As I kissed her, I nibbled on those lips with my teeth. She panted and opened her mouth which allowed me to thrust my tongue inside to taste her. She tasted like cherries and the drink she'd had. I devoured her.

My hands weren't stationary while I kissed her. I was running them all up and down her ribs and waist, then around to her ass. I grabbed it. She had a plump ass. She moaned. I hoisted her up in my arms. She automatically put her arms around my shoulders and her legs around my waist. I ground my hard cock into her pussy. Jesus, if I didn't slow down, I'd come in my jeans like a teenager with his first girl.

I laid her down on the bed and started to strip her. I needed to taste more than her lips. I kicked off my boots and stripped off my socks and shirt as I worked on her clothes. I wanted to feel her skin against mine. What I could feel, felt like the softest thing I'd ever felt. When she was naked, I saw her look uncertain. Her hands tried to cover her breasts and pussy. I grabbed them.

"No, baby girl, don't cover up that picture. God, you're so fucking sexy," I told her. As she relaxed, I lowered myself down to suck one of her breasts in my mouth. I laved it as I teased the other nipple. Both nipples were hard little beads. She was squirming a little by the time I was done. I kissed all the way down her ribs and across her stomach. It was soft and made me want to nuzzle into it.

The scent of her arousal was drifting up to me the closer I got to her pussy. I inhaled deeply. Jesus, she smelled so fucking good, like a combination of cherries, flowers, and musk. I eased her thighs open. I needed to push them wide in order to get my shoulders between them. I looked at the heaven that awaited me.

She was bare. Not a speck of hair was anywhere on her pussy. It was pale with the prettiest pink running down those inner lips. I groaned. "Baby, this is the prettiest thing ever." Before she could say anything, I lowered my head and took the first swipe. I think my eyes might have rolled to the back of my head at the taste! She not only smelled like cherries, she tasted like them, as well as a slight salty and musky taste.

I dived into eating her. My tongue swiped up and down her slit, going from her clit to her entrance and back. My fingers teased that nub and rim of her entrance. My teeth nibbled all over and I tapped my tongue against her clit in time to the thrusts I was doing into her pussy. Her damn vagina was so tight, it was hard to get two fingers inside of her. I'd have to stretch her more and get her nice and wet before

I sunk into there. She'd never be able to take me without it hurting. And I didn't want to hurt her. I was determined she'd have nothing but pleasure.

It took some time and a few orgasms before I felt like she could take me without too much discomfort. I stood up as she laid there, coming down from her last orgasm and took off my jeans. I didn't bother with underwear. It was a pain to wear. When she saw my cock, her eyes got large. I knew she was thinking it wouldn't fit.

I was large and I knew it, though I had yet to have a woman say it was too big and get up and leave. She wasn't going to be the first. If I didn't get inside of her, I might die. She bit her lip. I quickly donned a condom from my wallet and got down on top of her. I kissed where she'd bitten her lip. "Relax, babe. I promise you'll get nothing but pleasure." As I kissed her and she relaxed, I lifted her ass off the bed and started to push inside. Even after two orgasms and all the play and stretching, she was tight. I moaned as she hugged me tight as a fist.

I took it slow though it killed me. Her nails bit into my back as she clung to me. Her legs were wrapped around my hips. She was pushing up at me as I pressed down. When I was finally buried to the hilt, I had to stop and take a few breaths. She was panting. I took several breaths and then pulled back. As I slid into her again and her muscles squeezed around me tighter, I knew, my life was about to change!

I powered in and out of her depths. She was moaning and eventually begging me to let her come. I sped up and when she came screaming, I followed her into nirvana a couple of seconds later. It was the best orgasm of my fucking life. I couldn't stop coming as I filled that condom with my cum. Deep down, I wanted that barrier gone. I wanted to be in-

side of her bare. That would have to be a discussion for later.

As we both came back to earth, I pulled out and disposed of the condom then crawled back into bed. I hugged her close to me and kissed her. She yawned. I didn't say anything. I didn't want to ruin the moment. We fell asleep not long afterward. I woke up two more times throughout the night. Both times I took her again. I couldn't seem to get enough of her–the feel of being inside of her, her lips, those breasts, and that whole body. The feelings it churned up inside of me were incredible and new. As we drifted off after the third round, I knew something else. This woman wasn't going to be leaving in the morning. I was going to keep her.

Only that wasn't what had happened. When I woke up, it was to find her gone. I ran outside after pulling on my jeans. I looked around frantically, hoping I'd see her, but she was gone. Ever since, I'd been kicking myself for not getting her name, number, or something. I had no idea where to look to find her, and finding her was something I had to do. The last month had been hell. I'd thought constantly of her and despaired of ever finding her. To have her walk into that office had been like the answer to a prayer. No way in hell I was going to let her get away again! What I told her was the truth. If she ran, I'd find her. Skye Fulton was mine, whether she knew it or wanted to admit it. No way she didn't feel what I did. You didn't let something this good in life go.

Skye: Chapter 3

The party had been going well. I'd been nervous when we showed up. All these bikers made me nervous, but not as much as one did. Executioner had met us at the car as soon as we parked out front of what we found out later was the clubhouse. He hadn't been more than a couple of feet away since. I tried to ignore him, but his eyes seemed to be lasering into me. He'd found reasons to have to place his hand on me. Sometimes it was my arm, or my waist, and other times my hip. When I tried to slip away, he'd tighten his hold just a bit.

Now, we were talking to Sin, Lyric, Executioner, Boss, and his lady, Jenn, about the extortionist. They wanted to know details. We'd gotten to the part about what happened when we'd refused to pay. I knew how much Mom hated this part. It's what ultimately made her decide to give into their demands, despite me arguing that we shouldn't.

"Tell us what happened," Jenn said as she took my mom's hand. Mom blinked. I knew she was fighting not to cry.

"A few days later, Skye and my sons were coming home from the store. Their car was run off the road. A couple of men jumped out and dragged them out of the car. One of them made it very clear that if we didn't pay, something would happen to them or me."

The seat creaked as Executioner shifted his large frame on the seat. He was looking at me. "What the fuck did they say exactly, Skye? I want to know word for word," he growled. I sat up taller. Who was he to be making demands of me? I looked him in the eye, so he could see the defiance on my face.

"He said it would be horrible if someone were to break into our house at night and pay us a visit," I told him. He swore.

Mom told me, "Skye, tell him everything. His exact words were *it would be horrible if someone broke into our house at night and paid Skye a visit.* Then he touched her to make it clear what he meant." Executioner came jumping up off the bench we were seated on. He swore and had a look of absolute rage on his face. He marched around the table and bent down to look me in the face. I had to swallow the nervous lump that had crawled into my throat. God, did he look intimidating as hell. I was shocked.

"Where did he touch you?" he hissed between his teeth.

"It doesn't matter. What matters is—" I tried to argue, but he cut me off.

"It fucking matters. Where did he touch you, did they ever do something like that again, and who were the other guys with Marcos?" He fired off one question right after the other, not giving me a chance to answer him in between.

"If you must know, he grabbed my breast and squeezed, then tried to put his hand between my legs. The other two had the boys off to the side. Thank goodness, they didn't see or hear him. I slapped him and told him to go to hell. He laughed and kissed me. Then they left. When I got home and told Mom, she went crazy and said she couldn't risk her kids. So, the very next week, she started to pay them. It's been that way ever since. On the first of the month, they come around collecting.

I don't know the names of the other guys. I'd recognize them. One of them has a tattoo on his face. Does that tell you what you need to know?" I hurriedly explained and then threw in my defiant question at the end. He stood there staring at me, saying nothing for like a minute then he nodded.

"That tells me exactly what I need to know. Thank you, sugar." Then he stunned me when he leaned toward me and softly brushed his lips against mine and walked off. That tiny touch had me heating up like he'd kissed the hell out of me. Why had he kissed me, especially in front of his club, the other club, and my mom? She'd never let it rest until I told her everything.

Mom was sitting next to me speechless. Boss and Sin were looking at each other with smirks on their faces. Bet they thought it was funny he'd kissed me. Had he told them we'd hooked up? God, that would be humiliating. I was probably the talk of the club. Maybe some of the others would think they could get a piece of me too. After all, I'd slept with him and didn't know his name. They'd think I was a slut! I needed to get the hell out of here.

After that bombshell, the conversation turned to Tanner and what was going on at his school. I half listened as he explained. I interjected once or twice, but honestly. I had no idea what I said. When they were done, Mom and I walked off and sat in a quiet place alone. She looked at me.

"Skye, I want to know what the hell is going on with you and Executioner. Why did he kiss you? I saw your face. You didn't just meet him the other day, did you?"

"Mom, please, can we wait and do this at home? I can't talk about it here," I pleaded with her. I was about to lose it. I felt like eyes were all over me. Executioner had come back from wherever he'd gone, and he was standing not too far away, watching us. I made sure not to look directly at him.

"Fine, but as soon as we're home, you and I are going to talk. Now, let's mingle."

"Can't we leave?" I pleaded. She shook her head.

"No, we need to be neighborly. Give it another hour then we'll go." I sighed as she stepped away. I knew she wouldn't change her mind. My mom could be stubborn. As soon as she walked off, Executioner popped up beside me. I hadn't even seen him move. Shit, I was planning to get with a crowd of others to keep him away from me.

"We need to talk."

"No, we don't. We told you what they said and did. What more do you need to know?"

"I'm not talking about that, however, there is something else we need to talk about. But first, we need to talk about us." I walked off toward the others. He took a hold of my arm and steered me toward the front of the clubhouse. I could have put up a fight, but I didn't want to have even more scrutiny on me. I went with him reluctantly. When we were away from prying eyes, he backed me up against the wall of the clubhouse. His arms caged me in. He pushed up his sunglasses and those eyes were drilling into me. I tried not to squirm.

"I've been stopping by to see you at the shop. Every time I do, I'm told you're out. I don't believe that shit, Skye. Today, you've been trying your damnedest to avoid me. I want it to stop. Why are you so damn leery of me? Are you afraid of me?"

I could see that thought didn't sit well with him. "Executioner, I'm not afraid of you physically hurting me." Which wasn't a lie. I somehow knew he'd never do that. But it wasn't physical hurt I was worried about. It was the much worse kind—emotional—that had me terrified.

"Then why? I know we met under less-than-ideal cir-cumstances, but damn it, I know you have to feel what I do. It wasn't just a fuck and goodbye."

"That's exactly what it was. I don't know why you keep trying to make it more than it was," I practically pleaded. I prayed he couldn't see the lie on my face or hear it in my voice. For me, it had been much more. But to hear him say he thought it was more too had my hopes growing. I had to squash those. Nothing would come of falling for him. When he left in the end, I'd be left broken.

"Bullshit! It wasn't and you fucking know it. We con-nected that night. Do you know what it felt like to wake up the next morning and find you gone? I've been going crazy, trying to figure out a way to find you. Don't tell me you haven't thought of that night. How we were together and how right it felt." His mouth was almost grazing mine as he softly said the last part. I closed my eyes for a second. I had to be strong. I pushed on his chest, which did nothing to make him move. I opened my eyes.

"We had sex, Executioner. It was really good sex, but that's all. Don't tell me you've never had really good sex before. I don't believe it. It was a stolen night, but we're back in the real world. Time for us to get on with our lives. I'm not going to help you relive some kick you seem to have gotten out of it. There are plenty of women who can do that for you."

He growled and then sealed his mouth to mine. He

didn't let me escape as he kissed the hell out of me. When he let go of my mouth, I was panting, trying to catch my breath and beat down my arousal. I wanted to climb him like a tree and ride him all night, which was insane. I didn't think like that. He pressed his crotch into my stomach. I could feel his hard cock. Then he slipped his hand down and cupped me between the legs. He pressed into me. My clit was a hard nub, and I wondered if he could feel it even through my jeans.

"It was fucking more than a stolen night, and no other woman is going to be relieving this but you. I know if I slip my hands down inside these jeans, I'd find you soaked. You can feel how much I want you. It means something, Skye, and I'm not going to let you run because you're scared of it. I'll find out why. I promise, you'll never have to be afraid with me, baby girl. However, I'll give you a little time, but it won't be long. You need to be in my bed and my life, so, you need to come to grips with it."

"Screw you! I don't have to do any such thing. Who the hell do you think you are, telling me what I'm going to do? Fuck you," I snapped at him. He smirked.

"I'm the man who's claimed your ass. The man you're going to be with for a very long time. The man who'll kill anyone who tries to harm you. The man who'll protect you for the rest of your life. That's who I think I am. And yes, you'll be fucking me too. For now, we'll let this go. We need to get back to the party." He pressed a hard and quick kiss to my gaping mouth and then he tugged me with him as he went back around the clubhouse. I went with him like an idiot. My brain couldn't seem to function after his declaration.

He didn't leave my side once we got back to the

others. An hour or so later, Mom came to find me, and we said our goodbyes. When we left, he followed us home on his bike. I hated to think he now knew where we lived. He got off his bike as we parked. When we got out of the car, Mom walked over to him. "Thank you for the escort, but it wasn't necessary, Executioner."

"It was no problem. I wanted to be sure you got here alright and to know where you lived. I want to be sure you have our numbers in case anything happens. Don't hesitate to call, day or night. Let me see your phone." She took her phone out without a peep and he typed away. I heard a few pings come from her phone, then mine pinged. I pulled it out. The bastard had gotten my number out of Mom's phone and sent me his as well as a few others. "You both now have my number, Sin's, and Boss' as well. I can get you the others if you think you need them."

She smiled. "Thank you. This should be fine. Do you want to come in for a drink?"

"I'd love to, but I've got to get back to the party since we're hosting it. I'll take a raincheck if you don't mind." She nodded. Then he looked at me. "I'll see you later, Skye. Remember what I said." He fist bumped my brothers, gave Mom a kiss on the cheek and then got on his bike. After he sped off, I looked at Mom. She was staring intently at me. My brothers wandered to the door, unlocked it, and headed inside.

"Time to talk. Let's grab a drink and sit out back." I dreaded this. I had to confess to my mom that I'd acted out of character and slept with a man I didn't now. A man that I now knew lived in our town and was wanting to pick up where we left off. God, why didn't the ground open and swallow me?

All too soon, we were out back with our lemonade. She sat down and looked at me expectantly. Taking a deep breath, I dove in. I told her what had happened when I stayed in Fort Worth last month. To say she was staring at me incredulously afterward was an understatement. She was looking at me stunned. I could feel the heat in my cheeks.

"Skye, I don't know what to say. I mean, I know that you've never done that before, and you say you have no idea why you did that with him. Don't you think that it's worth figuring that out? I mean, take a step back. He seems intent on you two having something. Maybe it's just sex, but something tells me it's more than that. I don't want you to get hurt, sweetheart, but you have to at least try to live, too."

"Mom, I don't want to chance it. I know it's never going to be anything more than sex. Why set myself up to get hurt when he walks away and hooks up with someone else?"

"What makes you so sure he'll do that?"

"Because he's a man. They all do it eventually." She sighed and laid her hand on my leg.

"Baby, not all men are like that. I know your dad did a number on all of us. He was a selfish asshole that I should have kicked to the curb years before he left. I was a weak idiot. But it kills me that what I did has left you feeling like no man can stay around or be faithful." I could see the sadness on her face.

"Mom, it's not your fault. You tried your best. He just didn't want to be here. Why are you telling me not to let it affect me and how I look at men? It's done the same thing to you. You haven't gone on a date or been with a man since he left. Can you sit there and tell me it's not because you don't trust them?"

She sank back in her chair and got a pensive look on her face. She stayed quiet for a minute or two. "I don't know. I guess it has, but not consciously. I mean, I don't feel like all men are cheating, horrible assholes. I just haven't found someone who made me want to go out with them. I've been asked, but it never felt right."

"What about sex? Don't you miss it sometimes?" I knew most people would cringe to be asking their mom this, but me and my mom were usually open about things like this. It was unusual that I hadn't told her about Executioner. Hell, she knew right afterward when I'd lost my virginity. We'd talked the next day about it.

"I do. But like you, I don't have the urge to go out and just sleep with someone to ease that."

"But that's what I did! I acted like a slut and slept with a man I don't know," I cried out. She scooted over and hugged me tight to her.

"No, you didn't. You're not a slut. I refuse to believe you slept with him just to have sex. There's something that drew the two of you together. You owe it to yourself and him to find out what it is. Okay, I can tell you're ready to argue. I'll leave it alone for now, but promise me you'll seriously think about it." She gave me that intent mom look. Eventually, I nodded and sighed. She gave me a kiss and a pat. We sat out there not talking and just enjoying the day until it started to get cooler, then we went inside. There was work to be done, even though it was Saturday. I needed something to get my mind off of Executioner and what I was going to do about us.

Executioner: Chapter 4

The last week since the party had been a crazy full one for the club. Though I'd wanted to resolve this issue that was standing between me and Skye, there wasn't enough time. I texted her several times. At first, she wouldn't reply, then I threatened to show up at her door. That got her to respond.

We'd been exchanging bits of information. I wanted to get to know her and have her know me. So, I started out easy. Things like what was her favorite color, food, and season? What did she like to do to relax, and about her family? I shared the same information with her, even if she didn't ask. I found it interesting that she said nothing about her dad. That was something I knew I'd have to broach with her face-to-face.

I called her a few times as well. I needed to hear her voice. She'd answered because I'd texted that if she didn't, I'd be over. I hated to threaten her like that, but I was determined not to let her push me away. The sound of her voice made me want to curl up with her and hold her. Then I'd make love to her over and over again. I didn't know how much longer I could take not seeing her and being with her. I needed her where I could do both every day. I was quickly sinking into the same thing that had happened to Sin. I was fucking obsessed with a woman. No one else would do.

The bunnies at the clubhouse were now whispering when they saw me. Before that night with Skye, I'd been with all of them regularly. Hell, who wouldn't? But since her, I had no desire to touch a single one of them. No matter how horny I was, and believe me, I was horny as hell. I was jacking off a couple of times a day thinking about Skye. The bunnies were always coming over trying to hook up but I told them no.

This week I'd spoken to Omen. He was out of the hospital as of three weeks ago. They'd sent him to California for some reason for his rehab and recovery. They were still up in the air about whether to retire him or not. He'd sounded a little better. I prayed they'd just let him medically go. I was still chipping away at him to come here when he got out.

I was hoping that the weekend would give me time to see Skye. I wanted to take her out to dinner. It was Friday, and I was waiting for the end of the workday to call and talk to her. However, fate had other plans. Everything got shot to hell when I found out that her brother, Tanner, had been beaten on the way to school today. I'd rushed over to the school. I saw Skye running inside. I made sure to be right behind her. Saint and Boomer were with me.

She was legitimately upset when she saw him. I had gotten a little pissed when she said Drake had texted her to come get Tanner. Why in the fuck did Drake have her number? He and I would be having a talk. No one was going to move in on my woman. Not even a possible, soon-to-be brother.

Skye was busy touching Tanner's face, and he was trying to evade her and reassure her that he was fine. She didn't look happy. She was going off about who'd done it and tearing the school apart. Drake and Boss were questioning him. Lyric and Sin were sitting there watching. He calmed her down a little by telling us what happened. He'd been jumped by three guys in masks on the way to school.

That's when he confessed, he'd seen what might have been a drug deal the day before after school at the baseball field. Skye had chastised him for not saying anything to anyone. He said quickly, "I was going to tell Ms. Marsh today when I got to class, except when she ran into me in the hall and saw my face, she called in Drake and he called you. I think they weren't only threatening me but her too. You need to be careful," he told Lyric.

"Shit. Okay, you don't know the kid's name who you saw with them?" I asked him. He shook his head no.

Lyric thought she might be able to have Tanner point out the boy he saw at the baseball field in a yearbook. Boss said he was going to talk to Principal Andrews and try to get a judge to give him a warrant to search the school. I wasn't too sure that would happen. I was more worried about Tanner. Boss told him, "No walking to school, Tanner. No going anywhere alone. Hell, we might need to get someone on you like we have on Lyric," Boss mused.

"I can do it, Pres." I jumped in immediately to offer to Sin. I looked at Skye. She was giving me a death stare. *Oh, darling, you have no idea what all I'd do to get close to you,* I thought. I fought not to grin. She might take a swing at me if I did.

"Good idea, Ex. You work it out and then let me know the schedule. If you need help, let me know that too," Sin said with a satisfied smirk on his face. I knew I'd have to soon confess to him and my brothers what in the hell was going on with Skye and me.

Skye sputtered, "T-there's no reason for you to do that. I'll make sure to bring him to school and pick him up. He won't go anywhere after school alone. And when he's here, surely, you can keep an eye on him?" she asked the whole group.

"Sorry Skye but having you or your mom with him isn't enough. They could hurt you as well," Sin told her gently.

"Well, why does it have to be him?" She pointed at me scowling. This time I smirked.

"Because I'm the only one who's going to be watching your family. Get used to it. I'll bring him home and we can talk over dinner," I told her with a smile. This might just be the thing I needed to get her to let me see her. She growled and I think might have ground her teeth.

Sin quickly wound things up. As he did, I stood close to her, keeping watch. She acted like I wasn't there. When Sin and Boss were done, they left. I hung at the school to keep a watch and then I'd take Tanner home after school. When the last bell rang, he met me out front. I took him to my bike. He got an excited look on his face.

"Have you ever been on one of these?" He shook his head. I ran him through the safety measures then he got on behind me. As soon as he was set and holding on tight enough, I took off. I made sure not to get too crazy with him on there. Skye would kill me if anything happened to him. I didn't want to be responsible for hurting him either.

I made a detour before taking him home. We went to the compound. He gave me a questioning look when we stopped. "I need to get some things if I'm going to be keeping watch on you and your family. Come in with me. It shouldn't take long." We were outside where the members had their trailers. I went inside mine. It wasn't anything fancy, a two-bedroom, one-bath place, but it was new, clean and that's all I needed. He hung out in the living room while I packed a bag. Skye was going to shit when she found out I was going to be at their place. Ten minutes later, we were done and on our way to his house.

When I pulled into their driveway, his mom was waiting. She ran over and fussed over him. He tried to get her to stop. I laughed. I wondered where Skye was. Jackie answered that question for me. "Skye's at the shop. She stayed so I could be here when he got home. Thank you so much for doing this, Executioner."

I swung off my bike. "It's no problem, Jackie. We stopped to get some of my stuff. I'd feel better if I could stay and see if there's any trouble this weekend. Is that okay? I can sleep on the floor or the couch." She gave me a knowing look. Tanner had gone ahead inside.

"I'm sure you would. You're welcome to stay. No need to sleep on the floor. We have a pullout bed on the couch, though you might be more comfortable on the floor," she joked. I followed her inside with my bag. Last time I was here, I hadn't come inside. I looked around with interest. It was a basic house, nothing fancy about it. I could tell the furniture had seen better days, just like the house had. But everything was neat and clean.

"You can put your stuff in Tanner's room. It's the third door down on the left. When you're done, why don't you come keep me company in the kitchen?" I gave her a chin lift. I knew I was about to be grilled. That was fine. I'd gladly talk to her about her daughter. Maybe she'd have some ideas to help me win her over.

Five minutes later, I was in the kitchen. She handed me a glass of lemonade and pointed to a chair at the counter. I sat down and she got back to chopping vegetables. "Can I help you with anything?"

"No, that's fine. I've got this down to a science. But thank you for the offer. Now, tell me what it is you're thinking when it comes to my daughter? I won't have her hurt." She didn't beat around the bush. I decided I wouldn't either.

"I don't plan on hurting her. I want her to spend time with me and for us to see where this thing between us goes. I know it's obvious we'd met before that day in your office. Did she tell you that we had?"

"Oh, I know how you met. She told me after the party last weekend. You need to know that's not like my daughter at all to do something like that." I stopped her before she could say more.

"I never thought it was. I know that's not how you liked to hear your daughter met a man, but Jackie, I don't want you to think I'm looking for a hookup with Skye. It's much more than that. But she's determined to stay away from me."

"Where do you see this going, if she were to let you in?"

"I want it to go all the way," I confessed. She gave me a quizzical look. "That means her and I together as a couple. Us living together and having all those things other couples have." She looked surprised.

"You mean a house, marriage, and kids, or something else? I don't know what it's like in an MC. Do you all get married? I know Lyric and Sin are engaged. But is that normal? Are kids something you're allowed to have when you're in a club?"

I chuckled. "We make the rules on what is acceptable and not in our club. Some clubs might not believe in marriage or kids, I don't know. But I can guarantee you,

Sin and Lyric will be having some. Sara is already asking when. And yes, I think most would marry if they found the right woman. In the MC world, becoming an old lady is as binding or more so than marriage. I do want to have kids."

"Old lady? I've heard the term, though I don't understand it."

"It means you've claimed a woman as yours. She's seen as your wife by the club and in the MC world. You protect her like you'd protect your wife. Some don't think traditional marriage is needed if you have that. The only way someone is no longer your old lady is if one of you dies or the guy decides she's no longer his woman."

"Have you decided that many women are no longer your old lady?" she asked with a bite to her tone. I could see where her daughter got her backbone. I got the feeling if I said yes, she'd take that knife to me. Thankfully, I didn't need to lie to save myself.

"I've never claimed a woman as my old lady, and doing so isn't something I would do lightly. Nor would I walk away from one unless it was one helluva reason to do it."

"So, you think my daughter might be old lady material for you?"

"No." She shot me a pissed look. I hurried to explain. "I know she is. Jackie, I can't explain how I know, but she's been on my mind constantly since we met. I won't lie and say there's not a sexual component to it, of course, there is. But that's not all or even the biggest thing. She makes me feel something I've never felt before. That's what makes me sure she's the one."

"What does she make you feel?"

"Like I could conquer the world and I'd do anything to make sure she's happy and safe. I know I can make her happy. I just need her to give me the chance. She's got this wall I can't seem to get through, but I will."

She sighed and laid down the knife. "That's my fault. Has she told you anything about her dad?" I shook my head. She sat down on the chair beside me. Her face got a sad expression on it. "Her dad left us ten years ago. She was thirteen, Tanner was six, and Tyson four." I blinked. She'd just told me Skye was twenty-three. Shit, I was a whole damn decade older. Not that it mattered, but I thought she was older from the way she acted.

Jackie continued, "He was an outright asshole of a husband and father. He was always complaining about having to work. He didn't pay attention to the kids or me. He'd sit here when he wasn't working and drink as he watched sports. Looking back, I should have kicked his ass out when he started to act like this, which was after Tanner was born. Not that he paid a lot of attention to Skye when she was little, but he got worse, and the bitching started."

"Why didn't you tell him to leave, if you don't mind me asking?"

"I was raised that you got married once and it was for life. For better or worse is in the vows. I kept hoping it would get better. Only it didn't. Luckily, I had the shop to bring in the bulk of our money. He hated it too. He said I gave too much time to it and the kids and not to him. It had been my mother's and when she passed away, I inherited it. It's never made us rich, but we've survived. Anyway, one day, he just up and packed and said he was done. He walked out and we haven't seen or heard from him since."

"Not even when you got a divorce?" I couldn't fathom a man acting like that. I knew my dad had his demons and one of them killed him, but he'd always cared for his family.

"We never divorced. I had no idea where to find him to get one. As far as I know, he could be dead and I'm a widow."

"You mean he doesn't even pay support for his kids?"

She gave a humorless laugh. "Not a dime. If I could find him, I'd take his ass to court and have him pay for the boys and all the shit he should owe." I was glad to hear this. I knew a couple of guys who could help me find the bastard, because one thing was certain, if he was alive, she needed a divorce and he needed to pay for his kids. She didn't need to tell me that she and Skye were killing themselves to keep a roof over all their heads. Men like that made me want to put my fist through their faces.

"Don't be offended, but it's obvious you guys don't live large. How are you paying the extortion money every month?" Tears gathered in her eyes. She wiped them away with the back of her hand.

"Barely. We have to float the money we'd use for some bills to cover others and not pay all of them. It's a juggling act. Skye has taken on all the extra work she can but it's not enough. I thought about getting a second job too, but she insists one of us needs to be here for the boys. We cut other things as well." I stiffened.

"What kind of extra work does she do?"

"She does the books for several people who have their own businesses. Most are small ones, but it helps. However, she's burning both ends of the candle. She's going to collapse one of these days. I don't want that to happen. Some days I think I should just let the shop and the house go and we start over again. Maybe even leave Texas and see if we can be more successful somewhere else." I laid my hand down on hers.

"There's no need to sell the business or the house and move. No way do I want that. We'll get rid of these bastards and then we'll work on the other stuff. Is there anything you need help with right now?"

"Oh, no, Executioner. I didn't tell you this so you'd feel like you had to do something for us. The boys have what they need. We make sure of it."

"What about you and Skye? What do you need? I know you're not telling me everything." My gut was churning. My woman and her family were going without. I had plenty. No way I'd let this continue. She looked uncomfortable. I was about to ask her more when the front door opened. I guess Skye was home. I looked up and was surprised to see it was after six already. The shop closed at six.

Her coming home must have been a signal because Tanner and Tyson came into the kitchen. I sat back and waited to see what my baby girl would throw at me tonight. I was even more determined to make sure she let me into her life. She was meant to be mine. She came into the kitchen with a determined look on her face. I smiled. Let the games begin.

Skye: Chapter 5

I didn't want to go into the house. His damn bike was sitting in our driveway! What was he still doing here? I knew he was supposed to bring Tanner home after school, and he'd said Mom and I weren't enough protection, but I hadn't thought he'd really stay once Mom was here and they were all secure in the house. I guess I was wrong.

That seemed to be the story of my life since meeting him. I had thought I'd never see him again. Wrong. I thought I'd never have to confess I'd had a one-night stand. Wrong. I never thought I'd have to fight myself this hard not to do something I wanted to do. Wrong. He had no idea how badly he was testing my resolve.

I could deny it all day long, but I wanted Executioner. I wanted him in my bed. And if I was really honest, in my life. But I knew that was a pipe dream. Sure, he was willing to sleep with me, but it wouldn't end up being more than that. I was like most women. I wanted the happily ever after with a man who loved and adored me, hence, all those damn romance novels. Shaking off those depressing thoughts, I got out of the car and marched into the house. Time to face the dragon, or in this case, the executioner.

I could hear voices coming from the kitchen when I got in the door. As I entered the kitchen, I took in the scene. There was Mom preparing dinner. Tanner and Tyson were standing there already eager to eat, and Executioner was sitting at the counter. He was staring at me. I could see the challenge in his eyes. He was ready for my arguments. Ignoring him, I went to the sink and washed my hands.

"How was the shop after I left?" Mom asked.

"It was fine. That wedding order got picked up and I took a few more orders. Nothing strenuous."

"Anyone stop in that shouldn't have?" Ex asked.

I shot a look at the boys. Tanner knew more of what was going on than Tyson, but neither of them knew I had been threatened. I threw Executioner a warning look. "No, everything was good. What can I do, Mom?" I asked her as I stood next to her. She pushed over the chicken. I laughed.

Mom hated to touch raw chicken. Hell, I didn't like to do it either. Tonight, we were having what looked like chicken fried rice. With the rice, it would go a long way with very little meat. The boys would fill up, though, if Executioner stayed, we might have to add more rice. From the size of him and what I saw at the party, the man could eat. I grimaced as I looked at it.

Executioner got up and went to the sink. I looked at Mom. I had to tease her. "Really, this is what you leave me? I think I might throw up. Tanner, you're on chicken duty!" He laughed and backed up. I knew he'd do it, but I was only playing with him.

Suddenly, I was picked up and set out of the way. As I looked on in astonishment, Executioner took my spot and picked up the knife. "What're you doing? I was just playing!" I protested. He smiled down at Mom who was smiling up at him. My gut swirled. I didn't like him smiling at her like that. Like they had a secret. God, I was losing my mind.

"How do you want this cut, Jackie?"

"Just cube it into small bite-size pieces. It's going to

go into fried rice," she told him all happily. I watched as he got to chopping. They were bantering back and forth as they worked. They looked so good working together. An unwanted thought came to my mind. Mom was an attractive woman in her mid-forties. He had to be in his early to mid-thirties. What if he was attracted to her? The thought made me ill. I hurried out of the kitchen without a word and down to my room.

After shutting the door, I went into my bathroom. I kneeled on the floor and hung over the toilet. I was seriously feeling like I could throw up! Wow, he was killing me. Now, I was jealous of my own mom. They seemed to get along great, unlike him and me. What if they got together? How would I stand to be around the man I'd been with? I knew I couldn't. That would be the one thing that would have me moving out of the house.

Out of nowhere, I became airborne. Huge, strong arms were wrapped around me and carrying me to my bed. I gaped at Executioner. I hadn't even heard him come into my room. As soon as my ass hit the bed, he was hovering over me. I went to blast him, but never got the chance, since his mouth sealed around mine. He kissed the hell outta me. I tried not to respond, but it was impossible. My mouth was kissing him back. When he broke the seal, he stared intently down at me with a frown on his face.

"I don't ever want to see that look on your face again, Baby Girl," he growled.

"What look? And why're you in my room? Get out!"

"The look I saw in the kitchen. The one where you were wondering if I'm attracted to your mom. She's a great woman, but she's not you, Skye. You're the only woman I want." His hands were running down my sides. I pushed up on his chest.

"You don't know what I was thinking. I was sickened by that raw chicken. Why did you kiss me? For all you knew, I could have just puked."

"It wasn't the raw chicken that put that look there. And if you'd puked, so what? I needed to kiss that stupid thought out of your head. Now, get up and come back to the kitchen, because if you don't, I'll be staying in here and we'll be doing more than kissing, baby." He gave me one more quick kiss, then reluctantly got up, pulling me to my feet. I didn't argue with him. It was too dangerous to be in my room like this.

Though I tried to get free, he held my hand all the way back to the kitchen. Mom gave me a concerned look when we came in. I knew she'd be asking me about my behavior later. Shit! Executioner pulled out a chair and sat me down on it. "Where are the glasses, Jackie?" Mom pointed to the cabinet. I watched as he got one out and went to the fridge. He filled it with ice and then poured tea from the jug we kept in there. He came back to the counter and sat it down in front of me. "Drink," he ordered.

I wanted to not do it just to be contrary, but I did need one. My throat felt parched. I narrowed my eyes at him as I took a swallow. He chuckled and then kissed the top of my head. I could see the looks on my brothers' faces. They were wondering what in the hell was going on. I hoped they wouldn't ask. I decided to divert them.

"What is it going to be tonight, Tyson?" It was Friday night. We usually had family game night. Tonight, it was Tyson's turn to pick the game. He gave me a wicked grin. Damn, I knew what he was going to say. I groaned as he said, "*Monopoly.*" Tanner and Mom groaned too.

Executioner gave us a puzzled look.

"*Monopoly*?"

"Friday night we do game night. It's Tyson's turn to pick. He knows we all suck at *Monopoly*, so he almost always picks it." Tanner groused as he shoved Tyson. Ty just laughed at us. The little shit, I'd have to get him back.

"Well, if you want him to get his ass beat, you're going to have to let me play then, because I'm the king of *Monopoly*," Executioner said with a grin. Tanner got an excited look on his face. He gave Executioner a high five.

"Yeah! Absolutely, you can. After all, you're staying tonight. We're not going to make you watch." I jerked.

"What do you mean, he's staying?"

"Executioner is staying to be sure we don't have any more issues like this morning with Tanner, Mom said calmly. She watched to see how I would react. I shook my head.

"There's no need for him to stay! We're inside. The house is locked. We'll be fine," I protested. He came over and wrapped his arms around me and the chair.

He leaned over and whispered softly in my ear, "I'm staying. Get used to it. Don't worry, if you ask nicely, I'll stay in your room tonight." He nipped my ear with his teeth. I elbowed him in his rock-hard stomach. He just laughed as he stood back up. I rubbed my elbow. I swear, he was like a rock.

"As if," I hissed at him. He was smiling his ass off. Mom had a little one on her face and the boys were giving me funny looks. "Well, you all have fun. I have work to do tonight, and then I have to get up early in the morning to work."

"What work do you have to do tonight? I thought you

were off tomorrow at the shop?" Tyson asked, looking bummed. I usually made time to play even if I did have work to do. I just would stay up later to get it done.

"I have a set of accounts to balance for the month, then tomorrow, I have a few more. So, it's not a shop day, but it's still a workday, Ty."

"Honey, you need to take a break. You've been working every night for the past week and a half. You're going to burn yourself out," Mom admonished me. I tried to protest, but she wouldn't allow it. "You're playing with us, Skye Marie Fulton." I knew now that she'd used my whole name, I wasn't going to get out of it. I might be a grown woman, but my mom could still lay down the law.

"Mom, we need to go to the grocery store soon," I reminded her as a last resort. Her stern look didn't waver. I sighed. "Fine. I'll play but let me make a quick call to Ben." I got up and walked out. Executioner watched me go with a pissed look on his face. What was he pissed about? He was getting his way and staying the night.

◄II► ◄II► ◄II► ◄II►

Executioner:

I watched her leave the room. She was killing me. First, with the look on her face when she'd hurried out of the room earlier. I knew she was thinking I was maybe interested in Jackie. I'd been quick to wash my hands and go after her. No way was I going to let her think that shit. Then she attempted to get rid of me and not play game night. She was going to play, even if I had to hold her in the chair.

Her remark about needing to go to the store soon made me wonder. Were they waiting to get stuff until more money came in? Jackie's remark about her working for the last ten days or more straight didn't sit well with me, and now she was going to go call some man named Ben. I wanted to demand to know who in the fuck Ben was. If she was seeing someone, she'd have to tell his ass goodbye, if I didn't kill him first.

As I turned to go after her, Jackie touched my arm. The boys had moved into the living room. "She'll be right back."

"Who's Ben? And what did she mean about the store?"

"Ben is Ben Bentley, Jack Bentley's son over at the real estate office. She does their books for them. It's a new account she just got. I think she told him she'd be done by tomorrow."

"She's not seeing him?"

Jackie laughed. "No, she's not. My daughter doesn't date, Executioner. She says she doesn't have the time nor the desire to."

"Well, then it's a good thing I don't want to date her. I'll just claim her, and we can skip dating since she doesn't do it." She laughed harder. "Yeah, that sounds like a plan. I can't wait to see what she does when you tell her that." I gave her a wink. It seemed like I might have an ally in this fight to get my woman.

"What did she mean about the store?" She got an uncomfortable look on her face.

"Oh, just that it's time to go grocery shopping is all." She tried to play it off, but I knew it was more than that. I'd noticed as I got in the fridge, it was mostly bare. The cabinet she used as a pantry hadn't been that full either. They were waiting to get more money in order to have more food in the fucking house! Jesus Christ, no way was that shit continuing. I knew if I said anything about giving them money, she'd turn it down. So, I didn't bother. I pulled my phone out of my rag and started typing. She watched me as I did it, though she didn't ask what I was doing. By the time I was done, Skye was back from her call.

"Was Ben alright with waiting?" I asked her. She gave me a startled look then she looked at her mom.

"He said Monday or Tuesday was fine. I just don't like putting off someone, especially when they're new. It sets a bad precedent."

"How many people do you do their accounts for?"

"Five at the moment, though I hope to get more."

"You do them every month and I assume you do the ones for your shop. Why don't you do that full-time? Do you have an accounting degree or are you just good with numbers?" I had more than one reason for asking. One was to learn more about her. Two, to find out if this is what she liked to do or was it just because of necessity.

"I got my associate accounting degree after high school. The school here has a program. If you go straight into it after graduation, they'll pay for two years. I've always been good with numbers, and I like them. As for why I don't do it full time, I don't have enough clients and Mom needs help at the shop." I knew that meant they couldn't afford to pay for the help. They were living closer to the edge than I'd first assumed.

I didn't push her by asking anymore, but I'd be talking to Sin. He bitched about the books at the various businesses. We were paying someone to do those. Why not have her do them instead? And with a few more clients, if she wanted to work as an accountant, she could. I'd help figure out the shop.

After this, we settled into just basic talk. I watched them prepare the fried rice. I had to admit, it looked and smelled delicious. They worked like a well-oiled machine in the kitchen. When it was close to time to eat, the boys set the table. All five of us sat down to a heaping wok of rice. I watched as they dipped up their portions. The boys got much bigger ones than Jackie. Skye wasn't putting any on her plate.

"Why aren't you eating, Baby Girl?"

"She's weird. She waits until we're all done first. She says otherwise watching us animals eat makes her sick," Tyson said as he laughed. I flicked a look at her face. She was trying to keep her face blank. My gut clenched as I realized why she didn't eat with her family. She waited to make sure everyone else had enough before she ate. How many times had she gone hungry because there wasn't enough to go around? The idea of her or any of them going hungry made me want to throw shit. I picked up her plate and scooped up a nice portion.

She tried to protest.

"Don't even go there. Eat. What did you have to eat today?" I asked. She swallowed. I knew right then she hadn't eaten at all today. My appetite fled. No way I'd sit and eat while she didn't. I sat back and crossed my arms.

"Eat, Executioner," she said as she pointed at my plate. I shook my head.

"Not until you do." We stared at each other for a minute or two. Finally, she sighed and gave in, taking a bite. I caught the smile on Jackie's face. I took a bite of mine. I had to groan. It was as good as some of the ones I'd had overseas, where fried rice was a staple. "Damn, this is fantastic. Where did you learn to make it like this? It puts the stuff you get here in the States to shame."

"We experimented a lot until we got it to where we liked it. *YouTube* is great for finding and learning things," Jackie told me with pride. By the time we were done, I was happy to see Skye had cleaned her plate. At one point, I'd added more to it. She'd glared but she ate it. I'd have to tell her I didn't want my woman losing her curves. No starving or dieting for her. I was a big guy. I needed my woman to be able to handle me without breaking. Especially in bed, where I liked to get a little energetic.

We'd just finished eating and were clearing the table when my phone dinged. I looked at it and saw it was Dash telling me he was out front. I excused myself and went out to meet him. Dash was one of our prospects. He'd been the one I'd asked to run the errand. Out in the driveway was my truck. I'd told him where to get my keys, so he could use it. I shook his hand. "Thanks for doing this, man."

"No problem." We got into the bed of the truck and began to pull out bags. When we both were weighed down, we headed inside. As we stepped into the kitchen, I saw Jackie and Skye's eyes grow round as we sat the bags down on the counter. They looked at them and then us.

"W-what in the world is this?" Skye sputtered.

"Take a look," I told her as we turned to go get more. We were at the back of the truck again when she came running outside.

"Stop! What are you doing? We don't need this stuff!" she yelled. I saw Jackie was coming out behind her with a pinched look on her face. The boys had stayed inside.

"Bullshit! You think I don't know what you do, Skye. You don't just not eat because the boys are animals. It's so they and your mom get enough. That's fucking bullshit and I'm not going to let it continue. Besides, I'm here to stay and I need food. I'm a damn big man. I eat a lot."

"You won't eat that much in two damn days! You don't know what you're talking about," she hissed.

"I don't plan to stay for only two days. You're stuck with me, baby. Your brothers are two growing boys. They need a shitload of food. And I don't want you losing those curves. I love them." She blushed as she looked at Dash and her mom, who were trying to act like they weren't listening to us. Dash grinned as he took more bags inside. Jackie was carrying a few too.

I tugged her into my arms even though she struggled to get away from me. "Settle down, Baby Girl. I knew if I asked, you'd both say you didn't need any. It's obvious you need these, but you're too proud to say it. Well, you didn't ask, I'm giving it."

CIARA ST JAMES

"We don't need some man to come in and take care of us!"

"No, you don't. But I'm not some man. I'm your man. That makes this my family now. I take care of my damn family, Skye."

"You're not my man. I'm not your woman and my family isn't yours."

"Keep telling yourself that. Now, you can stay here arguing to the air, or you can come inside and put this away." I gave her a hard peck on the mouth and let her go. She snarled as I grabbed more bags and walked off. I was happy to see her come inside right behind me carrying more bags. We all worked together to get the bags inside and then they got to unloading them. The boys jumped in to help. I could see the pleasure on their faces when they saw some of the stuff. I'd mainly asked Dash to get staples of fruits, vegetables, meat, dairy and bread, but in addition, there was pasta and other basic cooking and baking ingredients along with some junk food. Looking at it, I was almost sure Dash had asked Sara what to buy.

Tanner and Tyson were exclaiming over some chips that Dash had bought. It was obvious they hadn't had much in the way of junk food in a long time. It made my blood boil to think they struggled, and their dad was off somewhere living his damn life without a thought of how they were doing. Well, when we found him and was done with him, he wouldn't be living so nice.

When everything was put away, Dash bade us good-bye. I walked him out to my truck and thanked him again. Back inside, Skye still looked upset. Jackie waved to me to follow her. We went outside in the backyard. She sat down.

70

"I don't know how to repay this, Executioner. It's more than I ever expected anyone to do. I'm kind of embarrassed that you did it. I guess that you saw that it was needed. We try really hard, but there's never been a lot left over, and with this extra five hundred to pay every month, there's even less. I'm failing my family and I know it." She had tears in her eyes. I gave her a hug.

"No, you and Skye aren't failing your family. Your dirtbag husband is the failure. He should at least make sure his kids are taken care of until they reach adulthood. Even after that, he should still care. Don't be embarrassed with me. I'd do this for anyone I knew who was struggling, but this is Skye's family. Like I told her, this makes you, my family."

"You really mean that, don't you? You're not going to give up on her."

"No, I'm not. I told you where I want this to go, but I might need your help. She's stubborn and fighting me every step of the way."

She chuckled. "That's my girl. Okay, I'll help, as long as I see it's not going to hurt her in the long run."

"Deal." I held out my hand and she shook it. I now had my ally.

Executioner: Chapter 6

The weekend went a little better than I'd hoped. Skye had still tried to get me to leave, and she argued, but I stuck to my guns. The worst part was going to sleep on the pullout and not in bed with her. I ached to have her in my arms. One night was all it took to have me needing her in my bed and arms. I was praying she wouldn't make me wait too much longer. Jackie had turned into a great ally in my fight to win her daughter's heart. She found ways to throw us together alone. Skye was giving her mom death looks because of it.

Now, it was Monday again and the work week was in full swing. I dropped the boys off at school then went to work at the dealership while she was at the shop with her mom. I'd head over to the school to pick up the boys later. I'd arranged to bring them both to and from school. Dash had brought my truck back to their house yesterday evening.

In the afternoon, I got a text from Lyric saying she was meeting with Tanner after school, and she'd have her guards bring both boys home. That would work out, I could get another hour or so of work done before I headed to their house. It wasn't that much later when I got a text from Dash saying Sin wanted us all to get back to the compound 911. I hurried out of the dealership after telling the staff I was going home. My heart pounded all the way there. What in the hell had happened? Saint's text came later that said there was a mess at the high school, and he was bringing Tanner, Lyric, and a guest home and we needed to get there immediately and keep our traps shut as to why.

When I got to the compound, I could see my other brothers all streaming in. We all worked around town, so it made sense we'd all gotten here around the same time. I got out of my truck and raced over to them. "Does anyone know what the hell is going on?" They shook their heads. I saw that Saint, Sin, and Wrecker weren't here. Another text came in. This one was from Saint telling us to get our asses to Sin's house. We took off. I saw Blake at the gate looking wide-eyed. Dash, Linc, and Drake were nowhere in sight.

We all burst into Sin's house without a word. Around here, we didn't keep our doors locked or knocked. Sara hit the door right ahead of us. We found Sin, Boss, Saint, Lyric, and Tanner. Lyric was seated, looking very pale and Tanner not much better. Sara rushed over to hug both of them. We looked at our president for an explanation.

Torpedo growled out the question all of us were wondering. "What happened, Sin? All Saint said is there was a big mess at the high school, you were bringing Tanner, Lyric, and a guest home and we needed to get here ASAP and keep our mouths shut," Torpedo growled. Sin went into the kitchen and grabbed a couple of sodas and told the rest of us to get what we wanted.

I went over to Tanner. "Are you okay, Tanner?" He gave me a tiny nod. He looked like he was a little in shock. That only tightened my gut more. Sin handed a soda to Lyric and Tanner.

"Baby, I need you to drink this." When she took a drink, he launched into the explanation. "Fuck, where do I start? Dash came back to the compound thinking he was recalled by me, and I was sending someone else to stand guard with Linc. Only I didn't. He showed me a text and it sure as shit looked like it came from my number. Is that possible to do, Phantom?"

"Yeah, if you know how to do it, it's not hard. I'll see if I can trace it later."

"Fine. Anyway, when we realized someone had tricked him, I took off with Saint and Drake, had Dash contact you guys and then call Boss. Boss and Wrecker showed up with two other cops, Montez and Cardenas. Anyway, it looked like the school was deserted. We split up, sent the other two cops one way, and we went to see if Lyric might be in her classroom. When we got close, we could hear voices. I snuck a peek and saw her, Tanner, that douche Terry, and another guy. He had his face turned away. While we were deciding how to enter the room, the voices got loud and then we heard a gunshot." He stopped and took a breath. I knew why as he told us about Lyric shooting the gunman in front of Tanner and Terry.

"I didn't know who it was at first. I checked on Lyric while the others checked on Tanner and cuffed Terry. She started apologizing and crying. Boss called me over to take a look at the man she shot. Fuck, I don't know how else to say this other than to just say it. The guy on the floor was dead, and it was Linc."

Shouts rang out all over the room in disbelief. Had I fucking heard him right? Linc had tried to kill Lyric? No, I had to have heard him wrong. The others were swearing and exclaiming in disbelief, so they'd heard the same thing I had.

Then a soft voice broke through. "He hated me. He said I ruined everything with his club. That I had humiliated him when I broke his nose and then you guys sided with me. He resented it. Terry told me. Linc somehow figured out that Terry was involved with the drugs at school." This got a few more mutters. "He approached him, and they were working together somehow. Terry was supposed to take care of me, but he wasn't going to kill me." Lyric looked up at us with tears in her eyes.

She went on to explain how Terry had been mad at Linc for becoming impatient. That Terry planned to have her, and he'd been biding his time to make a move. Her hooking up with Sin had pushed him to move sooner than he planned. He had a huge plan to live somewhere else on the drug money he'd been saving. To hear Linc had planned to make it look like a school shooting enraged the hell out of me.

She took a moment to look at Tanner and say, "I'm sorry, Tanner. I had no idea this would happen. If I had, I'd have never asked you to come to my classroom after school."

He was quick to jump to her defense. He explained to us, "Ms. Marsh, it's not your fault. No one knew. And Linc was nuts. He was debating at first if he'd kill me too. He was considering not doing it because I didn't know who he was. But then he got a text and next thing we knew. Mr. Tolliver came in and they started talking. That's when they said they now had to kill both of us." His voice quivered as he spoke. I put a comforting hand on his shoulder.

"It was after that when things went crazy. They were talking about it. Terry kept wavering back and forth on whether Linc should kill me. He tried to convince Linc that he could still take me away. That I'd never be an issue because he'd keep me locked away. They were arguing. That's when I decided it was now or never. I was sitting right next to my desk and my purse was on the desk with my gun in it. They got so into their argument, that Linc looked away and his gun pointed away from both of us. I just reacted. I don't know how I got the gun out and shot him without him shooting me. I just don't know. It was like a dream and in slow motion. That's when you guys came crashing through the door," Lyric said as a sob broke out of her.

This broke Sin. He took her soda out of her hands and wrapped her in his arms, pulling her onto his lap and rocking her. "Angel, shh, it's going to be alright." Tears poured down her face as she looked at all of us. We were all still stunned.

"I'm sorry. I didn't know what else to do. Please, don't hate me." I jerked in surprise. Talon was the first to recover. He went over and sank down on his knees in front of her.

"Why in the world would we hate you, Lyric?" he asked in a puzzled voice.

"I killed one of yours. Linc was about to become an Infidel. Sin told me."

"Jesus Christ, really? Lyric, sure we liked Linc and thought he would make a good Infidel. Shows you how wrong we can be, even when we do extensive background checks. There had to be something wrong in his head for him to do this. But, honey, either way, there was no way Linc would have walked away from this, not even to go to jail. He was going to kill an old lady, and not just any old lady, but our president's lady. He signed his death warrant the moment he made that decision," Talon said with a steely look in his eyes. We all nodded.

"Maybe he could have gotten help." She sobbed. Talon shook his head.

"Not for this. Now, stop feeling guilty. You did the right thing. If you hadn't shot him, it could have ended with you and Tanner dead. How would that have felt for us?" he asked. He stood up to retake his seat.

"So, what now, Pres?" Boomer asked. Sin quickly got us situated. He was going to get Lyric settled and then have Sara stay with her. We had Terry to talk to, and he was at the Gallows with Boss's guys, Bug and Kitty, as well as Drake. He told us Boss and the others were getting things settled at the high school then would be over to help. He looked at me.

"Ex, I need you to go get Skye and bring her here so we can explain. Tanner doesn't want his mom to know yet." Sin told me. I gave him a chin lift. "The rest of you, I need you to act normal. If anyone asks, you came home early because we were celebrating our engagement. I don't think anyone will ask, though. I'll text you when it's time to go talk to our guest." We took turns hugging Lyric and checking on Tanner before we left them alone.

I hated to leave him, but I had to go get Skye without freaking out her and Jackie all to hell. I had no idea how in the hell I was going to accomplish that.

As I pulled into the parking lot of Blossoms, I took a deep breath. Here went nothing. As I walked in the door and the bell rang, I saw Skye look up from one of the display cases. She was stocking it. Behind the counter was Jackie. She gave me a smile. I fought to give her one back. I went over to Skye.

"Where's Tanner?" she asked right away.

"I need you to come with me, Skye. Tanner's fine, but I need you to come with me to the compound."

"Why? What the hell, Executioner? I'm not going to your compound. I'm busy." I didn't argue. I just hoisted her up and over my shoulder and started out the door. She yelled at me. I winked at Jackie as I did it. She grinned but didn't ask why, thankfully. I put a struggling, swearing, and pissed-off Skye in my truck. I made sure to put her in on my side and to slide right in, so she wouldn't jump out. She was smacking at me as I put the truck into gear.

"Goddamnit, I'm going to kill you, Executioner!" she screamed.

"We're alone, baby. It's Slade," I said to distract her more.

"Slade, really, you carry me off like a sack of potatoes and then all you can say is, *call me Slade*. I swear if I don't kill you, it'll be a miracle. What's the damn big deal? Why do I need to come to your compound?"

"I'll tell you once we get there." She muttered, swore, threw out more threats and smacked me a couple of times on the arm as I drove. All in all, it had gone much better than I'd imagined. When we got there, I took her inside the clubhouse. Tanner was already there with Sara. She ran over to him and started to ask him if he was okay and what was going on. He looked at me and I shook my head. He kept quiet other than to reassure her he was unharmed.

She was pacing the room when Sin and the others came through the door. She ran over to him. "Will you tell me what's going on? This neanderthal comes into the shop and tells me I need to get over here. He doesn't tell me why and then just carries me out to his truck. Then I get here, and my brother is here!" she shouted as she gave me a shitty look. I could tell Sin was trying not to laugh. I stood there looking at her with my arms crossed.

"Have a seat, Skye. We'll tell you what happened, but I need you to remain calm and let us get the whole story out before you ask any questions. Can you do that?" She gave a nod and sat down as I took a seat beside her. Sin started to tell her the story we'd all heard not long ago. By the time he was done, and Tanner had added a few comments. She sat there frozen in her chair. She was pale. Sin gave me a worried look.

"Baby Girl, say something," I said softly. She shot out of her chair.

"You mean that fucker, Mr. Toliver, and your guy, Linc, were going to kill my brother? They were behind him getting his ass beat the other day and all the shit with Lyric? Where is he? Where is that fucker Tolliver? I want to talk to him," she ranted.

"Babe, you need to calm down," I told her. She whipped around to glare at me.

"Don't think you can tell me what to do, Slade Ashton! Just because we—" she cut off the remark. "I want to make that fucker suffer! He deserves nothing but pain."

"And he'll get what he has coming to him, but you're not going to see him," I warned her. She stood there glaring at me more.

Tanner interrupted, "Sis, calm down. You're going to stroke out. We have bigger issues. We need to figure out what to tell Mom," Tanner told her.

"We're not going to tell her anything, Tan. She'll lose her shit. She'll be thinking she has to move or something. You know how she is. Right now, we keep this between us. I assume Boss is taking care of things?" We nodded. "Good. Let me know if you need me to tell anyone a story to back you up. How's Lyric?" Her quick change in thought had us looking at her slack-jawed. Sin told her Lyric was shaken and at the house resting with Sara.

"I assume you have stuff to take care of. A certain guest to talk to. Let me take Tanner with me. I'll check on Lyric and then we'll go home. Can someone give us a ride since I don't have my car?" She narrowed her eyes at me again.

"Yeah, just have Blake or Dash take you when you're ready. Are you sure you're alright, Skye?" I asked.

"I'll be fine. This isn't our first shitstorm. Just make sure that fucker doesn't have the chance to come back into any of our lives. Make him hurt for me," she growled.

"Don't worry, I'll make him pay for you, baby girl," I assured her. It would be my fucking pleasure.

"Good. And stop calling me, Baby Girl. I'm not your anything," she hissed as she grabbed Tanner's hand to go. I yanked her into my arms and laid a possessive kiss on her mouth. No way was she getting away with saying that shit! I made sure to make it a long one.

When I came up for air, I told her, "Like hell you're not. And you're going to accept it soon." She jerked out of my arms and stormed out with her brother. Sin looked at me with a questioning look on his face. I saw my other brothers had the same look.

"Dare I ask what the hell is going on with you two?"

"Maybe later. Right now, let's go talk to Terry. That woman thinks she's going to get away, but I have news for her, she's mine and I'm claiming and keeping what's mine," I growled. The rest of them laughed and told me good luck.

As evening came and we dealt with Terry, my excitement grew. Not only at the thought of what we'd be doing when we caught the others dealing drugs, but at the heated battle I'd be walking into when I went to her house tonight. I was tired of waiting. It was time for her to be mine. Baby girl and I were going to have a talk tonight, and hopefully a lot more.

Skye: Chapter 7

When I got Tanner home, we were happy to see Mom wasn't there yet. Shit, Tyson, he was supposed to be brought home by Executioner when he brought home Tanner. I rushed inside to find him sitting on the couch watching a movie. He glanced at me when I came in.

"I'm sorry, Tyson, things got mixed up, and I had to take Tanner somewhere and I forgot to tell Executioner to still pick you up."

He shrugged. "No big deal, I walked. I'm not sure why you guys are so worried. Why would whoever beat Tanner want to beat on me? I'm much friendlier than he is," he said with a cheeky grin as he looked over my shoulder. I knew he was looking at Tanner. Tyson was a joking, easy-to-make-friends type. Tanner was the quiet loner. I smacked him on the head.

"Hush, you're not as adorable as you seem to think you are. We're just being careful. Did you get a snack when you got home?" He nodded. "I'll get dinner started in a little bit. I need you to get on the grass. It's your turn." He groaned. The boys took turns keeping the lawn mowed and trimmed. They traded off every week. It was his turn, and I knew he hated to do it, but we all had to do our share. He grumbled as he hauled himself off the couch and out to the garage where we had an ancient mower.

With him out of earshot, I started to talk to Tanner. "We need to make sure we both act like everything is normal. Mom can't find out about Linc. If she does, she'll lose it. She's got enough on her plate as it is, Tan.

Can you do it?" I knew we'd already talked about it on the way home, but I had to be sure.

"Yes, Sis, I can. I told you. I'm more worried about you letting it out of the bag. The look on your face was frightening. I knew you were a little crazy, but not that crazy."

"When it comes to my family, you haven't seen crazy. Okay, you need to do your chores and then get to your homework. I'll get changed and then start making dinner. Mom should be home in an hour."

"When's Executioner getting here?"

"Executioner? Why would he be coming here tonight?"

"Come on, Skye, you think he's not? No way after today, he's not coming back to stay. I think you just need to face the truth."

"What truth is that?"

"The man wants you and he's not going to go away. I hate to say this, but you're just going to have to give him what he wants." He playfully shuddered. I stood speechless. Had my little brother just told me to have sex with Executioner?

"Get out of here, you shit! I'm not giving him anything. Jeez, where's your mind at?"

"In reality, unlike yours. Okay, pretend if you want, but he'll be here later. I'm willing to bet on it." He smirked as he left the room. I stood there a moment trying to decide if he was right. Would Ex come here tonight expecting to stay again?

I went to my room to get changed. As I did, I thought of the past weekend. I hated to admit it, but it had been fun to have him here. He fit in with the boys. Mom seemed to like him. It was only me who seemed to want him gone, and if I was honest with myself, I didn't actually want him gone. That's what sacred me. I wanted him here. Hell, I wanted him period. Not a good thing for me to want.

After I got changed, I went to the kitchen and started pulling things out to prep for dinner. It was nice to have so many things to choose from and not have to worry about how to make it stretch, though the fact he'd bought the food had rankled. Mom had been a little embarrassed, but then she seemed to get over it.

I had the potatoes scrubbed and ready to go into the oven once it heated up. There had been steaks in the groceries. We hadn't had those in a long time. I had put them in a marinade this morning. When it was time, we'd put them on the grill. I fixed a large salad. The boys would groan, but they needed to eat their vegetables. I also had asparagus to grill. As I looked at it and the clock, I decided to fix dessert.

All of us enjoyed our sweets when we could get them. I had enough time to make a really great pie. The crust was quick. I'd get it made and then everything baked before I did the potatoes. I grabbed the ingredients and got started. In no time, I had a Dutch apple pie ready to go in the hot oven. It was a favorite of my brothers. I was washing my hands when Mom came in the door. It was six thirty already and she looked tired. I gave her a hug. "How did the rest of the day go?"

"Fine. Not too crazy. How did your afternoon go with Executioner?" she asked with a sly grin on her face. I knew she was dying to find out why he'd carried me off like he had. I could kill him for doing that. Now, I had to come up with an excuse to tell my mom. I was racking my brain to find one when Tanner cut in. I had no idea he had walked into the kitchen.

"She was mad at him. I told her not to be. It was just a joke. I bet him that he wouldn't go in there and do it. He said he would. Next thing I knew, he came out carrying her over his shoulder." I had bitched about Ex doing it on our ride home to Tanner, so he knew what had happened. Mom chuckled and shook her head.

"Tanner, really! Your poor sister tried to beat him silly. Don't do that again. I hate to say it, I did think it was funny."

"Mom! Jeez, thanks. Next time some man comes in and carries me out like a sack of potatoes, I'll know not to expect any help from you."

They both just laughed. Tyson came in hot and sweaty from mowing. Mom told him to go shower. As he did that, we caught up on the shop and finished getting things set for dinner. Even if I told Tanner that Executioner wasn't coming over, I did make enough for him. I'd deny it was for him if anyone asked.

With everything that had gone on and chores plus homework, it was eight before dinner was ready. We were just setting it all on the table when I heard the front door open. I gave Mom a startled look. Who in the hell would be coming into our house? Damn, our gun was down the hall. I went to grab a knife out of the butcher block. I was about to go hide by the door to the kitchen when Executioner stepped through it. I sagged in relief. Then it hit me, and I got mad.

"Are you mental? I could have stabbed you! How in the hell did you get in our house? I know Mom didn't forget to lock the door!" I shouted at him. He gave me an amused then satisfied look as he looked at the knife I held.

"No, last time I checked my mental status was fine. The door was locked. I used a key. That's what most people do. I'm glad you thought to protect yourself, however, a gun would have been better. You have to get too close to use that."

I slammed it down on the counter before I was tempted to go ahead and use it anyway. "How the hell do you have a key to our house? What are you doing here? And I have a gun, but it's down the hall in my room, smartass."

He walked over to me. I watched him coming and wondered what he was going to do. I figured he was going to get in my space and say something smart. He did get in my space, but he didn't say anything. He yanked me into his hard chest and laid his lips to mine. I gasped at him and he took his opportunity to slip his tongue in my mouth. I pushed on him, but he didn't budge. He kissed me thoroughly and only lifted his head when he was ready. When he did, I was a breathless mess. I wanted to climb up him and take him to the floor. That would be a sight for my family to see.

"Hello, Baby Girl. Dinner smells terrific. Anything you need me to do?" He stepped away to wash his hands like he hadn't just kissed me in front of my family. A family that was trying not to laugh and had smiles on their faces. As I stared at them, Tanner caught my eye, winked, and mouthed the words, *I told you so.* I just glared at him.

When Ex finished washing his hands, he gave me an expectant look. I realized he was waiting for me to answer him. "There's nothing left to do but eat. Sit down. God, this place has gone mad. How did you get a key to the house, anyway?" We all took our seats. He made sure he was right beside me.

"I gave him one. It made sense if he's staying here and going to be in and out. What if we're not home to let him in?" Mom asked calmly. I sat there with my mouth hanging open. Was my whole family on his side? I decided not to respond. Serving plates were passed around and we got down to eating. The guys in particular were very complimentary. When they found out there was pie, I thought they were going to have a party.

We'd finished and the boys were cleaning up. I was putting away a few leftovers when Executioner came up behind me and slipped his arms around my waist. He leaned down and laid his chin on my shoulder. "That was an awesome meal and that pie, damn, Baby Girl. I'm definitely going to marry you."

I elbowed him in the stomach. "So, is that your criteria for a woman? If she can cook, you'll marry her? God, that sets women back decades." I snorted.

"No, I also want her to drive me insane, resist the shit out of me, meet me at the door with a weapon, threaten to kill anyone who messes with her family, make me work to get back inside of her sweet pussy and in general, fucking slay me. The cooking is just a bonus." He growled then he whipped me around and kissed me.

In the background, I heard Tyson saying something like, "Eww, not again." I wasn't sure though because I was lost in what Executioner made me feel. I was instantly hot and ready to tear off his clothes.

It was so good, I felt like I was floating. I was brought back to reality when my back hit something soft. I pulled away and looked around to see we were in my bedroom, and I was on my bed. Ex was hovering over top of me. His eyes were bright with desire. I started to wiggle out from underneath him. How in the hell had we gotten in here?

"Executioner, get off me. What in the hell are you thinking, bringing me down here and like that?" His hands ran up my arms, and he caressed my bottom lip. I could feel it was swollen from that kiss.

"I was thinking I needed to get my woman alone. I didn't want to be stripping her naked in front of her mom and brothers. I'm not going anywhere. It's time we talked, Skye. No more of this evading bullshit." His face had a serious look now. He eased back and laid down beside me on the bed. I was prevented from getting up by the steel bar of an arm he had across my middle.

I laid there and didn't say anything. Maybe if I waited long enough, he'd get tired and leave. Yeah, right. I was kidding myself. I could tell by the serious look on his face, he wasn't going to be distracted from this talk. It was time to face the piper. I needed to make him see that this pursuit of his had to stop. We weren't going to be together, not even for a little while.

"Fine, let's do this. You want to talk, then let me go first. We're not going to be anything together. I've told you this and you won't listen. That night in Fort Worth was just a chance for us to blow off steam and get laid. You were horny and so was I. There's no reason for you to be thinking there's going to be more of those sessions. I know you hook up with women a lot. I have the same freedom, too."

He went to say something, but I cut him off. "Why are you so determined that we sleep together again? It can't be because you can't get laid. Not to make your ego any bigger, but you're not exactly an ugly, unsexy man. Is it because I'm not willing to go there again that you see it as a challenge or something? Because it's not meant to be. This will never work. Please, you have to give up this campaign of yours."

"Are you done?" he asked. I nodded. "Good, now it's my turn. I don't for one second believe you go around having one-night stands with strange men. In fact, I don't think you go around sleeping with men you know. Yeah, I was horny that night and maybe you were too, but it was more than that for you to agree to go back to my room with me, Skye. And it sure as hell became more than that when we did." He got up and walked over to my window. He stared out of it.

"That night changed my fucking life. I had no idea there were women like you out there. That being with someone could feel like that. And I'm not talking about the sex part, though that was fucking amazing too. For the first time in my life, I wanted to fall asleep with a woman and wake up the next morning with her still there. When I woke up and you were gone, all I felt was panic. I had no idea who you were or where you lived. How in the hell was I going to find you?" I laid there with my mouth hanging open. Oh my God, was he really saying this stuff? Men like him didn't get all soft and sentimental.

"I came back home and all I thought about was you. Then we walk into Blossoms that day and I find you. That's not a chance, Baby Girl. That's fate, and I'm not going to mess with fate. You and I are meant to be together. Whatever I have to do to make that happen, I will do. Even if it includes convincing you." He turned around and looked back at me.

"Executioner, you—"

"Slade. We're alone. I told you to call me Slade."

"Okay, Slade, do you hear what you're saying? Come on, there's no way this can work. You'll be bored within a week and then off to the next woman. I don't need or want that in my life."

"I know you're worried about me or actually any man leaving you. I know about your dad. Your mom told me about him. She thinks you're afraid to let a guy in because of him. But, babe, all men aren't like him. He's a loser and a sad excuse for a man. I'm not looking for us to play house and then move on. I want us to see this to its natural conclusion."

"And what do you see as the natural conclusion?" I didn't touch what he said about my dad. That had come a little too close to the truth for comfort. He came back over and laid down beside me. He tugged until I was encircled by his arms and his face was inches from mine.

"I see it as being you and me in a committed, lasting relationship. One where we share our lives. You, me, your mom and brothers, and my club. We'd live together and you'd be my old lady. Hopefully, one day you could be my wife and the mother of my kids. That's what I see. I'm not going to hurt you, abandon you, or any of that shit. Things might not always be rainbows and unicorns, but we'll be together."

His words stunned the hell out of me. He was serious. He meant what I thought he did. And it was so damn close to what I secretly wanted, I could almost cry. God, what if I took this chance and he changed his mind? He said he wouldn't, but men did it every day. My dad wasn't the only one. What if he did that? Could I recover and go on from that kind of heartbreak? Because I knew without a doubt, I would be heartbroken if he left me or cheated on me. I already had feelings deep down that were too close to what I thought was love for him. Who fell in love with someone they'd only slept with once and had been around a total of less than a week out of the six weeks since they'd met? It was insane to even think about it.

As I laid there saying nothing and struggling to come to a decision, he lowered his head and lightly brushed his mouth over mine. He nibbled at them. "I can see the thoughts going through that beautiful head of yours. Please, Skye, take a chance. Don't push me away. I won't break you. You seem not to realize. You could just as easily break me. What if you were to decide to leave me? That you want someone else? It's a two-way street, baby. Women leave men too. I'm willing to take the risk. Take it with me," he whispered then latched onto my mouth.

Skye: Chapter 8

His taste and the feel of him made me get lost. I sank my hands into his long hair and kissed him back. Our lips, teeth, and tongues teased each other. Both of us moaned softly as we kissed over and over. My body was on fire and my hard nipples were pushing against the cups of my bra. My panties were damp as hell. I was close to tearing off our clothes and begging him to take me.

Abruptly, he pulled away. He sat up and pulled off his t-shirt. I looked at his huge chest. He was broad across his shoulders and the muscles were well defined. I saw the tats I'd seen the night we'd been together in Fort Worth. I'd spent time tracing them and kissing them. He had intricate tribal tats for the most part. They were from the front of both shoulders and ran to the back. His back, and his arms had them and there were ones running down his ribs. I couldn't help but to touch them. He shuddered at my touch.

"Jesus, baby, let me get those clothes off of you. I'm about to die." He reached out and tugged up my top and then pulled it off. I didn't stop him. I might regret this, but for a second time, I was going to go for something I wanted in life. Next, my bra went sailing. He was pulling off his socks and undoing the belt and snap on his jeans. I licked my lips as he pulled them down and off. Like last time, he didn't have any underwear on. His more than impressive cock was standing proud. I felt the wetness between my legs get slicker. He crawled back onto the bed and took a hold of the waist of my yoga pants. He jerked them down and off, taking my panties with them.

Now, both of us were naked. He could see the cream between my legs like I could see the precum on the head of his cock. He groaned and then got over top of me. His mouth and then a hand went to my breasts. He was sucking on my nipples and tugging on them with his fingers. Every once in a while, he'd knead them. I was panting. My hands were busy tracing those tats and teasing his nipples.

He eventually started to kiss his way down my body. He nibbled down my ribs and teased my belly button with the tip of his tongue. When he got to my pubic area, he eased my thighs apart and got between them. I took a deep breath. I knew what he was about to do. I'd dreamed about it since that night. He gave me a heated look then lowered his face. The first swipe of that magic tongue had me almost coming up off the bed.

He went at me like I was ice cream, and he was eating it. He twirled his tongue in circles, licked up and down, took the edge of his teeth to my folds and then sucked on my clit. I bit the side of my hand, so I wouldn't yell out and have my family hear us. Then he slid a finger inside of me. I was about to lose it. I could feel the tightening in my stomach and the tingling down in my toes and lower legs. I was going to come soon.

"Oh God, Slade, I'm going to come if you don't stop," I cried.

He lifted his head. "That's what I want, Baby Girl. Come on my tongue. Give me all that sugar. You taste like fucking cherries, baby. That's my favorite fruit. Give it to me." He growled and then he went back to my pussy. I gripped the back of his head and sank my fingers into his hair and then I ground my pussy on his mouth. He moaned and flicked my clit harder and thrust his fingers faster in and out of me. I went off. I bit my lip as I shook and quaked, coming in a burst of heat. I had no idea how long I came, but when I was finally able to see, he was sitting up and stroking his cock. He had a satisfied look on his face.

"Bastard," I said without heat. He laughed. I reached for him. "My turn. I want to suck that beast." He laughed again.

"I want you to suck him too, but not right now. Save it for round two. I need to be inside of you, Skye. No more waiting. It's been a long fucking six weeks." He bent down and picked up his jeans. He took out his wallet and got out a condom. He rolled it on and then got back on the bed. His arms caught my knees in the crook of his elbows. He lifted them up and apart, then he was pushing inside. I moaned as the sensation of him stretching me made me half delirious. When he got inside, he started to power in and out. It wasn't a nice, slow lovemaking session. It was raw, dirty, hard, and deep.

He pounded in and out of me like a jackhammer. He was rubbing across my G-spot and hitting my cervix as he bottomed out. I wrapped my legs around him and pushed back at him. He had a hold of my hips and was using them to slam me down on his cock harder. It was too much. I came a second time. He groaned as I squeezed the hell out of him.

"That's it. Come for me. God, that's fucking amazing. Get ready, I'm going to fill you up." As I slowly eased down from my orgasm, he sped up and was hammering me almost into the bed. His breath was coming out in pants. His eyes were blazing, and his face was sweating.

As I watched him, I deliberately clenched my core. He hissed and then he was coming. As he came, I watched a snarl come over his face. He held himself deep as he jerked and came. I could feel the cum filling the condom. Seeing him in so much pleasure made me come for a third time. He moaned as I milked his still jerking cock. He collapsed over me but kept his weight from crushing me. We sounded like two winded runners.

Eventually, our breathing slowed, and he eased out of me reluctantly. He tied the condom and dropped it in the trash can beside my bed. He pulled me into his arms and gave me a slow, gentle kiss. "Baby Girl, you just slayed me. There's no way I'm ever going to want anyone but you. God, I think my toes came." I laughed.

"Wow, that's a claim a girl wants to make. I made my man's toes come."

"Your man? I like the sound of that. And that's one helluva thing to brag about. Just like I know I'm the shit because I can get my woman to come more than once." I slapped him lightly on the ass. He chuckled.

"We'll get to that later. I need to rest. While we do, we do need to talk about something." His serious tone had me tensing up. Oh God, what was he going to say? "Don't look like that. We need to talk about contraception." I frowned.

"You used a condom, what is there to talk about?"

"I don't want to use one. I want to be inside of you bare."

"Slade, I don't know if that's a good idea."

"I'm clean. I know that. Other than that, what is there to worry about?"

"Well, if it's not sexually transmitted diseases and pregnancy, then nothing. But we'd have to be sure we were both clean."

"I am and I can show you the proof. I don't go without a condom, Skye. But with you, I need to be skin to skin. Will you get on the pill or something, so we don't have to use one?" He waited to see what I'd say. I thought about it for a minute. I had never been with anyone without one. I wondered how it would change things.

"Okay, if we can show we're both clean, then I'll do it. I can get my last test from my doctor. I haven't been with anyone but you since. You go get tested and we'll talk."

"I was already tested. It was seven or eight weeks ago. I'm clean."

"Well, that was seven or eight weeks ago. We need to make sure you haven't caught something since then."

"I didn't."

"How do you know you didn't?" I asked him miffed. What, he thought you could just look at someone and know?

"Because you're clean and I haven't been with anyone but you." I felt my mouth drop open. Was he kidding? No way he'd been without sex for eight weeks. Men didn't want to go a day without, let alone that long. And I knew there were plenty of women around who would give an arm and a leg to be in his bed even for a night.

"There's no way you've been celibate for the—" He stopped me with a hard kiss, then he raised up on his hands.

"Like hell there isn't. If I couldn't have you, then I didn't want it. I told you I was trying to figure out how to find you. I don't lie, Skye. That's one thing you'll discover about me. I'll tell it like it is, even if it's not what you want to hear. You've been it. Now, how long does it take to get on something?"

"I-I don't know. I'll have to go to the doctor and find out."

"Then we'll make the appointment as soon as possible. I'm not kidding. I want it to be us with nothing between us as soon as possible."

All I could say was, "Okay." I laid there in amazement. He rubbed up and down my arms. It was soothing and soon my eyes grew heavy. I had no idea when I drifted off to sleep, but when I did, he was right there with me.

Executioner:

The last week had been uneventful for all of us. After getting Skye to agree to give us a chance and then making love to her, we'd settled into a semi-routine. I'd moved more of my things to the house. She'd tried to tell me I didn't need to stay, but I told her, it didn't matter if they needed protection or not. I wasn't going to be sleeping away from my woman. If she wanted to come to the compound, then I'd settle for that.

She hadn't agreed to move there with me, though one night we'd stayed there at my place. I had to admit I liked it more because she could let loose and not try to stifle her responses. At her house, she was conscious that her family was down the hall and tried to be quiet. I wanted her to scream if she wanted. God knows there were times when I wanted to. That woman could make me see stars.

In addition to our relationship advancement, there was no blowback so far for Terry or Linc. Boss had done a great job in diverting attention to the theory of some kind of altercation with someone. There was the ever-slightest hint that Linc had been involved in something that had pissed off a partner. We hated it for his family, but we had to protect ours.

The explosion that Santa, Kitty and Bug had rigged for Terry had been all over the news. We had to bear seeing them do a memorial for him at the school. I don't know how Lyric had been able to do it. Kerrigan had been upset, but she wasn't in on the whole story of what had happened.

Jackie and Skye were getting ready for the next hurdle. They weren't going to pay the guys who came around at the first of the month. I was going to be there with a few of my brothers to see who we could catch. It was time to stop these assholes. We'd taken care of Marcos, but he wasn't the only one doing it. We needed to find the other guys. None of the business owners knew their names but had given us similar descriptions. But besides having a face tattoo, they were rather generic, and a lot of men could have fit them.

I should have known it was too quiet. Everything went to shit when we found out some men had taken Paula, Hook's woman. The Time Served guys had reached out to us for help. They had found out where she was, and we were the ones who were going to go in and get her. Not because they weren't willing, but this was more in our wheelhouse. They'd just storm in with guns blazing and say fuck it. We hoped to get in and out without any of us going to prison.

As we waited for Saint and a couple of the others to say if they found her in the warehouse at the old Air Force base, I kept watch. It wasn't long before Sin came across the radio saying she was found. I saw her running toward the truck we had at one of the rendezvous points. She got in the back and the rest of us piled in. She was lying on top of Torpedo as Stamp drove. She was acting all excited. Not what you expected from a recently kidnapped woman, but then again, Paula was hardly normal.

We'd all just found out not long ago that she was from a mafia family, and she was a trained doctor. That had been a mind fuck to find out. There wasn't much she wouldn't help with, and nothing seemed to be off the table when it came to protecting your friends and family in her book.

I choked back a laugh as she said with a thrill in her voice to Torpedo, "It's about goddamn time you showed up! I thought you guys were never going to fucking get there! That was fucking awesome! I'm a ninja now too, right? I want some clothes like yours. I can barely see any of you back there. Are you wearing makeup?"

We all laughed as Sin called in to Boss that we were clear. I listened as she and Saint argued about it not being makeup. She was of the mind that if you put it on to change your appearance, then it was makeup. She just thought our camouflage made us ninjas.

Then they got to talking about this guy inside who she apparently stabbed in the eye. Suddenly, Saint asked if she'd just cut him? That's when we found out she carried razor blade rings in her boots and bras, plus a knife in her boot. Pitbull in particular seemed fascinated with the rings. He was checking them out. She was explaining to him all the cool things you could do with them.

That's when he said to her, "You're one twisted little lady, Doc. If things don't work out with you and Hook, give me a call. I could use a woman like you in my life." He said it with a grin, but I knew he was half-serious. Paula quickly crushed those dreams.

"Nope. He's the one for me. You found me too late, buddy."

He grumbled, "That's the story of my life." It wasn't long after that we got back to Boss. They'd stayed on Pop's land at the junkyard, which backed up to the Air Force base. In fact, it had been a part of it at one time. Boss had thanked us more than once and told us if we ever needed anything, to just let him know. It felt good to help people and to even the score on some bad guys. There were way too many of them in the world for my liking, and way too many we were finding out were in our town. With the things Paula told us, we had figured out what was going on around town with all the mail thefts.

These bastards were smuggling drugs around the country. They'd ask various crafters to put a little box or gift they brought in the box with whatever they'd bought and send them together. If the crafter didn't want to do it, then it wasn't long until things began to disappear from their front porches, or their houses were broken into. Deliveries of materials the crafter used to mail their merchandise would come up missing, and they all had their names on it. So, if the drugs were found, the crafter would take the fall, not the drug dealers. It was really ingenious when you thought about it.

It was late when I came through the door at Skye's house. I made sure I was quiet so I wouldn't wake anyone. When I was passing the kitchen, I saw a faint glow of a light. I glanced in and saw Jackie sitting at the kitchen counter. She had a cup of what I thought was hot tea in front of her. I went in. "Why're you still up, Jackie? It's midnight. You have a long day tomorrow."

She shrugged and then sighed. "I'm worried about what's going to happen when they find out we're not going to pay anymore. I'm afraid of what they might do." I sat down and took her hand.

"They're not going to do anything to harm you or your kids. Me and my club and hell, the Time Served club will make sure of it. If shit gets a little hot, we'll move you all to the compound. Hell, that might be the answer," I mumbled.

"Answer to what?"

"To how I can get your daughter living with me. Please don't take this wrong, I love the fact you let me stay here and you seem cool with me staying in her room. I mean we're all adults, but most parents wouldn't like that. I just would love to have her living with me in our own place. Hell, getting her to stay that one night was like pulling teeth. I know she worries about you and the boys. We'd never leave the three of you unprotected, but I can't help wanting her there."

"I've not asked her anything about the two of you. I didn't want to rock the boat. But is living together where you see this going so soon?"

"I do. I know this kind of thing scares her. I'm trying to take it slow, but she's it for me. I want everything—house, kids, marriage, you name it. She's getting there, but this would help me to be more patient about the rest."

"Wow, you really do care for her."

"Don't tell her, but I love her. I'm waiting to drop that on her. I want to be sure she doesn't run for the hills. It kills me that guys are supposed to be the ones who are all scared of commitment. Your daughter sure shakes up that notion." She laughed. I spent a few more minutes talking to her and then she said she was going to bed. I tiptoed into Skye's bedroom. She was curled up in bed sound asleep. I'd showered at the compound, so I just stripped and slid under the covers with her. She rolled over and wrapped herself around me. She never woke up. I had to smile at her.

She was the one thing I'd never hoped for, but God had granted. I wish Mom and my sisters didn't live so far away. I wanted them to meet her. I planned to tell Mom about her when we had our next call. I usually called her the first of the month to catch up. She'd remarried two years after Dad died and then had my sisters Selena and Shana, one right after the other. I liked her husband, Randall. It had been tough the first few years, then I'd realized he wasn't trying to take my dad's place. Selena was now sixteen and Shana fifteen. Sometimes I was glad I didn't have to see them dating. I was a tad protective of them and my mom. Thinking of how my mom would react to the news I'd found someone had me smiling.

She'd probably jump on a plane to race over here to see for herself. She'd despaired over me ever settling down. I'd been hearing from her since I turned thirty how she wanted to have grandkids before she died. Hell, she was only fifty-five. She acted like she had one leg in the grave. Randall would grin and roll his eyes when she did it. I knew she just wanted me to find happiness, but I hadn't thought that was going to happen. At least I hadn't until some little dynamo came into my life and knocked me on my ass. Mom would love her, especially since she stood up to me and didn't take crap. Mom had never been one to take crap either, not even from my dad when he'd get on one of his kicks. I loved my dad, but I knew he had issues. Alcohol had been the main one. It was ultimately what killed him. He'd never been abusive, but he could get loud and holler. When he'd get like that, she'd lock him out of the house. He'd learned not to do it very often. Despite everything, he had loved her, and I knew she'd loved him. She just couldn't get him to seek the help he needed. I settled around Skye and my eyes got heavy. It felt damn good to have someone to hold as you fell asleep.

Executioner: Chapter 9

Things had been going really well with me and Skye for more than a week. It was our new record. I'd essentially moved into the house with her and her family. We went about our day doing our usual things. I'd work at the dealership while she was at the flower shop. In the evening, all of us were at the house for dinner, though a couple of times, I got her to come to the compound and hang out for the evening.

However, today, I wasn't at the dealership or the compound, I was at Blossoms. Sin, Drake, and Saint were with me. Today was the first of the month. The extortion money was due to be picked up. We were ready for whoever came to do it. I couldn't wait to get my hands on one of the bastards who'd ran Skye and Tanner off the road and threatened her. My fists itched to beat the hell out of them.

Instead of having our bikes sitting out front announcing we were here, we'd come in my truck and Drake's car, and we'd parked them down the street. As we waited, we kicked back in Jackie's office unless there were things to carry. I'd found they often were toting around boxes of shit way too heavy for them. As soon as Skye got more comfortable and we rearranged things at the shop, they were going to get some more help. Tanner and Tyson helped when they could, but they both had school and homework.

It was already two and there had been no sign of extortionists. Skye had told us they usually came between one and five. I wanted them to come now. I got up and paced to the door of the office and looked out into the storage area. Jackie and Skye were out front. We'd arranged for one of them to text me as soon as they saw one of the guys.

"If you pace any more, you're going to wear a hole in the tile," Sin told me with a grin.

"Shut up, you'd be pacing too if it was your old lady out there waiting for a damn threat."

"Ah, did you hear that, Saint? His old lady is out there. Did you know he had claimed an old lady?"

"Nope. I haven't heard that. Maybe he's confused," Saint said with a smirk on his face. They were getting a jab in at me. I hadn't officially claimed her in church or explained our whole backstory. I rolled my eyes.

"Fuck you two, you know she's been claimed. I plan to do it in church this week. We've been a bit busy with kidnappings, rescues, and shit. Do you think I'd move in with a woman I hadn't claimed?"

"Well, we thought you might be having some issues with your memory. Or maybe it's us, because I don't recall hearing how in the hell you and Skye met. It's obvious as hell it wasn't that day you came to the shop," Sin said with his brows raised. He was calling me to task and wanting to know. He'd been quiet long enough.

"Do you remember when I went to Fort Worth to see Omen at the end of February?" They all nodded. "Well, I stayed all night and came back the next day. That night I went to a bar to have a drink before going back to my hotel. I met her then."

"And let us guess, it wasn't just a conversation in the bar," Saint added.

"Yeah, it was more than a conversation in the bar. Only the next morning when I woke up, she was gone.

I had no idea who she was or where she lived." I wasn't going to give them the dirty details. That was between the two of us. If it had been just some hookup, then I wouldn't have cared.

"But you wanted to know?" Drake asked.

"Hell, yeah. I'd been going nuts trying to figure out how to find her for a month when I came in here, and there she was. You could have knocked me over with a feather. Sin knows what it's like when you find your one."

He nodded. "But she didn't seem too excited to renew that acquaintance," Sin observed.

"No, she wasn't. Seems my woman has trust issues because of her daddy. Bastard ran off ten years ago and left them to fend for themselves—no word or money to help. I'm going to ask Phantom to help me find him soon. I want his ass found. Jackie needs a divorce, and he needs to pay. Jesus, they didn't have enough money to eat right. Skye still tries not to eat until everyone else has. She got into that habit to make sure her brothers got enough." All three of them swore.

"But you've gotten her to see things from your viewpoint. I mean, you're living with her," Saint said with a smile.

"Yeah, but it wasn't easy. After we rescued Paula, she and I had it out."

"What's your plan? Are all of you going to continue to live at their house? Not that it matters, just curious," Sin asked.

"I want us to have a house like you and Lyric at the compound, but I know she won't want to leave her mom and brothers to manage the house alone. She works the shop and several bookkeeping jobs to help pay for everything. Honestly, she likes the accounting stuff. She went to school for it. However, they can't afford to pay other people to work here, so she can't do it full time." I hadn't talked to any of them about my idea to get her to do all of our books. That would be something we'd have to discuss as a club and vote on.

Sin and Saint looked at each other. There was some silent communication between them. All of us did it to various degrees, but they were the best at it. That was one of the things that made them such a great president and VP. Sin looked back at me.

"We have church tonight. Why don't we ask the others what they think of her doing our books for the businesses? I don't think they'll have a problem with it, as long as she's good at it. Then we can see about getting her free from working at the shop. If she needs more clients, then we'll see who else needs help."

I walked over and gave him a fist bump. "Thanks, Pres, I'd love that. I was going to see if the club would be all for it. Believe me, she knows her stuff. I looked at the books she does here. She chases it down to the last penny. She does a few people's books. The most recent are the ones for Jack Bentley's Real Estate office."

"Hell, if Jack let's her, then she has to be good. You know how anal he is. I swear, I'm shocked he's finally stepped down and let the boys run the business," Saint said.

"I couldn't blame him for not wanting to let Jonathan do it. He's always been something of a laze about," Drake popped in. He'd grown up around here like Sin. He knew most of the people. "But Ben has a good head on his shoulders. I have no damn clue how those two can be brothers."

"Well, you know what they say, you can't pick your family. And speaking of family, I have another idea," Sin said with a smile on his face. We all looked at him expectantly.

"You said Skye won't leave her mom and the boys alone to deal with their house. Why don't we take care of it for them? We can just as easily have another house built at the compound. They can have their own place but be near Skye and not have to worry about the financial drain. Hell, we have enough materials and shit to do it for practically nothing. I don't think the rest of the guys would mind. After all, they're Ares' family if they're Skye's. Jackie's a great woman. She deserves a break. And when we get time, we'll make sure jackass pays fucking support and gives that poor woman a divorce," he growled. All of us hated men who hurt women and kids and didn't stand by their obligations.

I felt my throat get tight. I hadn't ever expected them to offer this. I was about to thank Sin for suggesting it, even if the others didn't go for it, when we heard a shout and what sounded like a scuffle coming from the front of the shop. I hit the doorway running.

When we came through the door from the back, it was to find Skye sitting on a guy on the floor. He was swearing and trying to get her off him. Jackie was standing next to them with a glass vase in her hand. I think if he got loose, she was going to beat him over the head with it. All of us froze for a second then broke out laughing. They looked at us.

"When you're done having your laugh, do you want to come get him? He's kind of hard to hold down. He's wiggly as a damn worm," Skye snapped. As she spoke, he suddenly bucked up hard and sent her spilling to the floor. I was on him in a flash. I slammed my boot onto his back to hold him down and leaned down to offer her my hand.

"Are you okay, Baby Girl?" She took it and stood, dusting off the seat of her pants.

"I'm fine. Just pissed. Let's get him in the back. I don't want any customers coming in and seeing this. That's all we need." I eased up my foot. Drake jerked him to his feet. Jackie went to the front door and flipped the sign to *closed* and locked the door. All of us headed to the storage room. The guy struggled but he had no chance of getting away.

In the office, Drake slammed his ass down in one of the chairs. That's when we got a really good look at him. Jesus Christ, he was just a young punk. He looked like he was no more than eighteen or nineteen. His pimply face was white, and I could see he was scared to death. I gestured to him.

"Is he one of the ones who comes in here to do the pickup?" Both of the women shook their heads no.

"Then how do you know he's here for that?" God help us if they'd overreacted, and this was just some kid who'd come in to get flowers for his girl or mom.

"Well, when he came up to me and said he was here for the envelope, I kind of figured he wasn't here for flowers," Skye said sarcastically. I couldn't resist. I stepped over to her and gave her a kiss. When I broke it off, I tapped her on the lips with my finger.

"There, is that better? You get cranky when you've been too long without a kiss," I teased her. I loved when she got like this. She made me want to laugh. She shoved at me.

"Quit it, Ex. This is serious. And I'll show you cranky

if you keep pissing with me." Sin cleared his throat, getting us back on track. I turned back to our captive. He was still watching every move we made.

"Okay, let's get down to it. Who're you? And why did you come in here asking for an envelope?" He swallowed nervously, and his eyes darted around the room. Drake hunkered down in front of him. He pulled out his wallet and flipped it open. Even though he was off duty, the main reason we asked him to be here was to be able to show an official police presence. He showed the kid his badge. His eyes almost bugged out of his head.

"I'm Detective Marshall with the Tenillo Police Force. I suggest you answer the questions. It'll go much easier on you. Or do I have to place you under arrest?" As long as he wasn't arrested, Drake didn't need to read him his rights. That left us with a lot of leeway in the questioning.

"My name is Bobby Sims. I'm sorry, man, I didn't mean any harm."

"So, you go around extorting money out of people, but you don't mean any harm?" Saint asked. Bobby's face got paler which I didn't think was possible. He broke out in a sweat.

"E-extorting money? I don't know what you're talking about! I swear. Listen, dudes, I was told to come in here and to speak to one of the women behind the desk. I was to ask them for an envelope. No one said anything about money or extortion."

"What did you expect to be in the envelope, flower petals?" Skye sneered.

"I don't know. I didn't really think about it."

"Who sent you to pick it up?" Drake asked.

"Just some guy. I don't know his name. He paid me

fifty bucks to do it."

"Have you ever spoken to this man before? What does he look like? What were you supposed to do with the envelope once you got it?" Drake fired off one question right after the other. He was using a classic questioning technique of not letting the person think in between questions.

"I-I, no I haven't spoken to him before. He caught me down the street. Said he had to get back to work but his lady had an envelope for him. Asked if I'd get it for him. Then he gave me the money. He was kind of tall, maybe my height. His head was buzz cut, and he had a tattoo of a tear under his eye. He kind of looked Hispanic," he spewed out.

"And what were you supposed to do with the envelope?" Sin reminded him of the question.

"I was to hold on to it and meet him at the playground over at Crockett Elementary at six." Crocket was a few blocks over from Blossoms.

"Did he tell you anything else? Was there anyone with him?" Drake asked. He frowned. He was thinking the same thing I was.

"Only that I'd better not open the envelope and not stand him up. I didn't see anyone with him, but there were people walking by." Drake stood up and sighed.

"You stay right here, we'll be back." He gestured for the rest of us to follow him out into the storage area. He closed the door to the office. "Jesus, that's a dead end. They obviously suspected or knew we were here, so they sent in a decoy. If they were right about us being here, they'd be safe. If they were wrong, they'd get the envelope later."

"So, we should still go to the school at six, right?"

Skye asked.

"We can, but I expect they won't be there. They most likely had someone watching the shop to see if he left or not. Since he's been in here so long, they have to know we caught him. I don't imagine anyone will meet him at six. Shit!"

"What do we do with the boy?" Jackie asked. This was the first time she'd said a word since we found them. I could tell she was worried about him. Typical mom, she was thinking of her boys.

"We could take him in, but we can't charge him for being stupid. I suggest we get his information and then I'll take him home. I'll make sure he knows if he's contacted by anyone, to call me immediately. Don't worry, I'll scare him without scarring him for life. He needs to realize you have to be smarter than this. Otherwise, one of these days, someone is going to get him into trouble he can't get out of," Drake reassured her. I hated to let our one lead go, but Drake was right. He was a patsy.

"Do you think it would do us any good to have him and me talk to a sketch artist and see if we might get an idea of the guy we're looking for? The tat on the face sounds like the one guy I've seen and talked to," Skye asked. She was frowning.

"It's worth a try. Maybe you could tell them what you remember about the other guys. It's a longshot, but we don't have much else to go on right now. It might be a good idea to get some of the other business owners down to the department to do it as well," Drake mused. We talked another minute or so, then Drake went back in to talk to Bobby. The rest of us went back out to the front and reopened the shop. They couldn't afford to lose any business.

I took Skye in my arms. "Baby, we'll get them. I know it seems like we won't, but we will. It's almost three. I'm going to go kick back in the office unless you need me for carrying stuff. If anyone else comes in, text me, okay?" She nodded and gave me a quick kiss.

"I will. Go get some work done. I saw you had your laptop. I'll let you know if anyone comes in, but I doubt it. God, this is so frustrating." I let her walk over to her mom and they got started on stocking the display cases. I shook Sin and Saint's hands.

"Thanks for the help. Wish we'd gotten more. I'm staying here until they close for the day. Are you guys going with Drake or do you need a ride back to the compound?"

"I texted Dash to come pick us up. We'll see you later tonight for church. You have a lot to tell the guys," Sin said with a grin on his face. Saint smiled too. I chuckled and gave them a chin lift. It wasn't long before Drake and Bobby left and then they got picked up by Dash. After one more look around the shop, I went to the back. I needed to do a little work and then go to the clubhouse. It was time to officially claim Skye.

◄◄► ◄◄► ◄◄► ◄◄►

At seven that evening, we were all gathered around the table in church. The rest of the day had gone by without any more excitement. I'd dropped the women off at the house and told them I'd be back after church. It was family game night. I had to be there to challenge whoever was the champ of the game. It was Skye's turn to pick the game. Who would have thought a big badass biker would look forward to game night?

Sin had updated the guys on our stakeout. They all

groaned when they heard we hadn't caught any of the bad guys, just a dumb kid. Talon, our treasurer, had just gotten done updating us that he'd have April's financials for us by the next meeting. His talk of money was a perfect way to get the guys onto the discussions I wanted to have. Sin must have thought the same.

"Thanks, Talon. And that brings us to the other main topics for tonight's meeting. Our brother, Executioner, has some things he wants to say and ask. Ex, the floor is yours." I nodded my thanks and stood up. I looked around the room.

"I wanted to make it official and let you all know. I'm claiming Skye as my old lady. I know we usually vote and talk about it, so that's what I want to do." The room broke out in smiles. Pitbull was the first to say something.

"Well, I don't know, Ex. I mean, you just don't seem that serious about her. You only spend all your time outside of work with her, neglect your brothers, live in her house, and hang with her family. Are you sure it's serious?" He gave me a taunting look. The others all laughed.

I flipped him off which made him laugh harder. "Yeah, I'm sure, dipshit. I know you all wondered how I knew her because it's obvious we met before a month ago. Skye and I met two months ago, that night I was in Fort Worth visiting Omen. I'd been looking for her since and then found her when we went to the flower shop last month. Let's just say, she had some reservations about us, and I had to convince her they were unwarranted. Now, do I have your support on this? And the answer had better be yes, or you and I will be having a talk you won't like," I threatened. Not that I thought they'd say no, but it was nice to remind them who their enforcer was.

"Well shit, then I say yes. Don't want to meet Executioner in the fucking dark," Talon piped up. The others quickly voted yes as they teased me. It was official. Skye was my old lady. Thanking all of them, I got to the other part.

"That brings up another thing. You know I've essentially been living with them. I want us to build a house here like Sin and Lyric have."

They all shouted out, "Hell yeah."

I continued, "But she's not going to want to leave her mom and the boys alone. She helps them financially with the bills. In fact, she works all day at the shop and then works at night and on the weekends doing other people's accounting."

"Jesus, how does she have time to sleep?" Wrecker asked.

"She doesn't have a lot, although she does have more than one client. However, it's what she loves to do and went to school to learn. She just can't do it full time."

"Why not?" Phantom asked.

"Because they can't afford to pay anyone else to help in the shop. They barely skimp by as it is. The dad ran off ten years ago and left them high and dry—no word and certainly no support. It's all on Jackie and Skye."

Before I could get to asking about the second house, the club's books or tracking down the dad, Phantom responded. "Dirty bastard. Give me his name and shit, I'll find him. He'll pay or else." The guys all grumbled their agreement.

"Thanks, Phantom, I was going to ask if you could do that. And when we do find him, he needs to give Jackie a divorce too."

"What do the rest of you think of Skye taking over our books? I mean, if she's good, then I'd rather have family doing them than paying someone else," Talon chimed in.

"She has to be good. Ex says she chases it down to the penny, and she's taken over Jack Bentley's books recently," Sin added.

"Well shit, then we should do it," Boomer said excitedly.

"I wanted to ask you what you thought of that idea," I told them. Rampage rapped his knuckles on the table to get our attention.

"While we're at it, what do you all think of us not only getting Pop's construction crew working on a house for Ex and Skye, but a little one for Jackie and the boys? It could be one like Sara's house."

"Thanks, Rampage. That was what Sin had suggested earlier, but I don't want to do that unless you're all okay with it. I know we haven't talked about having others build and live here other than the club, the prospects, and the bunnies."

"Fuck, if we have bunnies living here, why not extended family? We have the room and it's not like we're moving in all our relatives. No way we'd want all those people living here, but Jackie, Tanner, and Tyson are cool. I like the idea of them being somewhere safe where we can help out," Torpedo muttered. Several of the guys had less than stellar upbringings and relationships with their families.

This kicked off a discussion. It took less than fifteen minutes for them all to decide we should do it. I couldn't tell them enough how much it meant to me. I knew it would be mind-blowing for Skye and Jackie. Before we ended the meeting, I told them, "I'll talk to Pop's guys about the houses. Don't say anything to Skye or her family until I do. As for the books, I'll talk to her about them. As for the dad, once you know where he is, Phantom, I'll tell them." They all agreed. I left the clubhouse for home to tell them part of the good news. I couldn't wait until they knew it all!

Skye: Chapter 10

I couldn't believe it. Executioner had come home Friday night and told me that the club wanted me to do all their accounting. That was seven more businesses. Along with Jack's real estate office, Maddie's Diner, Jitters, The Front Porch, and Feather's, a small clothing boutique, I was at twelve businesses. I thought back to that conversation and what had happened afterward.

He'd come home, and we'd spent time with the family playing a game. It was my turn to choose, so I chose *Scrabble*. My brothers had groaned. They hated it because they said Mom and I knew more words than them. That night, Executioner had scraped by the winner. I came in second. After that and a movie, we'd all retired to bed. We were in my room getting ready to shower when Executioner brought up the club's businesses.

"Baby, sit down for a minute before we take our bath." I eased down on the bed. He was looking so serious. I wondered what was up.

"You know I went to the club for church." I nodded. He'd explained last week they had it on Friday nights and what church meant. It was their word for a club meeting. "Well, I'd mentioned to Sin earlier when we were at the shop, how you do books for a few of the businesses around town. Tonight, I was talking to the guys about it. Talon suggested we let you do our books for the various businesses we own. I mean, he's our treasurer, but he doesn't keep them himself. He hires someone. Why not pay you to do them? The guys all thought it was a great idea. What do you think?"

I stared at him speechless. Had I heard him right? The

Infidels wanted me to do books for their seven businesses? I knew it was seven because he'd told me one night all the ones they owned. "Slade, did I hear you right? They want me to do the books?" He nodded. "But why? They have no idea if I'm even any good at it!"

"Of course they do. You not only have balanced books for ages for Blossoms, but you do Jack, Maddie, and Gigi's books. Jack alone tells them you know your shit." He sat down to wrap an arm around me. I sat there for a minute thinking. I hated to seem too eager, but if they were serious, I couldn't say no.

"If they're positive, then I'd love to do it. Not just because of the extra money, but because I love to do it. Wow, why did they decide that?"

"Babe, we'll always go with family over strangers or friends." I looked at him.

"Family? I'm not family." He gently pushed me until I was lying flat on the mattress. He hovered over top of me.

"What do you mean, you're not family? You're my old lady, that makes you family." He tenderly kissed my lips. I pushed him up.

"Old lady? What in the hell does that mean?"

"You've seen Sin with Lyric, Hook with Paula, and Boss with Jenn. That's an old lady. For bikers, the woman we're with and want to spend our damn life with is our old lady. It's the biker equivalent of a wife."

"And I'm your old lady?"

He growled. "Fuck yeah, you are. I told you I was all-in, Skye. That wasn't bullshit. I claimed you to the guys tonight. It's official. If you're going to try and argue that you're not, we're going to have one helluva argument to-night. You're my woman and I'm your man, period." As he looked at me with a frown on his face, I laid my hand up

CIARA ST JAMES

under his t-shirt. His skin was so damn hot.

"Well, then if you're my man, why don't you take off these clothes and let me show you how happy you just made me? Not only with the work, but especially with that old lady claim," I whispered as I scraped my nails lightly over his nipples. He shuddered and then sat up. In a flash he had his clothes off and was starting to tear at mine. I didn't stop him. I wanted him to be touching every square inch of me with his naked, chiseled body.

When he had both of us naked, he ran his eyes up and down the length of my body. His tongue sneaked out to lick his lips. He went to lower his head on my breasts, but I knew if I let him touch me, I wouldn't get my turn. I stopped him with a hand on his shoulder.

"Not yet. I want to have a chance to explore. Lie down on your back, Slade. Tonight, it's your turn to be pampered." His eyes flared, but he relaxed back onto his back. I started at his mouth and kissed from there down to his neck and chest, where I stopped long enough to flick each nipple with my tongue. Then I worked down his ribs and stomach until I got to the glorious beast he had between those legs.

I eased back so I could kneel between his legs. His cock was standing up proud against his stomach. I grasped him at the base and slowly moved my hand up and down twice. He moaned and his hips jerked. I ran my fingertips all over his sac and then up his length to circle the head. I made sure I didn't touch the head.

"Shit, baby, that's torture. Stop teasing me," he growled. I laughed but didn't stop. I wanted to drive him out of his mind like he did me every night. I lowered my head and licked around his balls. As he shivered, I sucked first one and then the other into my mouth and gently applied suction and lashed them with my tongue. This got a reaction.

He moaned louder and his hands fisted in the sheet. I was happy to see him liking it.

So far, I hadn't gone down on him. He was always so adamant about him pleasuring me and that I got off more than once before he did, not to say he didn't get any pleasure. If his shouts and words were anything to go by, he got a lot. But I wanted to give him more than that. Besides, I wanted to practice my skills. He had way more experience than me.

After I was done teasing his balls, I licked up his length to the head. I stopped and looked at his cock and then up at his face. He was watching me. His amber eyes were bright. As he watched, I stuck out my tongue and lightly flicked just the tip with it. He growled. I moaned. I could taste his precum on my tongue. It was slightly salty but otherwise had no taste. Gripping the base firmer, I opened my mouth and lowered it until the head was in my mouth. He filled my mouth and made it so I couldn't close it even a fraction. I slid my tongue around the head and sucked just a little.

"Jesus, Baby Girl, give me more. I'm going to fucking die if you don't," he groaned out. I couldn't smile with his cock in my mouth, but I wanted to. It looked like my man liked what I was doing, and I hadn't even gotten started.

Now, I'll admit, I'd been thinking of doing this to him. In the past, I'd only ever gone down on my previous boyfriend a couple of times. It never got far before he would tell me to stop. Then it was a couple of minutes of his fumbling and thrusting and he was done. It had been a disappointment. With Executioner, it was never like that. Sometimes, I couldn't think after we were done.

In preparation for when I got my chance, I'd been watching some videos online and reading a few articles. I wanted it to be the best experience for him as possible. I knew with practice I'd get better. I was also curious to find out what he tasted like.

I concentrated on taking more and more of him in my mouth. As I did, I made sure to caress and tease his balls and shaft. I licked and sucked when I'd pull back. Soon, I was lost in a rhythm. I was taking him deeper. Suddenly, he was hitting the back of my throat. I didn't gag. I was one of those people who couldn't even gag themselves to vomit. I was happy to see that this didn't do it either. He gave a shout as I kept pushing and he slipped further down the back of my throat.

His hands came down and he gripped my hair. He pulled on it slightly and hissed out, "Goddamn! That's fucking amazing. Jesus, take me, Baby Girl. I want that throat of yours tightening around me." I swallowed. I'd read that it squeezed a guy's cock and felt good. It must have been true, because he swore and then was thrusting his cock in and out of my mouth and throat. He was going faster. His breath was coming out in pants. I concentrated on sucking and taking him deeper. I tightened my mouth on him and massaged his tight sac in my hand.

"Do you want to swallow or not? If not, tell me, because I'm gonna blow," he hissed. I tightened my hand on his base and kept sucking. A few more thrusts and he stopped moving and held himself inside of me. He came, moaning my name as he jerked in my mouth. Cum filled my mouth, and I swallowed as fast as I could. He was coming so fast and so much, I was afraid it would leak out. The taste was saltier and had a slight sweet taste compared to the precum. I eagerly kept swallowing.

When he was finally done coming, I slid my tongue up and down, licking him and then sucked gently on the head. He came up off the bed and pulled me off him and up to his mouth. He took my mouth and sank his tongue inside. He moaned more as he tasted his cum in my mouth. I found the idea made me even hotter. He kissed the hell out of me and then he rolled me over and got between my legs. "My turn," he muttered and then he lowered his head.

He was like a wild animal. He licked, sucked, fondled, and bit at my folds and clit until I was mindless. My legs were starting to shake, and I knew I was close to coming. His fingers were thrusting in and out of my pussy. The sound of the wet suction was loud. I was too damn gone to care or be embarrassed. I grabbed his silky hair in my hand. It had come loose from his tie and was lying all over my thighs and stomach.

He looked up at me and thrust his fingers in and out a few times as he watched my face. My eyes grew heavy. I was about to come. He latched onto my clit and sucked then flicked it with his tongue. I came in a blinding flash. I bit my lip to keep from screaming and letting the whole house know what we were doing. He grunted in pleasure and lapped up all the cream gushing out of me. When I could finally think, he'd kissed his way up my body and kissed me. I eagerly kissed him back.

Afterward, we had laid there for a while just basking in the aftermath, then he took me to get that shower. In there, he proceeded to take me up against the tile wall. I'd fallen asleep almost as soon as my head hit the pillow. That was three days ago.

It was now Monday, and I was back at work. He was at the dealership. He'd wanted to stay with us to be sure no one bothered us, but I told him it wasn't necessary. I didn't think they'd do anything during the middle of the day, when anyone could walk in and see it. He'd gone to work but not before making sure I had the whole club's numbers as well as Boss' and his guys.

I checked the clock. It was almost one. I needed to head out if I was going to make my appointment. I went to find Mom. She was in the back unpacking some materials. "Mom, I'm heading out. I'll be back as soon as I can."

"Alright, honey. See you later. Be careful." She gave me a hug and I left. As I pulled into the parking lot of my appointment, I thought about how different everything was in just a few months. It was kind of crazy to think of the differences. I grabbed my purse and got out of the car then headed inside. I couldn't miss this.

As I pulled into the parking lot of the club's Harley dealership, I took a deep breath to calm myself. I'd left my appointment and came straight here. I needed to tell Executioner about it. I'd had two appointments this afternoon, but it was the last one that had been the most surprising. Lord, everything was in crazy mode, and overnight my accounting business seemed to be exploding.

I walked into the showroom. Behind the desk was one of the girls who worked there along with Sin's mom, Sara. When I got to the desk, Sara looked up and smiled at me. "Hello, Skye, it's good to see you, honey. I expect you're here to see Executioner. Go on back, he's in his office." She pointed toward the door that must lead to the back office.

"Thank you, Sara. Good to see you, too." As I walked off, I saw the young woman beside her give me a dirty look. What in the hell was up with that? I pushed the door open and saw it led to a short hallway. There were a couple of doors off to the left and one at the end of the hall. That was the one with the sign on it saying, *office*. I headed for it. As I got close, I saw the door wasn't all the way closed. I could hear Ex's voice. He was talking to someone. Maybe he was in a meeting. I hesitated as I tried to decide if I should knock or not. That's when what he was saying became clear.

"Omen, man, I can't tell you how happy that makes me." Then there was a pause. I didn't hear anything, so he had to be on the phone. I knew Omen was an old Marine buddy of his. I turned around to go wait in the front for him to get done. I'd text him and tell him I was here. Just as I turned around, I heard him saying more.

"You won't regret it. When you get here, we'll have a helluva party. We'll make sure to have the alcohol flowing and the women lined up. I can't wait for us to have our usual fun. Remember that night we were in Thailand? This will put that to shame. Be prepared for us not to be able to move the next day."

My heart dropped and I felt slightly faint. Was he seriously talking about him and Omen hooking up with other women when he got here? I had to be mistaken. I got closer to the door.

"Skye? Yeah, she'll be around but not all the time. We'll still have time to do our thing. You know, manly stuff that she doesn't need to know about." I stepped back. He was talking about it, and it sounded like he thought he'd be doing it and hiding that from me. Well, too bad for him, I'd heard his plan. I turned and rushed back to the front. When I came out of the back, Sara was nowhere in sight, but the other girl was. She gave me a smirk as I rushed out.

I got in my car and sat for a moment, waiting to stop

shaking. Oh my God, I'd messed up. I'd let him in, and he was just like most men. He was just another cheating and lying bastard! I turned on the car and squealed out of the parking lot. Jesus, I needed to think. No way I was going to be with someone who would do that. All thoughts of telling him about my day fled my mind.

I had a couple of hours before he was supposed to stop by the shop, and we'd go home. I had to get myself in order. I wouldn't belittle myself by breaking down in front of him or telling him I knew what he was up to. I drove until I came to the park not far from our house. I went to the parking area under the trees and stopped. I laid my head down on my steering wheel. Tears started to run down my cheeks. Sobs were loud in the car. I had to wrap my arms around my stomach. It hurt and I felt sick.

I sat there for over an hour. It took me that long to get myself somewhat calm. But by the time I dried my tears, I had the beginning of a plan. A plan that didn't include Slade Ashton. I headed home rather than back to the shop. I'd texted Mom and she said it was quiet. I let her know I was going to go home instead of back there.

Back at the house, I went to my room and grabbed my laptop. It was time to do a little research. It was just after six when my phone dinged, alerting me that I had a text. I glanced at it. It was Executioner.

Executioner: I'm at the shop, why did you go home alone and not tell me?

I wanted to tell him to go screw himself, but I didn't. I sent him a short text back.

Me: My appointments ran long and it wasn't worth going back. I got involved in work and forgot.

A few seconds later came his response.

Executioner: I'm on my way home. Don't leave.

I sneered at the phone. He had no idea what was coming his way.

Me: Okay.

I went back to working. It was twenty minutes later that I heard his truck roar into the driveway. I steeled myself to face him. He came striding into the kitchen where I was set up working at the table. He came straight to me.

"Skye, what the hell, you should've gone back to the shop? You know I don't want any of you here alone. It's dangerous. Those guys haven't been caught yet." I knew he was worried about them. I was too, but right now that wasn't my main concern. I fought down my urge to scream at him and hit him.

"I simply got caught up. I wanted to get started on my new client. Hal hired me to do the books for the hardware store."

He sat down and took my hand. "Baby, that's great. I know how much you want to be able to do that more. But please, don't come here alone. Not until we catch them." It killed me to see what you would think was concern in his eyes. He was a really good actor. I'd been taken in.

I casually moved my hand back to close my laptop. "I won't forget. I didn't know it was so late until you texted. I need to start dinner, then I have a lot of work to do." I got up and started to pull things out of the fridge. He sat there frowning.

"Are you okay, Baby Girl? You seem off."

"I'm fine. Just thinking about what I need to do first. You know, I'm going to be really busy, why don't you go to the club tonight and hang with the guys? You haven't been there in a few days." I wanted to get him out of the house. He got up and came to stand behind me. His lips skimmed my neck.

"I'd rather stay here with you," he whispered. I could feel his erection growing as he pressed into me. I wanted to puke. No way I could let him touch me. Not knowing he was going to be with other women. Hell, he might have already been doing it. I wasn't with him all the time. I gritted my teeth.

"I know and I'd like you to too, but I'm not going to be done until at least midnight. Why don't you go and come back around then? The boys will have a lot of homework and Mom will be doing whatever. Go, have fun. I don't want your brothers to think I'm keeping you away from them."

After a few more minutes of back and forth, I got him to agree to go. It was all I could do to get through dinner while he laughed and talked with my family. He acted like he was in his element. When he left at eight, I let him kiss me. I responded enough so he wouldn't get suspicious. As soon as he was gone, I raced to my room. I had to get this done before he got back.

I quickly grabbed clothes from the closet and my dresser, then I went into the bathroom to get my stuff there. I wanted to cry seeing his stuff sitting and hanging alongside mine. When I came back out, Mom was standing by my bed looking at my suitcase. She looked at me in confusion and surprise.

"Skye, what in the world are you doing? Are you and Executioner going to the compound? You guys didn't say anything, though I'm not surprised he wants you to live there with him." I held up my hand to stop her from saying anything else. Each word was like a blade to my heart.

"I'm not going to the compound. I need to get out of here. I need to think, and I can't do that with him in my face." She gasped and grabbed my hand.

"What is going on? What happened?" Seeing her concern caused my tears to form. Next thing I knew, I was sitting on the bed and spilling out everything to her. When I was done, she was rocking me and trying to explain how I must be wrong.

"Honey, I don't know what to say, but there's just no way he'd do that. You had to have misheard him. He loves you, Skye. I don't think it's fair for you to leave without giving him a chance to explain."

"I don't want to hear his lies. He's a master at fooling people. He sure fooled me into thinking he was different. But he's not. He's just like dad. And I'm not going to take that from anyone. Please, I know you don't like this, but I need you to be my support in this. I just need a few days and then I'll be able to tell you what I'm going to do," I begged her.

Her face was sad, and she looked like she was going to cry. I hated to do this to her, but I had to do it. Otherwise, I'd end up living a nightmare. My worst nightmare if I was honest. Reluctantly, she nodded. "Okay, I'll support you. But don't stay away too long. If you're not home in a week, I'm coming after you. I want you to call me every day."

"Mom, if I do, he'll want to talk to me."

"He doesn't need to know where you are. I'll tell him I haven't heard from you. Because, sweetheart, if he is doing or planning to do what you said, he doesn't deserve to be a part of our lives. What do you want me to tell him when he comes back tonight?"

"Tell him I needed space and I'll be in touch when I'm ready."

"Nothing else?"

"No, absolutely nothing else." She hugged me, then she helped me to finish packing. I hoped to get out the door without the boys being any wiser. My luck wasn't that good. When we came out of my room, Tanner was standing in the hall with an angry look on his face. He stomped up to me.

"I'm going to kill him." I cringed. Shit, he'd heard what I had told Mom—at least some of it anyway.

"No, you're not. You're going to keep your mouth shut and let me handle this. You can't tell him anything about what you heard, Tanner. Promise me."

He stood looking belligerent. My heart sank and then he sighed.

"Whatever. I won't tell him what I heard, but don't stay away long. We'll deal with him like we always do, as a family. Take care, Sis." He hugged me. That had the tears ready to flow again. After a quick kiss on his cheek, I went out to my car. Mom stood and watched as I backed out of the driveway. I wish I could have told Tyson goodbye, but that would have broken my resolve, and I'd need all of it. The night stretched out in front of me as I took the highway toward Wichita Falls.

Executioner: Chapter 11

When I pulled into the driveway at the house, the feeling I'd had all night came over me a hundred times worse. Something was wrong. My gut had been nagging me since I'd come home from work and talked to Skye. She had seemed off, and I'd let her talk me into going to the clubhouse for a few hours. She said it was so she could work, but now, I was certain it wasn't. I got off my bike and rushed inside. As I unlocked and opened the door, I was surprised to see Tanner standing in the entryway. He had his arms crossed and a pissed look on his face. I shut the door.

"What's wrong, Tanner?"

"Get your stuff and get out."

"What? What in the hell? Where's your sister?"

"It doesn't matter. I'm the man of the house, and I say you need to leave. Get your stuff and go. We don't want you here. Don't bother to come around the shop either. We'll take care of our family. We don't need lying ass-holes in our lives," he half-yelled.

I grabbed him by the shoulders. He struggled to get away, but he was no match for me. I gave him a tiny shake to get him to look at me. "Tell me what is going on. Where's Skye and your mom?"

"I'm right here," I heard softly. Jackie stepped into the dim light. I could see her face was drawn, and she looked tired. My heart began to pound.

"Jackie, what's going on? Where's Skye? What in the hell is Tanner talking about?"

"She's not here. She left for a while. We want you to

leave," she told me. My legs got weak. *Skye left. When? Why? Where?* All that raced through my mind as I stared at her.

"Why did she leave? Where is she?" I almost shouted. I saw her flinch. Shit, I was scaring her. I tried to calm down.

"She left and told me to tell you that she needs space and she'll be in touch when she's ready."

I stumbled over to the couch and sat down. "Where is she? I need to talk to her. She can't leave me."

"Executioner, please just go. It's not going to do anyone any good for you to stay here. My daughter will decide what she wants, and we'll back that. Right now, she wants space and time. We're giving that to her."

"What am I supposed to do while she's off somewhere getting her space and time?" I growled. I was close to losing my cool. Not that I'd hurt them, but I certainly wanted to put my fist through something.

"Why don't you go back to your club and screw one or all those women you keep there. That's what you do after all, isn't it?" Tanner yelled. His words hit me like a ton of bricks. I jumped to my feet and stomped over to him.

"I don't touch anyone but your sister. What the fuck is wrong with you? Why would you even say that?" He looked at his mom. She was giving him a pleading look, but she didn't seem to be surprised at his accusation like I was. As that fact registered, a sick feeling came over me. God, please don't tell me Skye thinks I'm cheating on her.

"Jackie, she doesn't think I'm cheating on her, does she?" She didn't answer me, which was an answer. "Why? Damnit, why would she ever think that?" I was tugging on my hair. My head was whirling. Surely, this was a nightmare, and I would wake up soon, but her next words confirmed it was very real.

"Because you proved you can't be trusted. That's all we're saying. Leave. I know calling the cops won't do any good, but if you don't then we'll leave." I didn't want to leave. I wanted to make them tell me what I did to prove I couldn't be trusted, but the expressions on their faces told me they weren't going to tell me. They'd closed ranks to protect Skye, to protect her from me. I had no idea why. I reluctantly nodded.

"Let me get my stuff." It killed me to say that. Both of them escorted me to her room and watched as I packed the few things I'd brought and left here. As I did, I noticed some of her clothes were missing along with her girly stuff in the bathroom. Wherever she'd gone, it looked like she planned to be gone for a while.

I was back outside and got on my bike in under ten minutes. As I did, I looked at the two of them. "I didn't cheat on her, and I'm not giving up. You tell her that. Tell her we're not done." I started my bike and took off. It took me less time than usual to get to the compound. As soon as I got there, I went straight for Phantom's trailer. His place was across from mine. I could see a faint light on. I pounded on the door with my fist. If he was with one of the bunnies, tough shit. This took precedence.

When he opened his door a minute later, I saw that he was alone. He was in sweats and peering at me like I was nuts. "What in the hell are you doing, beating down my door at one in the fucking morning?" I pushed past him and stepped inside.

"I need your help. It's Skye." His whole demeanor

changed.

"What happened to her? Where is she?"

"I don't know! She's gone. I went back to the house. She's left and no one will tell me why or where. All Tanner and Jackie said was I'm a liar and cheater. Jesus Christ, Phantom, they all but confirmed she thinks I'm cheating on her. She went somewhere to have space and time to think. She's fucking left me, and I don't know why. I'm not cheating on her. Fuck, she's my old lady. I love her!" I was half-shouting at this point. He pushed me toward a chair.

"Sit down." He went to the counter and picked up a bottle of tequila. He opened it and poured me a shot. He handed it to me. "Take this. It'll help." I threw it back. "Now, start at the beginning and tell me everything." I launched into the details of how she was before I left and then what happened when I went back tonight. He was frowning when I got done.

"I need to grab my laptop. Stay here. We might want to let the others know she's gone too, but first, let me get it." He went down the hall and came back less than a minute later. He sat down and typed on his laptop. "Did anything unusual happen earlier today or yesterday? Anything that might explain her running off."

I racked my brain but came up blank. "Nothing. She had a couple of appointments this afternoon. She got Hal's account. That's what she was going to work on while I was gone. Damnit, Phantom, there's nothing. This came out of nowhere. I need to find her. I need to find out why she thinks this and set her straight. God, I was in the process of building us and her family houses."

"Does she know that?" I shook my head. I had wanted

to surprise her with it when I also gave her the property rag I was having made.

He was looking at his laptop and frowning. "What is it?" I asked, afraid of his answer.

"I can't find her. I was trying to run a search for her phone, but it's not showing."

"What does that mean?"

"It means she's got it off or something is interfering with the signal. Do you know of any place she might go? Anyone she's close to besides her mom and brothers?"

I thought over the conversations we'd had since getting together. I shook my head. "No, she doesn't really have any friends. She doesn't usually leave town, but I got the impression that she's not in town."

"But you met her in Fort Worth. Why was she there? She stayed there, maybe she knows someone and would go to them." I jumped up.

"Fuck, I don't know! She never mentioned anyone, and it's not like I can ask her family." My tirade came to an end when I heard a knock at the door.

Phantom yelled, "Come in." The door opened and in came my brothers one after the other. I looked at Phantom. He shrugged. "They need to know what's happening. I texted them."

"What's happening? Why're you here, Ex and not at home with Skye?" Sin asked me, frowning.

Swallowing the lump in my throat, I gave them a rundown on what had happened. All of them looked frustrated by the time I was done.

"Shit! That blows. And you have no idea how she came to that conclusion? Jeez, Ex, what can we do?" Saint asked me. The others were all nodding.

"I don't know but I know one thing, I'm not giving

up on us. She has to come back, eventually. We need to make sure we have eyes on her family, but I also want to know if Phantom can track her using her phone like he said."

"If she turns it on and leaves it on long enough, then yeah, I should be able to do it. Maybe Preacher has other tricks he knows that can help," he mused. Preacher was the hacker guy for Boss' club. He was a well-known conspiracy theorist and Phantom's idol.

"Do what you need to do to set up for tracing her phone. As soon as it's a more reasonable hour, call Preacher and let him know. It's all-hands-on-deck for this. We need to find our brother's woman, and we'll keep an eye on her family. Not only to be sure she doesn't come back and we don't know it, but also because they're still at risk from those extortionists. They've not made a peep, and it's been four days since they didn't get their money. I don't see them letting that go," Sin said with a dark look on his face.

A few more minutes of talking and we had the start of a plan. I wanted to go roaring off and look for her, but I knew that wouldn't do any good. She could literally be anywhere. Everyone agreed to meet back at the clubhouse at ten. It was Saturday and most weren't working today. I reluctantly went back to my trailer after I thanked all of them.

I sank down on the bed without even bothering to get undressed. I laid there and all I could think about was her. Could I have lost the best thing to ever happen to me? And if I did, why? What made her think I was cheating? How would I be able to stand not being with her for the rest of my life? A month of not knowing who she was almost made me nuts. A lifetime would drive me insane.

⫷❂⫸ ⫷❂⫸ ⫷❂⫸ ⫷❂⫸

By the following afternoon, I was about to go to Blossoms and demand Jackie tell me where Skye was. She hadn't turned on her phone, so Phantom couldn't trace her. He had Preacher helping, and they were digging into seeing if she had a credit card and where she used it, but they were a bust. She didn't seem to have one. Since they had no idea where she went, they couldn't look on traffic cameras or into hotel systems to see if she was staying at one. We were getting nowhere.

I hadn't bothered to go into work today. There was no way I'd be able to concentrate on what was going on. I'd been thinking over every conversation we'd had trying to figure out what had changed her mind about trusting me. Hell, I hadn't looked at a woman since the night I met her, let alone fucked one. It seemed my cock only got hard for one woman. Not that I'd ever try to cheat on her.

I drank down my third cup of coffee for the day. I knew I'd pay for it later and not sleep. But I didn't want to sleep, just in case they got a lead and I needed to run it down. As the club's enforcer, I was used to doing stuff. I protected my club in any way necessary. I wasn't the kind of guy to sit around and do nothing.

Dash and Blake were keeping a watch on the shop and at the house, just in case she came back. I'd texted them dozens of times today to check in. I knew I had to be making them crazy, but they had no idea how important finding her was. The only one who did was Sin. He had Lyric and loved her like crazy. He'd be the same way if Lyric was gone.

As time wore on and evening came, I went back to my trailer. I couldn't stand to see the looks the guys were giving me. It was a mix of pity and concern. They knew I was on edge and all it would take is one little thing to tip me over it.

I was up, blindly watching a show on the television and thinking when a text came over my phone. It was Sin, and he told me to get my ass to the clubhouse. I ran out of there like my ass was on fire. Had they found her? When I came crashing through the clubhouse door, I saw most of my brothers were gathered there. Sin came over to me immediately.

"We didn't find her yet." My stomach clenched in disappointment. "But we do have a problem. Sit down for a second." I took a seat at one of the tables. He sat down as well as Saint and Rampage. The others remained standing around us.

"I got a call from Boss. One of his guys called him. There was a break-in tonight in town. It looks like someone vandalized the flower shop. He's calling Jackie. I texted Blake to follow them to the shop. You know she's going to want to see what the damage is. I figured you'd want to be there, even if Skye's not. This is her family."

I stood up and kicked my chair back into the wall. "Fuck yeah, I'll be there. No way I'm going to let them face this shit alone. Even if they're not helping me find her right now, they're hers. That makes them mine. I'm outta here." I went for the door. Boots thundered behind me.

It took me only a couple of minutes to get my stuff and get on my bike. When I pulled out of the compound, I had an escort. All of my brothers were with me. It warmed the hell out of me to know they had my back.

138

When we pulled into the parking spots in front of the flower shop, I saw Blake pull in right behind Jackie's car. She stopped and then jumped out of the car. Both boys were with her. They all started to run for the shop. I got in front of them. I caught Jackie as Saint and Torpedo caught the boys.

"Jackie, hold on a minute. We don't know if the cops cleared it yet or not. Let me ask one of them."

"I need to know what they did, Executioner. This is because we stopped paying. I knew they'd do something." She practically was crying and trying to get away from me. Tanner was struggling with Saint, but Tyson was standing still, looking like he didn't know what to do. Tanner turned his head to look at me.

"What're you doing here? This doesn't concern you," he snapped.

"Boy, I know you're upset about your sister, but don't think I'll take your mouth. I'm here because you and your family need support. Whether you believe me or not, I'm going to find your sister and we're going to be together. This bullshit about me cheating on her will be laid to rest." As he glared at me, Jackie sagged a little in my arms and laid her forehead down on my chest.

"What are we going to do? The shop is all we have. If we lose it, then that's it. We're done. Maybe Skye is right. We should just sell it and leave. It'll solve so many problems," she whispered. Hearing her say Skye wanted them all to leave sent a flash of pain through my chest. No! No, I wouldn't let it come to that.

Before I could say anything, a guy, who was obviously a detective because of his dress clothes, came over to us. "Mrs. Fulton, I'm Detective Marcus Clinton. I'm handling this case. I need to ask you some questions. Would you come with me?" He studiously ignored me and my brothers. I looked around and caught Wrecker's eyes. He was watching Clinton with narrowed eyes. When he saw me, he shook his head. Ah, this must be one of the ones Boss didn't trust.

"How about you give her a chance to see what was done to her shop? Has it been dusted for prints?" I asked him. His eyes darted to the left to look at me for a second then he was looking back at Jackie.

"We can go down to the station where it's more private to talk about this. There's too many people here," he told her. His attitude was starting to piss me off. I gently handed Jackie off to Pitbull, then I stepped up to get in the detective's face.

"She's not going anywhere without me or one of my brothers. You can talk to her after we see what damage was done. This is her livelihood. We need to know what needs to be repaired and figure out how quickly we can do it so she can open her doors. Why don't you concentrate on finding out who did it?"

He finally looked at me. I could see the disdain and dislike on his face. I didn't know if it was because I was a biker, or if he disliked me telling him what to do. Well, tough shit, he wasn't going to come in here and dictate. If Boss didn't trust him, then I sure as hell wasn't.

"And what is your relationship to Mrs. Fulton, Mr.," he glanced at my rag, "Executioner." He snorted a little as he said it.

"She's my family so that makes this my business. Her daughter is my fiancée. She's not here at the moment, so that leaves me to make sure her mom and brothers are alright. My club is helping with that. We aren't going to let anything happen to them."

"What in the world do you think is going to happen to them? It's simply a bunch of kids who had to cause some trouble because they were bored."

"Really? And you know this how?" Wrecker asked as he joined us. Detective Clinton looked even more angry at seeing him. You could feel the dislike coming off Wrecker and vice versa.

"I've got this, Detective Dickerson. If this involves your gang, I think that's a conflict of interest," he said spitefully. I was about to introduce him to my fist when a car pulled in and Boss got out. He came straight over to us.

"What in the hell is going on here, Clinton?" He didn't ask the rest of us. I got the feeling Wrecker had texted him about the situation here.

Clinton told Boss. "I need Mrs. Fulton to come to the station so I can ask her some questions. This guy here," he gestured to me and said, "is obstructing my investigation."

I laughed. "All I said is she doesn't go anywhere alone, and that we wanted to see what the damage was. You know the situation we're in, Boss. Clinton here also seemed to think since Wrecker and Drake are part of our club, that there's some kind of conflict of interest. I don't know how he got that idea."

Boss stared at Clinton. He didn't say a word, just gave him a hard look. Boss had this presence about him that made most men step back and get the hell out of his way. "Clinton, get the techs down here and check it out. Then we'll let Jackie in to see if anything is missing and what the damage is. The Infidels are her escorts unless I say otherwise. Don't worry about detectives Dickerson or Marshall. I know I can trust them to be impartial and to do their job." Even though he didn't say it, you could tell he didn't have that confidence in Clinton. Clinton's face got red, and he gave a curt nod and stormed off. Boss shook his head.

"I wish I could prove he's a dirty bastard so I could get rid of his ass. But so far, he's slithering under the radar. Jackie, we'll get you in there as soon as possible. It might take a few hours. Why don't you go home and one of us will call you when it's okay to come back? I know we don't know for sure, but my guess is this has to do with you not paying that extortion money."

"I think so too. I don't know what to do. If I don't open the shop, we can't pay the bills. I'll lose everything. Please, see if we can get it cleaned up enough to open as soon as possible," she begged. I could see she was about to crack.

"We won't let that happen. Come with us and we're going back to the house." She didn't put up a fight, which I was thankful for. "Boss, thanks for the help. We appreciate it. Let me know when I can bring her back."

"No problem, Ex. I know you have enough shit on your plate to deal with. It's the least I can do." He clapped me on the shoulder and then went to speak to his other officers. Sin came up to me.

"You take them home. Take Torpedo, Pitbull, and Boomer with you just in case they get any ideas to pay them a visit there. Call me if you need anything. Maybe you'll get lucky and find something." I knew he was now talking about Skye and not the vandals.

"Thanks, Pres. Talk to you later." We got Jackie and the boys back in her car. I took the lead with her behind me and then my brothers riding on each side and behind her. It didn't take long to get to the house. Once we were in the house, I went to the kitchen and started a kettle of water. Jackie liked to drink hot tea, just like Skye.

"Tanner, Tyson, why don't you guys try to get some sleep? You have school tomorrow. Or I guess, I should say today."

"You're not my boss. I'll decide if I go to bed or not," Tanner said snarkily. I didn't hesitate. I walked over to him, grabbed him by the arm, and marched him down the hall to his room. I could hear Jackie asking what I was going to do. I should beat his ass for acting like a brat, but I wouldn't. He was acting hateful because he still thought I'd hurt his sister. I slammed the door shut. He was watching me warily now.

"I'm only going to say this one more time. I didn't cheat on your sister. I have no clue what made her think that, but once I get her back here, we'll straighten that up. Which means, you and I are going to be family whether you like it or not. I know you're upset, but this isn't going to do any good. So, before we go back out there, get it all out of your system."

He flopped down on the end of his bed. "You might not have cheated on her, but you were going to. She heard you. How could you? I thought you loved my sister. Hell, she's not going to come back anyway. She's looking for a job somewhere else. Once she gets one, we're out of here."

I paced around the room. "How do you know that?"

"I heard her on the phone telling Mom that last night. She's not going to be here where she might run into you. Mom told her she needed to think about it more and not do anything out of anger. She cried on the phone. Said it would be too much to bear, seeing you and having no contact."

I sat down beside him and put my head in my hands. It just kept getting worse. "Where is she, Tanner? Please, you have to tell me. I can make this right. I just need a chance to talk to her, to find out what I did or said that made her think I 'm cheating. Jesus Christ, I love her! I want to marry her and spend the rest of my life with her. She doesn't know it, but I'm even having a house built for her and I hope one for you guys. Why would I do all that if I didn't love her?"

He stared at me with his mouth hanging open in astonishment. He blinked a couple of times then stuttered, "Y-you're building houses? Where? Why would you do that? We have a house."

"Because she wouldn't be happy leaving you here. This house is a drain on your family. Your mom and sister work way too hard to keep everything going. In a few years, you'll be out of school and maybe in college or possibly living somewhere else. I want to make sure my woman is happy, That means I take care of her family, and living at our compound like Sin and Lyric is safer."

"She's going to be pissed, but I think the two of you need to talk. If what you just said is true, then this whole thing is a huge misunderstanding. There's no need for you to build us a house." I turned to find Jackie in the doorway.

"It's my need, Jackie, to have you close to us. When we have kids one day, I want them to be able to run over to their grandma's house any time they want. Tell me where she is. As soon as we check out the shop, I'll go get her. She's coming back."

"Okay, I'll tell you as soon as we see the shop. Please, Executioner, don't make me regret this. She's going to be upset with me. If you turn out to be a bastard, she'll never forgive me," she pleaded. I could tell she was torn.

"I swear on everything I hold holy that I won't do that." She gave me one last look then left the room. I had to beat down my excitement and the need to rush the cops through their investigation. I needed to go get Skye and bring her back home.

Skye: Chapter 12

I tried to shake off the nerves. I was back in Tenillo trying to get in and out before Executioner even knew I was here. I should have stayed away, but when Tanner told me what had happened at the shop, I knew that Mom needed me. I was positive I could get in to see her and then leave before anyone was the wiser.

When I got on the outskirts of town, I turned on my phone. I needed to call her and find out if she was at home or the shop. It was five in the morning, but I doubted she was asleep after what happened. As soon as I had a signal, I dialed her number. She answered on the second ring.

"Skye, what in the world are you doing up this early?" I could hear the strain in her voice.

"I'm almost home. Are you there or at the shop?"

"Home? What do you mean? Why would you be home? I thought you were going to stay in Wichita Falls."

"I was but then Tanner called and told me about the break-in at the shop. You should have told me, Mom!"

"I'm going to beat that boy! I told him not to tell you. I can handle this, Skye. You don't need any more stress right now. Get yourself situated."

"I'm not leaving my family to do this alone. It's bad enough I took off and left you shorthanded. I wasn't thinking clearly. I think we need to sit down and talk about selling the shop. This just shows that we need a fresh start. If we leave, then no one will be forcing us to pay them money."

"And you won't have to face Executioner," she said softly. I sighed.

"Mom, I know you think I should talk to him, but I can't. It's too much. I can't take that right now. Please, can we not talk about him?"

She gave a long and weary sigh. "I'm at the shop. The cops have left. Why don't you come here? The boys are with me."

"Okay, I'll be there in ten minutes. Bye." I gripped the steering wheel harder after I hung up. Talking about Executioner made my heart hurt. Like it was being torn from my chest. Even two days later and I was crying at the drop of a hat. I'd gone and done what I thought I'd never do—fall for a guy and then have him be unfaithful. Or at least planning to be.

When I parked behind the flower shop, it was eerily quiet. The only vehicle I saw was Mom's. It was still dark, and all the stores were closed. Not a soul was out and about. I grabbed my purse and hurried inside. I'd barely made it through the back door when I was grabbed and picked up in huge, hard arms. I screamed and lashed out with my feet. Oh God, they'd come back! What had they done to my mom and brothers?

"Skye! Stop it, it's me, Slade. Calm down. I'm sorry, I didn't mean to scare you," a deep voice said urgently. I froze. Executioner was here? The lights flared on and there stood Mom, Tanner, Tyson, Torpedo, Pitbull, and Boomer. Mom was giving me a guilty look.

"You told him? You told him I was here? Why?" I cried out to her. She gave me a pleading look.

"You two need to talk. He was with me when you called, Skye. You need to talk like two adults and figure this out. The shop can wait. He said he has no idea what you're talking about. He needs to know." She gave me a stern look. Damn, she was going to pull the, *I'm the mom, you do what I say look.* I hated that. It still worked on me even though I was a damn adult.

He was still holding me up off the floor. His arms were like hard bands around my ribs and chest. His breath was fanning my hair on my neck. "Put me down. Let's get this over with. And I don't want an audience either," I snapped at him. Maybe it was time to clear the air and get this closure.

Everyone slowly cleared the back room. Ex didn't set me down until we were in the office, and he'd shut the door. As soon as he did, I hurried over to stand behind the desk. I wanted as much distance as possible between us. Just being in his arms for a few minutes had shaken me. I'd wanted to curl up in his arms, cry, and beg him to make it all okay. That only happened in fairy tales and dreams.

"I don't know why she thinks this is necessary but get on with it. Tell me what you want to say. I need to get things straightened out here and then go."

He marched over and stood in front of the desk. He leaned over it. "You're leaving over my dead fucking body! I know you're thinking of selling the shop and the house and moving. Well, I have news for you, Baby Girl. You're not going anywhere but to your house or the compound. And I'm going to be with you. This bullshit stops now. What in the hell were you thinking, running off like that?"

"I was thinking I needed to get away from a lying bastard before I did something I couldn't take back. Like killing his ass and burying him. Don't stand there act-ing all pissed and like you're butt hurt. You did this, not me!" I shouted back. Seeing him and hearing his voice had my blood pressure rising.

"Butt hurt! I'm fucking dying here. You left me, Skye. You left and never said a word. I had to find out from your family. And what do they tell me? That you said I was planning on cheating on you, and you didn't know if I might have already done it. Where the fuck did that come from?" he yelled back. His eyes were lit with anger. That caused mine to flare.

I marched around the desk and got in his face. He might stand a good foot taller, but I wasn't going to take his shit. "I got it straight from your damn mouth. I heard you, Executioner. I heard your big plans to have fun. There's no way in hell I was going to stay with you after hearing that. I can do this on my own. I don't need a man. All men do is let you down and tear out your fucking heart."

"I never said I was going to cheat on you! You've lost your mind. When did I say it?"

"So, you deny that you and your good buddy, Omen, aren't planning to have a big party when he gets here?"

He looked at me for a moment. "How did you know he was coming? I didn't tell you."

"Oh, I see. It was supposed to be a secret, was it? I heard you on the phone at the dealership that day. I came to talk to you, and you had the door cracked. I was going to go wait out front until I heard all your plans for drinking and having the women lined up. I believe you were going to relive a good time you two had in Thailand."

He rocked back and looked at me in astonishment. Ah ha, he remembers now, I bet. I turned around and went toward the door. We were done talking. He now knew what clued me in. As I went, I told him, "It's over. I'm not going to spend my life with a cheater and a liar, for however long that would be. You'll be moving on soon, anyway. I'm not going to live with resentment and hate. I know what that's like."

As my hand grabbed the door handle, he jerked me back and turned me around. I tried to shove him away, but it was no use. He didn't budge an inch. "Jesus Christ, Skye, stop trying to leave. God, Baby Girl, why didn't you tell me you heard that? You misunderstood it."

I gave a humorless laugh. "Oh, I misunderstood what women lined up means? Silly me. How dumb. Just let it go. Just walk away. We can pretend we never met. I'm not going to stay here. You won't have to see us. I don't want anything from you." I was now almost sobbing.

"I'm not going to forget you! Yes, Omen is coming, and I was going to throw him a party. There's going to be alcohol and of course the bunnies, but I wasn't going to be fucking them."

"If that's true, why did you say I wouldn't be around all the time? Why would it matter if I was if you weren't going to be with them?"

"He asked if you were living at the compound with me, and if I'd be able to spend time with him since I was head over heels for you. That's why I said that. God, Skye, I can't believe this. Please believe me. I wasn't going to cheat on you." He backed me up to the wall. His mouth came down on mine and he kissed me like we were never going to kiss again. I tried like hell not to respond. It would only make it harder. He gripped my face, nipped at my lips, and teased me with his tongue. I kept my mouth clamped tight. Finally, he drew back.

"Kiss me. Let me inside that mouth. It's been almost

three days of hell. Kiss me," he whispered. I shook my head no. The tears were gathering in my eyes. I was about to break. Everything in me wanted to believe I was mistaken and that he only wanted me, but I couldn't be sure. As he leaned toward me again, I ducked and squeezed between him and the wall. I ran to the door and jerked it open. I was racing toward the front when he caught me. I screamed. As I struggled and he begged me to calm down, Mom and the others ran in. She looked at me in horror.

"Skye, stop fighting him. You're going to hurt the baby!" she yelled. She realized what she'd said as soon as it came out of her mouth. I heard surprised gasps, and Executioner froze. His breath caught. I closed my eyes in defeat. Damn it, now he knew. He sat me gently down on my feet and turned me around to face him. I didn't look up.

"Is it true? Are you pregnant?" I remained mute. He grabbed my chin and raised my head so I had to look at him. I closed my eyes. He hissed, "Fuck! You're pregnant with my baby and you weren't going to tell me! That's fucked up!" he growled. I opened my eyes and glared at him.

"Who said it was yours?" His eyes got big then he narrowed them. He pulled me tight to his chest.

"I know you better than that. You haven't been with anyone but me."

"Maybe I lied." I didn't get a chance to say more, because he kissed me again and this time, he forced his tongue into my mouth. He kissed me with anger and hunger. I vaguely heard the others leave the room again. When he was done, he raised his head.

"You wouldn't lie about something like that. Jesus,

why wouldn't you tell me? Is it because you thought I was going to cheat? Baby Girl, this is my kid. I'm going to take care of it." I felt the tears run down my cheeks. He was doing exactly what I had dreaded.

"No, you're not. I'm not doing this, Ex. I'm not going to be with a man just because I happened to get knocked up, and have my kid grow up in a house filled with resentment, anger, and even hate. I'm not. No kid deserves that. I can take care of this baby on my own. I have Mom and my brothers. We'll be fine. You don't have to change your life. It's not like it was a few decades ago where you stayed together for the kid's sake. That's bullshit. All that does is lead to more pain."

He looked at me in stunned silence, then I saw something sweep across his face. It got dark. He lifted me and took me back into the office. This time, he sat me down on a couch we kept there. He held me on his lap even though I tried to slide off. He tightened his grip.

"Look at me. What did your dad do, Skye?" I squirmed. I didn't want to talk about my dad. To me, he was as good as dead. I hoped he was rotting somewhere.

"I don't know what you mean. Let me up, Ex."

"Stop calling me Ex. You know my name. I know he did something. All that stuff you just spewed came from somewhere. I could hear the fucking hurt in your voice. Why would you think I'd stay with you just for this baby and then there'd be resentment, anger, and hate in our relationship because of it? What did he do?"

He stared at me. I could see he wasn't going to let it go. Taking a deep breath, I told him my worst memories and fear. "Because he told me. He hated the fact that Mom had me. He said I took her attention away from him. It only got worse when Tanner was born. He got even uglier toward us. Tyson was the final straw. He made sure he didn't do it in front of Mom, but when she wasn't around, he told us how we'd ruined his life. That we were just a burden he had to bear. How he wished he'd never gotten her pregnant. If he hadn't, he'd have left."

I gulped as I sucked in air. This was killing me to say. Even Mom didn't know all of this. It would have devastated her. "He told me that I was going to be miserable too, because I'd try this bullshit on some man one day and find out what it was like to trap someone into a life they didn't want. Into kids they didn't want. After all, I was a girl, we did that kind of stuff." I broke down sobbing.

He tugged me to his chest and held me. His lips skimmed my hair, and he rubbed my back. I felt his lips on my cheek. He kissed over to my mouth where he gave me the gentlest kiss I'd ever had. With his lips on mine, he whispered to me, "Baby Girl, you're not trapping anyone. I fucking love you, Skye. I want to marry you. Hell, I have Pop's construction guys getting stuff together to build us a house and one for your mom out at the compound. I wanted to surprise you. God, babe, I could never hate or resent you. This baby is a fucking miracle and gift. Unless…" He moved me away from his chest so he could see my face. "Unless you don't want this baby. Is that it? Are you going to resent having one?" His face was filled with dread.

"No! Of course, I won't resent my baby. I'll love him or her to death. But men aren't like women. Men are meant to stay free and do whatever they feel like doing. Women drag you down with all this domestication," I told him. It's what my dad had told me.

"Jesus Christ, that bastard did a number on you! Skye, there are some men like that, I won't disagree. But there are a lot more who aren't. Who want to have a wife and kids. Who would thank God for bringing someone to love into his life. That's me. I know we didn't plan on having a baby, but this is amazing. God, Skye, don't let his mind games destroy us. I'm not going to cheat. I'm not going to leave you. I'm not going to resent or hate you or our kids. I'm going to love you every day for the rest of eternity. Please, I can't let you go."

The pain and dread in his eyes and voice shredded the last of my resolve. He had what looked like tears in his eyes. His hand was lightly rubbing across my stomach, right where the baby was, even though you couldn't tell I was pregnant. I touched his face and then ran my fingertips over his lips. He sighed. I raised up and kissed him. This time he let me take control. I kissed him with all the desperation, fear, and love I was feeling. When we had to take a breath, he smiled at me.

"Does that mean you're not going to leave?"

"It means, we'll try. But Slade, please, you have to be sure. If you're even a tiny bit unsure, we can't do this. I know what it turns into. It's not pretty. I won't have my child subjected to that kind of mental abuse."

"I'm one hundred percent positive I want this. Baby, I'm sorry you had to go through that. Did he do more than mentally abuse you?" I could see anger in his eyes this time.

"He hit me a couple of times, then told me if I told Mom, he'd smother Tanner or Tyson in their sleep. Luckily, they were young and didn't get much of his tirades or don't remember them. Tanner was six and Tyson was four when he left. That was the best day of our lives. We might struggle to pay for things, but he's not here. That's a win in my book."

"Forget about that bastard. He'll get what he deserves. Why don't we go home? I need to be with my baby girl."

"I need to check out the damage first. And I should talk to Mom."

"We already checked it. We were about to leave when you called. Our prospects will be here shortly to clean up the mess. The window is boarded up already. As soon as we can get new glass, it'll be replaced. I told your mom to close for the day today so we can work, then she can open up tomorrow."

"Slade, what's all that going to cost? We don't have any money to pay for all those repairs. I need to wait until I get paid for my accounting work," I told him, mentally calculating what I thought it would cost and how much I should get for my accounts.

"I'm taking care of it," he said. I shook my head.

"No, you're not. It's our store, we'll do it. I need to see where I can float the cash from."

He stood up and carried me out of the office. He went to the front. "Where are you taking me?"

"You're going to say goodbye to your mom and then you're coming back to the compound with me. I need to have alone time with you. You can forget the repairs. They're already paid for by me. If you insist on paying for it, we're going to have to negotiate what that payment plan is." His lips smirked. I knew he was thinking of something sexual.

Mom, the boys, and his brothers were all standing around when we came out of the back. Mom hurried over to me. "Is she okay? Why are you carrying her?

Honey, I'm sorry. I shouldn't have said it."

"Mom, it's fine. I'm okay. He just seems to think he needs to carry me," I reassured her.

"Are you mad at me?"

"No, I'm not mad. I know it was an accident."

"Jackie, I'm going to have one of my brothers take the three of you home. Someone from the club will stay with you. I'm taking Skye back to the compound. I'll bring her over to the house later." Mom smiled at us and nodded.

It took a matter of a couple of minutes, and they were out the door. Torpedo was going to stay with them. Executioner carried me out to my car. I looked around. I didn't see his bike anywhere. "Where are you parked?"

"I moved it over a block when your mom said you were coming. I was afraid you'd see it and run."

"Oh, Slade, I'm sorry. Let me take you over so you can get it." He put me in the car, but on the passenger side. He got in and rearranged my seat and drove to where he'd parked his bike. When he got out, he kissed me. "I'll be right behind you. We're going to the compound." I nodded. I think he was worried I'd try and run. I reset my seat. It was a quick drive to his place. I was starting to get anxious about our make-up session. Would he feel different about having sex with me now that he knew I was pregnant? God, more shit keeps whirling around in this screwed up head of mine.

Executioner: Chapter 13

As we drove back to the compound, my mind was going over what I'd learned. It was more than I'd imagined. I now had even more reason to find her dad and make that fucker pay. He'd mentally and physically abused his own daughter, all because he wasn't man enough to live up to his responsibilities. He'd blamed his innocent children for the life he was living. A life he didn't want according to Skye.

I couldn't imagine feeling like that. Even if you didn't love the woman, those were your kids. I'd never do that. I'd protect them as fiercely as I planned to protect Skye. That brought me to the other big revelation. I was going to be a father. I didn't know what to think. When Jackie had blurted it out, I'd been stunned. I thought at first, I'd heard her wrong.

I couldn't wait to get Skye alone. I wanted to know everything. When did she find out? How did it happen? When did it happen? How was she feeling? I knew she was going to have to slow down. No more working the shop and then doing all those books. She needs to rest. A baby took a lot out of a woman.

The gate opened when I pushed the remote. I stopped outside of my trailer. She parked beside me. I opened her door, unhooked her seatbelt, and swept her out. She laughed at me. "Do you plan to carry me around for the next several months? Your back is going to give out when I get bigger."

I snorted. "Baby Girl, you don't weigh shit, and adding a few pounds of baby won't make a damn difference.

I deadlift three hundred and fifty pounds. I think I can handle you."

She ran a hand up my bicep and squeezed. "I think I need to check out this body to be sure it's in tip-top shape."

I growled. "Let me get you inside and you can check anything out you want. But I get to return the favor. I hope you've rested while you were away. I plan to keep you awake for a while." I opened the door and carried her inside. I didn't stop until we were standing in the middle of my bedroom. I laid her gently down on the bed and toed off my boots. The talking could wait until much later. Right now, I needed her desperately. Even a couple of days without her had been unbearable.

I didn't stop with my boots. I tugged off her shoes and then got back to my clothes. She laid there propped up on her elbows watching me. Though I wanted her something fierce, I decided to tease her just a little. I wanted her to be as fired up as I was. I slowly inched up my shirt. I made sure to reveal inch after inch of my abs then my chest. When I had gotten it all the way off, she was sitting up on the bed. I could see the heat in her eyes had gotten a smidge darker.

"Wanna see something else, Baby Girl?" I asked as I put my hand on the button to my jeans. I didn't undo it. I just held still. She inched closer to the edge of the bed. Her eyes were glued to my hand. She didn't say a word, just nodded. I unsnapped them and waited. She glanced up at me.

"Are you going to tease me the whole time to get those off?"

"Oh yeah, I am, baby. I have to make sure you're just as ready for this as I am, because I'm not going to be able to go slow the first time. It's been a few days and I need you too much. I want you to be nice and wet. Tell me what to do next."

She whimpered. "Undo your belt, honey."

I took my time undoing my belt. She was now at the edge of the bed and her breathing had picked up a bit.

"Unzip your jeans and take them off, Slade." I unzipped them but only pushed them down enough for my cock and balls to show, then I stopped. I didn't have to wait long for her reaction. Only she didn't tell me what to do. She slid off the bed onto her knees and grabbed my jeans to yank them to my ankles. She tapped my foot and I raised one then the other, so she could take them all the way off.

"Baby Girl, get off the floor. It's too hard down there for you." I didn't want her to be uncomfortable. She ignored me and took my cock into her warm hand. I sighed. Her hand felt so damn soft on me. She slid it around my balls then stroked up and down once on my cock. I was rock hard, and the precum was all over the head. I moaned.

Then she made me really moan because she quickly lowered her head and sucked me inside that hot, wet mouth of hers. Jesus Christ, she knew the perfect amount of suction. I grabbed her hair and held it back so I could watch her go down on me. The sight of my cock stretching her mouth so wide made my cock jerk in anticipation. I knew I wouldn't be able to stand much of this without blowing my load, but I'd let her play until I couldn't stand it any longer.

She massaged my balls and tugged gently on them, rolling them between her fingers as she held my cock tight and took me deep. I could feel the back of her throat and then she was swallowing me. God, I'd never met a woman without a gag reflex. She was squeezing the sensitive head over and over as she swallowed.

As she pulled back, I couldn't help but to slide back in and down her throat again. She was looking up at me as she swallowed. Seeing the tiny bit of drool coming out of her mouth and the way her eyes were lit up, I knew it was time to stop. I pulled out. She reached for me like she was going to take me back inside. I stopped her.

"Skye, no more. I'm too close. I don't want to come down your throat, babe. At least not this time. I need to be inside of you." I quickly stripped off her clothes then picked her up under her arms and sat her back on the bed, then I pressed her down on her back. As she relaxed back, I tugged her legs apart and looked at her pussy. She was gleaming with the cream coming out of her. I blew across her clit. She shivered and her hips bucked up off the bed.

I could see it was hard and peeking out from underneath its hood. I spread her lips and then latched onto it, sucking hard. She sat up and screamed as she sank her hand into my hair. I took that as a good sign and didn't let up. I licked, sucked, and bit, all up and down her lips and thrust my tongue inside of her. It took her maybe two minutes until she came, crying out her orgasm as she shook on the bed.

I didn't wait for her to fully recover. I hooked her knees over my elbows and lifted her ass off the bed, then I slid home in one long, continuous thrust. She was slightly resistant, like every time I entered her. It made it feel like she had a fist around me. I groaned.

"God, Baby Girl, that feels fucking amazing." As soon as I bottomed out, I pulled back, then I slowly slid back inside.

I did this a couple of times before she asked, "Slade, why are you going so slow? Baby, I want you to take me hard and fast. I need it."

"I don't want to hurt the baby."

"You won't. You've been doing it for weeks and I was pregnant. It's going to take more than that to hurt this baby." I realized she was right. She had been pregnant all along.

"Promise if anything feels wrong or hurts, you'll tell me."

"I will. Now, fuck me before I die!"

I slammed back into her. As I hammered in and out and listened to her moan, I told her, "I'm not fucking you, Skye. This is me making love to you. I love you, baby. So damn much." I groaned as she clenched down on me. She leaned up and touched my cheek.

"I love you too, Slade." Hearing her say those words made my fucking life perfect. It only took a few more thrusts, and she was coming. She clamped down tight on me and as I pushed through her grip, it only took me a couple more strokes before I shouted and came. I came long and hard with her milking everything out of me. I had enough sense left not to fall on top of her. I laid over her with my elbows, propping myself up until I softened, then I laid down beside her and held her against my chest.

"I meant it, I do love you. I couldn't be fucking happier about us having a baby. It might not have been planned, but this baby is very much wanted." I gave her a slow, gentle kiss. She kissed me back.

"I love you too. And I agree. Not planned but I can't wait for us to have this baby, though I'm not sure what your brothers are going to think of it and me. What if they think I did it on purpose to trap you?" I saw anxiety fill her face.

"Not one of them would ever think that. They know I'm gone on you, baby. You didn't have to do anything like this to trap me. I was trapped the moment I saw you. As for what anyone else thinks, fuck 'em. I do have some questions though. Maybe we can talk about those while we rest up for the next round."

She smiled. "Oh, next round, huh? Okay, ask away." I thought about the questions that had come to mind after her mom blurted out that she was pregnant.

"When did you find out?"

She sighed. "The day I left. I'd gone to the doctor to get on birth control like we talked about. They do a pregnancy test before they'll prescribe anything. They told me. I left there and went to the dealership to tell you. I had no idea what you would think. Then I heard that conversation with Omen and I couldn't do it."

"God, Skye, that conversation is going to be the worst day of my life. I can only imagine how bad it sounded to you and I understand why you thought what you did. But, baby, you have to swear you won't take off again. No matter what you hear or think, you come to me. We'll talk it out. I'm never going to leave you or cheat, so there's nothing we shouldn't be able to fix. Promise?"

She nodded. "I promise. I'm sorry, I know I over-reacted. Even if it were true, I owed it to you to tell you about the baby. But I wasn't lying about not having my kid being resented and hated by its father. That would have never been allowed. I'd have taken you to court and if that didn't work, I'd have found a way to disappear," she warned me. I thanked God she hadn't done either of those.

"You never have to worry about that. But if it had happened, all you had to do was tell my brothers. No way they'd let that shit stand. They'd have beaten the hell out of me. Fuck, who knows, they might have kicked me out of the club, and I know they would have looked out for you and the baby. If anything ever happens to me, they'll be here for you."

"Don't talk about anything happening to you! I can't even think of it without wanting to puke."

"Okay, I won't, but remember it. As for puking, is the baby making you sick?"

"I'm doing okay. Some nausea and I've hurled a few times, but not too bad. Mostly, I'm tired."

I decided not to tell her she had to stop working. I'd hold that one until I finished asking my other questions. "Do you know how far along you are? I mean, how soon can they tell?"

"They can tell much earlier, usually within two weeks of conception." I thought back. It had been three weeks since we got back together. She added, "By my blood levels, they're positive I got pregnant our first time together. Guess that condom had a hole in it. Right now, they think my due date is November twentieth. I'll find out for sure at my first real OB appointment. It's on May nineteenth. That puts me at twelve weeks right now, according to their calculations."

Shit, she was already three months along. I looked down at her belly. Other than maybe the tiniest softening, I saw nothing that even indicated she was pregnant. I laid my hand on her stomach. "Babe, are you sure you're alright? You're not even showing! Shouldn't you be? We need to have the doctor see you sooner. I want them to do one of those picture things so we can see the baby. You're not big enough to be three months pregnant." I frowned. I was starting to worry. She'd not been eating right until I brought in those groceries. She laid her hand on top of mine.

"I'm fine, Slade. Not all women show quickly. My mom didn't with us, though after the first, you do show sooner the next time. My tummy muscles are nice and tight now. Wait until I have this one. There's no need to go sooner. They'll do a sonogram at that appointment. I asked. I'm taking my vitamins already."

I leaned down to kiss her tummy then I raised up to kiss her lips. "Okay, but if you start to feel bad, we're going sooner. Which brings me to something else." She raised her eyebrows at me. "You can't be working two jobs. It's too much." She sat up.

"Slade, I need to do that. Mom needs the help at the shop, and we need the extra money, even if we're not paying those guys," she protested.

"No, you don't. We'll figure out something for your mom's shop since I know you really want to do the accounting work."

"It's not a matter of finding someone. It's a matter of affording them."

"I know, and I'll take care of it."

"You're not paying for it, Slade! It's my family's problem." I pressed her back on the bed and hovered over her. I stared into her eyes.

"Are you my woman?" She nodded. "Then it makes this my problem. This is my family now too. I'm not going to fight about it. Your mom will agree with me anyway. She hates you working so much. I'm not going to have you running yourself or the baby down. I want a

164

healthy baby and mommy. Understand?"

She stayed quiet for a minute. I waited to see if she'd fight me. Finally, she relaxed and sighed. "Fine, I'll cut back, but don't think you can tell me what to do all the time, Slade Ashton! You're not my boss."

I grinned at her. "No, I'm your man, and I'll make sure you're safe and healthy. Now, why don't we see about round two and then maybe we'll go over to the club-house and share our good news." I nudged her with my cock. Arguing with her had gotten me hard. She laughed as she spread her legs.

"I can get with that idea."

⟨‖⟩ ⟨‖⟩ ⟨‖⟩ ⟨‖⟩

We didn't leave the bed and head over to the club-house until it was evening. That gave us time to get in a few rounds of lovemaking and a decent amount of sleep. She had to be tired, and I knew I was. It was seven o'clock when we rolled in the door. Since it was after work hours, all the guys were there. I saw Sara and Lyric were too. Good, that would make it perfect for our an-nouncement. I couldn't wait to tell them.

I led Skye over to one of the tables and sat her down. "What do you want to drink, baby?"

"Do they have any water? Plain is fine. I don't think they have the flavored kind." I made a mental note to have them start to stock some. She didn't like the plain kind I'd found. Also, I needed to get one of those books on pregnancies so I knew what she should and shouldn't eat or drink.

"Blake, get me a beer and a bottle of water. And next time you guys do a run to the store, get some of those flavored waters for Skye, would ya? She likes any kind of berry best, just no fruit punch."

"Sure thing, Ex. I'll put it on the list in the back. Here you go." He handed me our drinks. Before I could go back to Skye, Sin came up to me. He looked over at Skye talking to Lyric and Sara.

"Looks like things worked out. I heard it was a little tense this morning at the shop."

"Did you hear anything else?" I asked, wondering if they already knew about the baby. He frowned.

"Like what?"

"Maybe about Skye and me."

"No, not anything other than she showed, and you two ended up getting a little loud and talked. Why, what should I know?" I smiled. At least I knew Pitbull, Boomer, and Torpedo hadn't run back and blabbed. I wanted to be the one to tell the rest of my brothers.

"Will you get all the guys' attention and let them know I need to talk to them? It can be out here with Lyric and your mom." He nodded while giving me a puzzled look. As I went to our table, he gave out an ear-ringing whistle.

"Listen up, you bastards. Executioner needs the floor for a minute!" he hollered. The guys all got quiet and stopped whatever they were doing to look at me. I sat down our drinks at the table and took Skye's hand. I had her stand up. I could tell she was a little uncomfortable being the center of everyone's attention with me. I wrapped an arm around her.

"As you all can see, Skye's back and we've sorted out our misunderstanding." They broke into whistling and clapping. She turned pink. I held up my hand so they'd quiet down. "Yeah, yeah, quiet, you assholes. While I'm happy as hell she did, because I was about to go find her ass, I wanted to let you know something I found out today." They got silent and were looking at me then at each other.

"I know a few of you already heard it. Thanks for not saying anything." I nodded to the three who'd been at the shop. "Skye and I are going to be parents in about six months. So, by Thanksgiving, the first Infidel spawn will be here." It took them a second or two to respond, then they were all rushing over to us with stunned looks on their faces along with happy ones. There were hugs and kisses, mainly for Skye. The ladies kissed me, but the guys kept their lips to themselves. That damn Boomer acted like he was going to kiss me. I punched him in the gut lightly. He backed off with a grin on his face.

"Keep your lips off my damn woman, you bastards. She's mine. I was the one smart enough to knock her up," I growled at the ones who'd kissed her. They gave me shit-eating grins.

Suddenly, Wrecker spoke up, "Wait a minute. You said by November. That means—"

"Yeah, I knocked her up the first time I touched her. Let's see any of you do that while still wearing a party hat. That takes super sperm and a real man. None of you are capable of that shit," I said with pride and a smirk on my face. Skye smacked me in the stomach with the back of her hand.

"All that says, Mr. Super Sperm, is there was a tiny hole somewhere in that condom. Or maybe I'm just fertile as hell." Lyric high-fived her. The guys all roared with laughter. I gave her a mock growl and kissed her. When I let her go, I smacked her ass.

"Nope. It's all the sperm, baby. Your man is a stud."

She rolled her eyes.

"Well, Mr. Stud, wait until that baby gets here and see if you feel like you're still one. I'm not doing all the night feedings and diapers. You'll be just as sleep deprived as me," she warned.

"Baby Girl, I wouldn't have it any other way. I'm going to be a hands-on guy with our kids. You have nothing to worry about on that score," I promised her. I knew that wasn't how a lot of guys thought, but I did. She gave me such a look of love, I wanted to carry her back to my place and make love to her all over again.

As we settled in to talk with the club, I watched her with Lyric. Lyric and Sin were getting married in two months on the Fourth of July. That made me think of me and Skye. She was my old lady, but like my brother Sin, I wanted to make it even more official than that. I needed to tell my mom and sisters about her and then I was going to get a ring on her finger and her in front of a minister or judge as fast as I could. Well, at least I was after I talked to Jackie. As her mom, I wanted her to know how serious I was about her daughter.

We didn't stay past nine. She insisted she had to go into the shop tomorrow, so I wanted her to get a good night's sleep. After I had my way with her again, of course. When I got her back to the trailer, I stripped her slowly and took my time with her. By the time I was done, we were both worn out. After a quick shower, we fell into bed and into a deep sleep. The best sleep I'd had in days.

Skye: Chapter 14

The last two days of the work week flew by after I came back to Tenillo. We hadn't seen or heard a peep out of the ones who'd sent in Bobby Sims to get the money that day. This made all of us nervous, especially Executioner. He was in ultra-protective mode, and me being pregnant made him worse. I went nowhere without an escort of at least one if not two of his club members. It was either prospects or brothers.

The club also had someone stay with us at the shop. When the boys were in school, they were okay, we thought, but if they were at the house and Mom and I weren't, they got a guard, too. I hated the strain I knew it was placing on the club. So, as much as possible, we had them come to the shop after school and stay until we all could go home. At night, Ex was staying with us, giving the guys a break at least.

It was Saturday and the club had decided while I was gone, they needed to have a party. Apparently, Ex told them to go ahead and plan it because he'd intended to have me back before then. The man was nothing if not persistent. They invited the Time Served gang and my family as well. We were going to have a barbeque outside and then relax.

Mom and I helped make some of the food, though Sara and Lyric told us it wasn't necessary. They did a lot of it as well and then their restaurant, The Hangout, helped with the rest. It wasn't a gourmet place, since it had a big bar attached, but they could more than help with this kind of event.

As Mom and I were getting ready at Ex's trailer and the boys were already out hanging and helping the guys, I thought about the conversation he'd had with my mom and then his call last night to his mom in England.

After we told the club Wednesday night about the baby, Executioner had pulled Mom aside at the shop the next day. He went into her office, and they were behind closed doors for a while. When he came out, he looked happy and so did my mom. He'd kissed me and said he'd see me after work. As soon as he left, I cornered my mom.

"What did he want to talk to you about, Mom? Why did he not want me to hear?"

She smiled. "Are you sure you don't want to ask him?"

"No, I'm asking you. Is something wrong?"

"Other than the man is head over heels in love with my daughter, no. He just wanted to be sure I was okay with the two of you being in a relationship. He assured me he loved you and would always take care of you and the baby."

"Why couldn't he say that in front of me?"

"In case I had objections, I think. I reassured him that as long as he never physically or mentally hurt you and took care of you and my grandchild, we wouldn't have issues. However, if he doesn't, his ass is mine." I had to laugh. The image of my five-foot-one mom kicking his six-foot-six ass was hilarious. She narrowed her eyes at me. She knew what I was thinking.

"Mom, he won't. He told me if he ever abused me or didn't take care of our child, his own club would beat his ass and probably kick him to the curb."

"I knew I liked those guys for a reason. Now, let's get to work. I understand we have a party to go to on Saturday."

That had ended our discussion. That night I made sure to thank him thoroughly for telling my mom what he did. Then last night, he'd called his mom. They were like six hours ahead of us in Manchester, England where his mom lived. I'd gotten off early from the shop and we called them around five o'clock. He'd told me more about his mom, his stepdad, and his sisters, Selena and Shana.

He'd gotten on the phone and started out the conversation asking his mom how they were doing. She chatted for a little bit. Then he brought the conversation around to us. I was sitting there on pins and needles. She didn't know he had her on speakerphone.

"How are you doing Slade?"

"I'm doing really well. Are the girls and Randall there?"

"Yeah, why?" I could hear the hesitation in her voice.

"Will you ask them to come get on the phone for a minute?"

"Slade, what's wrong?" Her voice got higher.

"Nothing's wrong, Mom. I just want to tell you all something." She grumbled but got them to quickly come to the phone. After he greeted all of them, he got down to the point. I was clutching my hands so tightly; my knuckles were white. Maybe I should let him talk to them alone. I went to stand up, but he stopped me by pulling me onto his lap. He rubbed my hands soothingly.

"I wanted to tell you all something great. I met someone. Her name is Skye." I heard them all gasp and then the excited chatter started. They were all talking over each other asking him where he met me? Who I was? How old was I? How long ago had we met? He finally got them to quiet down. I was hoping he wouldn't tell them we'd started as a one-night stand.

"Now that you've shut up, I'll tell you," he teased. "She's twenty-three and works in her family's flower shop, but she

also has her accounting degree and does books for various businesses here in town. We met in Fort Worth."

"You really like this woman, don't you? Otherwise, you'd never be telling us about her. You've never told us about any woman, Slade," his mom said excitedly.

"I've never been serious about a woman, Mom, but I am about Skye. In fact, I'm so serious I've claimed her as my old lady." I heard four gasps.

"What? You're serious?" his sister, I think it was Selena asked.

"Hell yeah, I'm serious. And there's more news."

"What?" his mom asked.

"You're going to be a grandma and you two brats, aunts."

There was a moment of silence, then his mom responded. "Son, you're not doing this because she's pregnant, are you? Because if you are, that's not a good solid basis to be with someone," she cautioned him. My stomach dropped. I tried to stand up. I didn't want to hear anymore. He should have told them without me here, though I was glad I knew they probably weren't going to like me. They were thinking what a lot of people would probably think.

"Fuck no! I claimed her before we ever knew she was pregnant, Mom. I love her and she loves me. I'm stoked about this baby. Yeah, it wasn't planned, but I don't care. I'm ready to have a family and she's the only one I want that with." He kissed my neck as he held me in place. I could hear a note of anger in his voice. "I thought you'd be happy for me."

"We are! We just don't want you to get hurt. Please, don't be mad. If she's the one and you're happy, then we are," his mom rushed to reassure him. His sisters were exclaiming the same thing in the background. I didn't hear his stepdad say anything.

"She's my damn life, Mom. I love my club, but she's more important than it." I heard a swift inhale on the other end of the line. "I know you'll love her. She's way too good for me, but I lucked out and she loves and wants me anyway. I really hope you'll give her a chance when you meet her."

"Of course, we will, Slade. We're just all shocked. When we talked to you last month, you never mentioned seeing anyone. Now, you're going to be a dad and claimed someone. Tell us more about her. You said she works in her family's flower shop. What're they like? And when is the baby due? How far along is she?" This came from his stepdad. He sounded like he was happy for him.

"Okay, I can understand why you'd be shocked, Randall, but I do love her and we're going to spend the rest of our lives together, no matter what I have to do to keep her happy. She's three months along, but we just found out a few days ago. The baby should be due around November twentieth. We don't know yet what we're having. They won't be able to tell for at least another six weeks or so when they do an ultrasound. But if we do certain blood test that looks for things like Down Syndrome and a couple of other things, they can tell the sex because it'll show if there is a Y chromosome or not. They can do that starting at ten weeks." I was shocked he knew that. I didn't even know about the blood test. Apparently, he'd been doing research.

"Will you get that done? And what if it shows something like Down Syndrome?" I heard the distress in his mom's voice.

"I plan on talking to Skye to see if she wants to do the test. But it doesn't matter what it shows, Mom. We'd never abort our child. I'd just love to know now what we're having. I can't set up a nursery without it. And speaking of a nursery, we're going to be building a house here on the compound like Sin has. Already got the local construction company working to start it. We're hoping her mom and her younger brothers will move onto the compound and into a small house, too."

"Really? When can we talk to her? I want to know more about her family," his mom replied.

"Give me a second and I'll get her." He put them on mute. "Baby, I didn't tell them you were on here because I wanted you to hear what they said. I knew they'd never trash you. I knew they'd be stunned. Please don't think bad of them for asking if I was doing it only because of the baby."

"Slade, I don't think bad of them. Hell, that's what most people are going to think. I just want them to like me."

"Screw what other people think. As long as you know why I'm with you. They're going to love you." I waved at the phone.

"Let me talk to them." When we got back on, they all greeted and acted like they were thrilled about the baby. They asked about my family and some other things. Time flew by and before I knew it, we were saying goodbye. They promised they'd come soon to see us. I'd be happy if they got to come after the baby came.

Mom touched my arm, bringing me out of my thoughts. "Are you okay, honey? You've been awfully quiet."

"Just thinking about the phone call with Executioner's family last night." I'd told her earlier about it.

"You're still worrying they won't like you and think you two are together because of the baby, aren't you?" I nodded. "Honey, as soon as they see the two of you together, they're going to know that's bullshit. The love the two of you have for each other is written all over your faces. Now, stop thinking that and let's get out there. I'm ready to party and celebrate. Are you guys announcing the pregnancy to Boss and his guys today?"

"I think so. He said he wanted to start telling others. I told him I was fine with it. I think something else is happening too. He didn't say what, but he and the guys had church last night and he seemed happy about something."

"Even more reason to get out there. Come on." She tugged on my hand. I gave myself one last look in the mirror and then let her drag me outside. While we got ready, I'd heard a large group of motorcycles come in about ten minutes ago. We hurried over to the barbeque area that sat between the back of the clubhouse and the trailers the members lived in. I saw a sea of leather, tats, and sexy men. I nudged my mom.

"Maybe you can find yourself a sexy biker man. Boss' guys are all single I think except him and Hook." She blushed and elbowed me.

"I'm not looking for a man. I'm too old for that."

"Mom, you're only forty-five. You're in the prime of your life. Don't rule it out. Just let yourself have fun." She rolled her eyes at me. I decided to let it go, but I would be thrilled if she found someone. If anyone deserved a happily ever after, it was my mom. We looked around and I found Ex in the crowd. He was with a few of Boss' guys, Wrecker, Pitbull and another guy I didn't recognize. I wondered who he was? I tugged her in their direction. They all smiled when they saw us. Time to get this show on the road.

⊲‖⊳ ⊲‖⊳ ⊲‖⊳ ⊲‖⊳

Executioner:

I watched her make her way over to us with her mom. She took my breath away. She was just so damn beautiful, both inside and outside. I had no idea how in the hell I'd gotten this lucky. I curled my arm around her waist and hugged her to my side. She looked up so I could place a kiss on her lips. I made sure it wasn't a tiny one either. When I let her go, the guys were laughing and Jackie was smiling.

"Hello, Baby Girl. I was just about to come get you. I want to introduce you. You know Santa and Preacher." He indicted the two Time Served guys. I smiled at them and nodded. They greeted me and Mom. Then he turned to the guy standing next to them that I didn't know. He was looking at me closely. I couldn't read his expression.

He was a big guy, maybe a few inches shorter than Ex. He was muscular, though he looked like he might have recently lost weight. He looked like he was in his thirties or even close to forty. He had a short military-looking haircut with some white at the temples. His face was deeply tanned like he spent a lot of time in the sun and there were lines around his eyes from squinting. He had the prettiest blue eyes. He had a closely cropped beard and mustache.

I stared back at him. No way was I letting him intimidate me. Executioner got my attention. "And Skye, baby, this is my friend from the Marines, Omen." I stiffened when I heard the name. This was the one who he had been talking to when the comment I misunderstood was made. I fought not to frown. It wasn't his fault I misunderstood. I held out my hand to him.

"Hello, Omen, it's nice to meet you."

He took it and raised it to his lips. He kissed the back of my hand. "The pleasure is all mine, dawlin'," he said. He was smiling and winked at me. Executioner took my hand out of his.

"Keep that Cajun charm to yourself, buddy. She's taken. Omen, this is Jackie, she's Skye's mom." Omen gave my mom an appreciative look which had her blushing. He took her hand and kissed it as well.

"Another beautiful woman for me to admire. No way you're old enough to be her mom. Her sister, maybe, but not her mom. Are you taken, love?" Mom blushed more and shook her head.

"No, I'm not, but don't get any ideas. I don't fall for smooth-talking men." This got all the guys laughing. Omen winked at her and let go of her hand, but he made sure to stay beside her. I had no idea if he liked her or wanted to see what she'd do.

"How're you feeling, Omen? Executioner said you got hurt pretty bad. I think he said your leg and chest." He shrugged.

"It's better. I'm still doing some therapy, and it hurts like hell when it rains, but other than that, I'm fine. Glad to be able to get back to working out and doing stuff."

"Are you here long for a visit?" I asked him.

He glanced at Ex, and Executioner answered, "He's here for good. He finally got mustered out of the Marines. He's decided to give the Infidels a try. He's going to be prospecting with us. There's someone else here I want you to meet. He's going to be prospecting as well. I'll find him in a bit."

"Wow, I didn't know. Congratulations. I think you're

going to love it here." I told him with a smile. We spent a few more minutes talking before Ex excused the three of us to go find the other person he wanted me to meet. Obviously, he was another military man, He had been a Marine with Pitbull I found out. He was probably in his thirties as well. He was a little more reserved than Omen. I was happy to see they were getting more guys. That would get them to five prospects. Executioner introduced him as Brennan, another new prospect.

After that introduction, Sin called us all to order. He got up on one of the picnic tables so we all could see him. "Thank you all for coming. I hope everyone got a chance to meet Omen and Brennan, our two new prospects." He pointed at them. Everyone cheered. Sin grinned. "Let the torture begin." That got a big laugh. "But that's not the only thing we asked all of you here for today. We'd like to make something else official. Drake, come over here."

I saw Drake make his way to Sin. As he did, Saint stepped up next to Sin. He had his hands behind his back. "Drake, this is a little overdue because of all the shit that's been happening lately. But you've been doing a great job not only for the club, but Boss says at the department. So, I'd like to offer you this." He reached over to Saint, who handed him something leather. As Sin opened it, I could see it was a rag. It had the club's logo and name on the back, but it didn't say prospect. The whistles and clapping started. Drake stripped off the one he had on, and Sin took it so he could put on the new one. As he admired it, Sin yelled, "Say hello to the newest member of the Ares' Infidels, Cuffs."

Drake grinned hearing his road name. I thought it was appropriate given his job. Everyone congratulated him. As that died down, Sin continued, "As if that's not enough, my brother Executioner wants to talk." He waved Ex up. Executioner made sure I went with him. I guess this was when we were going to tell everyone about the baby. I had butterflies in my stomach. Ex got up on the picnic table.

"I know you all have met Skye, and I know you all know she's my old lady. But it's not official until she's fully claimed." I looked at him puzzled. What in the world was he talking about? "Baby, I love you and you know I'm going to spend the rest of my life with you. Will you wear this for me, so everyone knows you're mine?" He held out a piece of leather that Saint had slipped into his hand. He jumped down to help me put it on. As I did, I saw it said on the back, *Property of Executioner*. On the front was stitched, *Baby Girl*. I felt the tears well up. I hugged him as I kissed him. That got a lot of wolf whistles.

I whispered to him as we parted, "I'll gladly wear this, Slade. I love being your old lady." I was thrilled to have an official property rag like Lyric had. She was smiling at me. As things got quieter, Executioner got back up on the table, but this time he took me up there with him. He held onto me tightly.

"One last thing you all should know. In six months, the Infidels will be welcoming their first spawn. Skye and I are happy to announce that we're having a baby." This floored those who didn't know. It was deafening the response this got. It took forever to get free of everyone wanting to congratulate us. I knew as we talked to everyone, this day couldn't get any better.

I was introduced to two women I didn't know. They were here with the Time Served guys. One older woman was introduced as Brea. She was Hook's best friend and worked for Pop. With her was her daughter, Sis. I gauged her to be close to my age, or a few years younger. She was hilarious to talk to. The afternoon and evening flew by. When it was getting late, the bunnies came out. That's when I called it a night. I didn't want to see them hooking up, and I sure didn't want my impressionable brothers to see it. Executioner offered for Mom and the boys to stay, but they wanted to go home. Blake said he'd go with them. I kissed them and watched them leave, then we went to his place. We had some celebrating of our own to do.

Executioner: Chapter 15

I was happy to get away from the party. I'd been wanting to make love to Skye ever since she slipped on her property cut this afternoon. Something about seeing my name on her made me even more crazy for her. Once she had the baby, I hoped like hell she'd be willing to get my name tattooed on her as well.

When we entered my place, I started kissing her immediately. She didn't hold back and was devouring my mouth as much as I was hers. I stopped long enough to get off our boots then took her to the bedroom. I backed her to the wall inside the door and pinned her there. She was looking into my eyes.

"Baby Girl, I've been wanting to ask you something all day."

"What, Slade?"

"After you have the baby, will you consider getting a tattoo with my name on it? I'd love to have you wear that as well."

"Do you want Slade or Executioner?"

I thought about it for a minute. "Can I get both? Even if you don't, I'm going to have Phantom put yours on me. I'd love to have both of yours, Skye and Baby Girl. But you don't have to if you don't like it. I know some people don't want tats." Even if I knew she loved mine, that was different from getting them yourself.

"I have no objection, Slade. I think I'd like it to have both Slade and Executioner in it."

I gave her another kiss. "Enough talk, I have a woman to pleasure. I want to hear and watch you come over and over, Skye." I growled as I slid my hand up under her top. It became a flurry of clothes as we both shed ours. When we were both naked, I took her to the bed and spread her out. Her hair was spread across the sheets and her pale skin shone in the light. Her nipples were hard, and she was kneading them. I was hard and ready to go, but first she needed to come on my tongue.

I crawled between her legs and took in the sight. I loved to see her wet and her pussy all pink and puffy. I hungrily took her clit into my mouth and sucked. She hissed. I proceeded to eat her like she was my last meal. I was proud that I lasted long enough to get her off not once but twice with my mouth and fingers.

As she settled down from the last one, I flipped her over onto her stomach. I rummaged in my nightstand as I told her, "Ass in the air, baby. I need it here now, before I lose my fucking mind." As she raised up, I gripped her hips and slammed into her. She cried out in pleasure as I groaned. God, I could die right now and be utterly happy. I powered in and out of her over and over. She was already whimpering, but I wanted her mindless.

I reached down and picked up the bottle of lube I'd gotten out of my drawer. I squeezed some out and let it run down the crack of her ass. She shivered and looked over her shoulder at me. I worked my finger through it and into her ass. She moaned and pushed back. As I fucked her slower, I worked her ass, stretching her. When I thought she was stretched enough, I picked up the second thing I had. I showed it to her.

Her eyes got a little wider. It was a set of anal beads. They weren't too big, but it would fill her ass more than a finger did. I wanted her to get used to them and then eventually, I hoped she'd be willing to let me in there.

"I want to see if you like these. Are you willing to try them?" She nodded. Her breath was coming faster. She'd clenched down on me when she saw them. I slicked them up and then started to work them into her. It took a minute and I stopped moving inside of her to do it. When they were all the way in, I got back to business. I knew it must feel a little weird to her, but I had something in mind.

Sooner than I wanted, she was getting close and so was I. I sped up and as I hammered into her, she started to shake. She screamed, "Slade," as she came. I roared as I came right after her. I kept thrusting and every time I pulled back, I tugged, pulling the anal beads, one at a time, out of her ass. She amazingly tightened down on me harder. By the time I got all four of them out of her, I was drained and ready to collapse. She was lying on her stomach, moaning. I pulled out.

I laid down beside her and rubbed her back. "Alright, Baby Girl?" She nodded with her eyes closed. I chuckled. I knew that look. She was ready for a nap. But I knew she'd be eager for another round soon. I scooped her up and took her to the bathroom for a quick shower. We'd just gotten out of the shower and dried off when my phone rang. I grabbed it and saw it was Blake. I answered it with dread in my stomach. "What's wrong?"

"Executioner, I need you to come to the house. You have to see this shit. Jackie and the boys are fine, but they came home to a mess. We stopped at the store on the way back." I was pulling on my clothes as he talked. Skye was looking worried.

"Did you call anyone else?"

"No," he said.

"I'll text them. Did you search the house?" I watched

Skye stiffen.

"As soon as I saw it, I made them wait in the locked car and I did. It's clear. I have them locked inside with me right now and we're all in the living room."

"Keep them inside until we get there. If it looks like trouble, get them the hell out of there and back here."

As I hung up, she started asking, "What happened, Slade? I know it's my mom. What's wrong at the house?" I typed out a message and hit send.

"Baby, I need you to calm down. Your mom and brothers are fine. Yes, that was Blake. They got home and found the place had been broken into. I need to get over there. I want you to stay here and rest. I'll be sending them back here to stay." She was dashing around picking up her clothes.

"No! I'm coming with you. I need to be there for them." I stopped her in the middle of dressing.

"Baby, please, this is too much stress. Stay here."

"I'll be more stressed if I stay." She gave me a pleading look. I sighed as I gave in. She was probably right about the stress. My phone pinged with the guys responding they'd go with me. I knew a lot of them were still partying. I hated to disrupt their fun, but this needed attention. I answered them back.

"Okay, get dressed. We'll take my truck. Be ready in five minutes." She nodded.

In five minutes, we were out the door. The sounds of the party had drastically diminished since I sent the text. A whole crowd stood waiting for us. I saw it wasn't just my brothers. Most of the Time Served guys were still here too. They glanced at Skye.

"She's going to worry herself sick if I leave her here. Let me get the truck and we'll head over." They nodded.

I took her around the clubhouse.

"Honey, why are we taking the truck and not your bike?"

"You're not on that bike until after this baby gets here. It's too damn dangerous. I'm not going to risk you or the baby getting hurt," I explained as I helped her in and then I got in after I took off my rag and laid it on the seat.

"Why do you do that when you get in a car or truck?"

"It's disrespectful to wear it in one. Our colors are meant to be seen and respected. I don't ever lay it on the floor or ground either. You'll need to do the same with yours." I was happy to see she'd slipped hers on. She didn't say anything, just nodded and took hers off as well. I could tell she was worried by the way she held herself. I took her hand in mine. The night was loud with the roar of bikes behind and in front of us. "Try to relax. Nothing we find is going to be something we can't fix."

Since it was late, there was hardly any traffic, and we were pulling into her place within ten minutes. I saw Blake's bike and Jackie's car in the driveway. I pulled in front of the house and the others found spots to park. I bet the neighbors were loving this, but I didn't give a shit. I got out and opened Skye's door, helping her down. I held onto her as we went to the front door. Blake was waiting for us and let us inside. I could see the living room from the entryway. It was trashed—furniture overturned, things strewn across the floor, and a few items broken. Skye gasped. She took off to hug her mom.

"Does the whole place look like this?"

"Yep. But it's Skye's room you need to see. Don't let her in there, Executioner," Blake warned me.

"Keep her here if she tries to come down the hall." He nodded. I took off with the guys on my heels. When I stepped into her room and saw what he'd meant, I wanted to kill someone. They'd not only wrecked the room, they'd slashed her clothes, and written on the wall a message. *Sorry we missed you. See you soon, sweetheart. We warned you what would happen.* I fought not to lose it. Omen had come with us. He walked over to look at her bed. He wrinkled his nose and then yanked back the comforter. I heard him swear.

"Fuck, Ex, you have to see this. That's some sick shit." I went over to see what he was looking at. Someone had jacked off all over her sheets. I almost gagged. Wrecker pushed in between us and the bed.

"Jesus Christ! Okay, let me get a team in here. Don't touch anything. We'll get samples and shit. Executioner, get them out of here and back to the compound."

"Can they take anything with them?" He thought for a minute. "Let me and Cuffs go with them, and we'll make sure they don't touch anything they shouldn't. Put on these gloves and pack some of her stuff if you want." I shook my head.

"I'm not letting her wear anything they may have touched. Fuck it, don't bother. If they need shit, I'll take them shopping. None of them need to wear it. Once you're done, I'll see about getting things cleaned up and shit boxed. They're not coming back here. Not as long as those bastards are still out there. Looks like we're getting a new family moving onto the compound sooner than we thought."

Sin had come with us. He nodded. "Did you talk to Jackie about the house for her yet?"

"No, I planned to do it soon."

"Well, let's do that tomorrow, or I guess later today. No use them having to keep going back and forth between here and the compound. For now, we'll get them back there and situated. I expect they need to destress a bit too."

"Thanks, Sin." I went out to them. Skye was anxiously watching the hall. Blake was standing at the head of it with his arms crossed. When I came up behind him, he looked over his shoulder.

"Thank God, I think your old lady was about to tackle my ass. She's a mean little thing." She wrinkled her nose at him and rolled her eyes.

"Yeah, she's a handful. Thanks." She came over to me.

"What's going on? Why wouldn't Blake, soon-to-be-dead Blake," she looked at him and he smirked, "let me down the hall?"

"Babe, I told him not to. They did a number on your room. You don't need to see that shit. Let's get everyone out of here and back to the compound."

"What about our clothes?"

"Forget it. If you need stuff, we'll get more. I don't want you wearing the shit they touched." I should have known she wouldn't let that stand. Before I knew what she planned, she darted around me and ran down the hall. I shouted at her to stop, but she kept going. I raced after her. I caught her right after she got inside her room, as I heard her cry out. When I got in the room, she was down on her knees staring at the message on the wall.

I crouched down beside her. She began to rock with her arms around her middle. "Why? Why would they do this? My God, all because of some money." She sobbed. I picked her up. She cried on my shoulder. I turned to take her out when she raised her head. "What is that on the bed?" I swore. Her face got white as she realized what it was, then she was shoving at my chest.

"Put me down, Ex, put me down!" she said frantically.

"No, you need to stay right where you are."

"I'm going to be sick!" she shouted. I quickly took her into her bathroom and sat her down beside the toilet. I was just in time, as she puked into it. I grabbed a washcloth and wet it as she vomited. When she was done, I wiped her face and mouth. Jackie was in there by then. She and I helped Skye clean up and brush her teeth. When she was done, I picked her up and carried her out of there. That was it, she was going back home. The sight of that shit had made her sick. Something else I'd make the fuckers responsible pay for when we found them.

I left Wrecker and Cuffs there with a couple of Boss's guys. As I got ready to pull out, Boss pulled in with Saint. I got out to brief them. They looked pissed. "Wrecker said the house was broken into. Anything else I should know?" Boss asked me.

"Yeah, take a look at Skye's room. Boss, you're the law, but hear me when I say, this isn't going to be something the law is going to take care of. These kinds of people don't learn. If I get to them first, they're dead." Maybe not the smartest thing to tell the chief of police, but he'd done the same to the guy who'd hurt Jenn. Hell, Jenn had killed a woman bent on killing her.

"I hear ya, Executioner. Let me see what's happening. Take your family home. Skye should be resting. I'll stop by later and we can talk." They both clapped me on the shoulder and then went inside. I got back in the truck with Skye. She was sitting there listless. I hurried to get us back to the compound. She needed to lie down. This couldn't be good for her or the baby. I worried the whole way back.

"Skye, baby, look at me." She glanced over at me. "I swear we'll take care of them. No one's going to hurt you or your family. We're going to find them. And when we do, they'll regret ever targeting you or anyone else." She didn't say anything for a few moments.

"Slade, I think I know what you're saying. So, let me be clear." I tensed. Shit, she was going to tell me not to kill 'em. I couldn't promise her that. "You make them pay for everything they've done to all of us. Make it hurt." Her face got hard. I was stunned. Maybe she was harder than I thought.

"I will, babe, I will. We're here. I think you need to rest, but I know you won't yet. Your mom can stay in the spare room at my place and the boys can bunk out in the living room. Later, we'll figure something else out for them long term."

"Okay," is all she said. When we made it back to the compound, I took them straight to the trailer. Jackie and the boys were right behind us. I got out and helped Skye out. Tanner got his mom's door.

"Jackie, you and the boys can stay here tonight. Then we'll see about finding you something more comfortable for all of you. Guys, I'll get a couple of sleeping cots we have at the clubhouse. They're not great, but they're sure better than the floor."

"Ex, anything is fine. I hate that we're pushing in on you, but I do feel safer here than at the house," Jackie said.

"It's not pushing. Later, I have something I've been wanting to talk to you about anyway, but that can wait.

Baby, get inside with your family and I'll be right back."
I gave Skye a quick kiss and then went to the clubhouse.
I was digging around in one of our storage rooms when
someone came in. I turned around to find Sara standing
there. She had a worried look on her face. I gave her a
hug.

"Are Jackie and the boys, okay? I knew you guys tore
out of here to go to their house."

"They're fine. The house is a mess, and we don't want
them to stay there. They're going to stay with me tonight and then we'll see about getting them in a more
comfortable place to stay here. I'm getting cots out for
Tanner and Tyson to sleep on." I went back to rumma-
ging.

"They can stay with me if they want, Ex. I have two
extra bedrooms. The boys would have to share, but that
one has two beds in it." I stopped searching.

"Seriously? Are you sure, Sara? I mean, I can find
them something else. I just don't want to put them up in
the clubhouse."

"Of course I'm sure. I wouldn't have offered if I
wasn't. I agree this isn't the place for any of them. Besides, they're family now along with Skye. We take care
of family." I had to give her another hug and then a kiss.
She smacked me on the chest. "Behave. I expect Skye
wants them close tonight. Bring them over tomorrow
after you talk to them. Get some rest yourself." She went
for the door.

"Thanks, Sara. Love ya," I told her. She grinned as she
left. With that figured out, I hurried to grab the cots and
get back to them. I hoped they'd be happy to go to Sara's
house. If not, I'd find somewhere else.

When I walked into the trailer, I saw everyone was in

the living room. I was happy to see Skye had changed into pajamas. It looked like she'd given a pair of hers to her mom. The boys I'd have to figure out something until I could take them shopping. I was serious about them not wearing anything those fuckers had touched. It was just the boys were smaller than any of us guys. They were tall but not filled out. I put the cots down.

"I found them. By the way, I ran into Sara while I was getting these. Jackie, she said she'd love to have the three of you stay with her. She has two extra bedrooms, and one has two beds in it. You guys would have to share, but not sleep with each other," I teased Tanner and Tyson. They both groaned as I grinned at them. I wanted to ease their tension.

"Oh, Ex, that's so kind of her. Is she sure? I hate to invade her sanctuary with these two monsters."

"She wouldn't offer unless she was. And she can handle these two. She handles all of us with no problem." Skye got up and came over to hug me close. She kissed my neck.

"Thank you, honey. I know you need to go talk to the guys. They should be back soon. Why don't you do that and let me and mom get things arranged here?"

"Do you promise to lie down soon and get some rest? I don't want you lying here and worrying about it."

"I promise. Go. If we need anything, I'll text." Jackie caught my eye and nodded. I knew she'd make sure she rested. I gave Skye a deep kiss then went outside. Time to shake some shit up.

Executioner: Chapter 16

It was after two by the time my brothers and Boss made it to the compound. I'd paced the common room and picked up a few things. The bunnies had been there looking pissed that they were alone. Vonnie gave me a suggestive look that I ignored. She'd better not pull any of her shit like she did with Sin on me. She was on thin ice. In fact, I was surprised she hadn't left. She kept whining about having to clean and cook. That was the best damn idea ever.

Omen came over to me as soon as they came inside. "Damn, *mon ami*, I had no idea how exciting it was going to be here! How's your *chéri*?"

"She's okay. Her mom is keeping an eye on her to make sure she rests."

"Ah, the beautiful Jackie. Those are two gorgeous women."

I glared at him. "Don't get any ideas, buddy. I'm not going to have you sweet talking your way into my future mother-in-law's pants for a piece of ass. There's plenty around if you want it." I pointed out the bunnies who were looking at him like he was fresh meat. "She's had enough shit from men in her life," I warned him.

"I'm not looking for a piece of ass, as you put it, from her. And what do you mean she's had enough shit from men?" He had a funny look on his face.

"I'll tell you about her husband, Skye's dad, later. That's a whole lot of fucked up right there. He's on my list to find and take care of, but first, I want to know what Boss and the guys found out." He nodded and we went over to them. Sin told the bunnies to get lost, and they stomped out. We all sat down at a few tables.

"Did your techs find anything, Boss?"

"They took prints, which we'll get samples from Skye and her family, and I guess you. Plus, anyone else who's been in the house lately. And they took samples of the mess left in Skye's room. Sick motherfuckers to do that shit. They can go back and get stuff if they need it. Heard you wanted to move them here."

"Yeah, I do want to move them. I plan to talk to Jackie later today about building a house here on the compound, next to the one I want to build for me and Skye. Since it looks like we need to wait to see if anyone pops up in the system, what're we going to do about the extortionists? We know they're still active with some businesses. People are too afraid to stop paying. And those that haven't will see escalations I think after this. They wanted to make a point with Skye."

"Why would they single her out?" Omen asked. I quickly told him about what happened months ago when they didn't pay, and the threat made against Skye. He stood up. "That shit's not happening. We need to figure out how to set a trap. They know you're waiting for them. I assume they know you guys, but they don't know me and Brennan. How about we go undercover at one of the other businesses where they do pay? We could pretend to work there and watch for one or more of them. I assume you tried to catch them that way?"

"Not yet, since the first of the month has passed. We just found out they were on to us last week. It's not a bad idea. You would have to not hang here. Do you think we can get someone to let us do it?" I asked Sin and the others. We all sat there thinking. Saint snapped his fingers.

"It would have to be somewhere a couple of buff guys wouldn't stand out. I think Seth at the Grain & Kernel feed store and Abe over at Bubbles strip club would do it. They always need help. One of you can be a bouncer or bartender and the other whatever Seth needs."

"I call dibs on the strip club." Brennan smirked.

"I don't care who does which, I just want to get them to agree. But just so you know, Abe doesn't let his guys mess with his girls. How soon do you think we can find out? It would be better to get these two in place ahead of the first of the month," I told them.

"I can talk to Abe if you'll talk to Seth, Sin?" Boss volunteered.

"Sure. Not a problem. They don't like paying and the only reason they do is Seth's worried about his family and Abe about his girls. He's like a damn father to those women. Let's plan to speak to both of them by the end of the day on Tuesday. In the meantime, we get Jackie and the boys moved here. Any idea where they can stay long term until the house is done?"

"Yeah, your mom took care of it. She told me they can stay with her. I think they're going to do it."

"I should have known she'd do that. The woman keeps us sorted," he said with a grin. Sara did treat all of us like we were her sons. At times it could be a tad annoying, but most of the time it was a godsend. With this settled, we all broke for a few hours of sleep. We'd get back together later in the day.

I made sure Omen was settled into his room at the clubhouse and then went to mine. It was quiet when I got inside. The boys were sacked out on the cots, dead to the world. Jackie, I assumed was the same in her room.

I tiptoed to ours. I eased inside and saw Skye was curled up in bed sound asleep. I was happy to see she was sleeping. I hurried and stripped then crawled in with her. She rolled over and flung her arm and leg over me.

"Everything okay?" she mumbled. She didn't even open her eyes. I kissed her softly.

"Everything's fine. Go back to sleep. We'll talk later." She drifted right back to sleep. It didn't take too long for me to do the same. I was too tired to think anymore right now.

◄‖► ◄‖► ◄‖► ◄‖►

We slept until almost noon. When we got up, Jackie was in the kitchen cooking lunch. We sat down at the table. This looked like a good time to tell her about the house idea. "Jackie, I wanted to talk to you about something. I mentioned it to Skye, and I need your approval."

She gave me a puzzled look. "Okay, what is it?"

"I've got the guys over at Pop's construction business getting started on materials to build us a house here on the compound. I know I briefly told you about wanting to build a house here for you. You told me no, but I want to talk about it again. It's something I really want you to do."

She sighed. "Ex, I love that you're willing to do this, but it's too much. You and Skye have a house and a baby to take care of. I'm not adding that to your plate. The only way I'd consider it is if we sell my house and I pay for this one to be built. It doesn't need to be huge."

I didn't want her to pay for it, but maybe this would be the only way to get her to agree. And if it should happen when it was done, the house was already paid for, she and I could battle it out then. Sneaky I know, but worth it. "Okay, let's do that. You sell your house and build here. When it's done, you can pay what is owed on it. Deal?" I asked as I stuck out my hand. She looked at me like she knew there was a trap, but she had no idea what it was. After a few seconds, she shook my hand.

"Deal. Now, let's eat. My grandbaby needs some food. Skye, did you take your vitamins? If not, you need to take them now. If they make you sick, try taking them at bedtime with food. That always helped me."

"Yes, Mom, I took them. But they do make me queasy, good idea," she told her mom lovingly. With Jackie around, I'd have to worry about her less. She and Skye were setting the table when there was a knock at the door. I yelled for whoever it was to come in. The door opened and in strolled Omen.

"You're just in time for lunch. What's up?" I asked. He greeted the ladies before he sat down. The boys came in from the living room. I was going to have to make sure they had stuff to keep them entertained when they weren't in school or working at the shop. We'd have to go shopping today before school and work tomorrow.

"I just came to see if you all wanted me to do anything today. I talked to Sin. Me and Brennan will be rolling out tonight. We'll stay in town." That's all he said in front of the ladies. He knew enough not to get into anything that might be considered club business in front of them.

"Not that I can think of. Thanks."

"Why're you two staying in town?" Jackie asked as she took her seat. He glanced at me. I didn't see any problem telling them this. They needed to know not to act like they knew them if they ran into them in town anyway.

"I can't go into too many details, but they're going to help us with the extortionist situation. In order to do that, they can't be seen associating with us. So, if you see them, you can't act like you know them," I warned them.

"We'll make sure to not give it away. Right boys?" Jackie asked.

"Yeah, Mom, we know. Hey, Executioner, we have school tomorrow. Are we going to the house to get some of our stuff?" Tyson asked.

"I thought we'd go shopping. I'd rather not have you wearing what they touched."

"Honey, that's sweet, but as long as we wash it, we'll be fine. I need to see what can be salvaged. I'd like to go to the house if we can," Jackie added. I could tell by the look on her face, she wasn't going to budge on the clothing thing.

"Shit, okay, I guess we can do that. It's a good thing to get started anyway. We can box things and throw out stuff as we go. You'll be just one step closer to moving into the new house," I said with a smile. She rolled her eyes.

"House? Are you moving somewhere?" Omen asked all smooth as if he had no idea. I'd have to keep an eye on him. He wasn't opposed to women older than him, and Jackie didn't look or act her age. He caught me watching him and winked. I showed him my teeth.

"Ex wants us to build a house here next to him and Skye. He's bribed me with the vision of my grandkids running over to see me all the time. He doesn't fight fair."

"Yeah, well neither do you nor your daughter. Besides, I need to make sure to keep the men from beating down your door." She blushed and shook her head.

"You're so silly. Eat. I want to go to the house." We all fell silent as we inhaled lunch. Once it was done and the mess cleaned up, we got ready to go. Since Omen couldn't be seen with us, I asked Dash and Cuffs to come with us. We left a half hour later.

I hated the idea of Skye having to see the house again. Drake had pulled me aside and said they had the message painted over already after taking pictures, and the disgusting bedding was gone. It made it a little better, but not much.

When we went inside, I watched Jackie get teary eyed. She scanned the rooms, looking lost. I gave her a hug as I held on to Skye. Once she was back under control, we got started. She'd seen it last night but in the harsh light of day, it looked so much worse. They packed the clothes that weren't destroyed along with their personal stuff. The rest we'd work on packing and storing. It took us a couple of hours.

When we left, I made sure to lock up though it seemed to be a waste. They'd broken in before; they could do it again. Before heading back, we stopped to check on the store. It looked like it was fine. We'd upgraded the security system there and added more cameras. If anyone tried to mess with it, we'd likely see who it was. Back at the compound, we took them over to Sara's. She was ready for them. Jackie was thanking her again for offering her house and making sure she wouldn't mind.

"Hell, I'd love the company. Too much testosterone around here. I'm trying to get all these boys to settle down so I can have daughters. Smelly men all the time get to be too much." She elbowed me in the ribs as she said it. I pretended like it hurt.

"God, you're getting meaner every day. Does Sin know how mean his mom is?"

"Yes, he does. Now, why don't you, Tyson, and Tanner go bring in their stuff? It needs to be washed. Jackie, Skye, and I are going to have a chat and sit a spell." I knew when I was told to get lost. We went to do as she said. I loved to see Skye fitting in so well. We spent an hour there and then left them to get busy.

At my place, we sorted her clothes and got them started in the wash. "Are you sure you won't let me buy you all new stuff, baby?"

"No, there's no need. I can wash them. But you know, you could help me with something else while these wash?"

"What's that?"

"Well, I seem to have this ache that I think only you can help me with," she said coyly. As she said it, she inched her top up and off. Then her hands went behind her back to unhook her bra. I was instantly getting hard. I walked over and helped her discard it and cupped her breasts in my hands. I ran my thumbs over her nipples, making them stand up.

"I think I can most definitely help you with that ache, darling. And you can help me with this." I took her hand and placed it on my cock. She gave me a squeeze.

"I'd love to." I swung her up and carried her off to our bedroom. I had a job to do, and no way was I going to do less than a satisfactory one. I stripped her down to her panties then worked to get my clothes and boots off. She wiggled out of those panties as I undressed then flung them at me. I grabbed them and held them to my nose. I could smell her cherry scent. I growled.

She tried to run as I stalked her. I caught her on the other side of the bed and gently threw her down on it. She squealed as she bounced. I jumped on top of her. "Ready for me to take care of both our problems, Baby Girl?"

"Oh, I'm more than ready. Work away." She spread her legs and let me see her cream. I moaned and then got down to work on pleasuring my woman and myself. It didn't take long to have her screaming my name and then for me to fill her with my cum. When we were done, she was dozing in the bed, and I felt like I needed to take a short nap. She could wring me out like no one else ever could.

Skye: Chapter 17

It had been a week since our house had been vandalized. It still made me sick to think of the words written on my bedroom wall and the cum left on my sheets. Thankfully, when we went to get our things, someone had painted over the words and the bedding had been removed. I knew it had to have been Executioner's brothers who did it. It made me love them even more.

Mom and my brothers had settled in at Sara's house. The guard duty had been kept up in light of the incident. Only now, someone was outside of the school while the boys were there. It was something I found they had done just a matter of weeks ago when Lyric was in danger. Brennan and Omen had started to work in town at the strip club and the feed store. I hadn't seen them yet, but I knew I had to act like they were strangers.

My hours at the shop had been decreased. If Ex his way, I wouldn't be working there at all. He'd gone behind my back and worked with Mom to hire another employee. She was a friend of Sis', Brea's daughter. Her name was Debbi. She seemed to be nice enough. I guess time would tell if she stuck it out. My worry was the cost, but they had assured me that with us not paying the extra five hundred a month, me not being at home and the family at the compound, it would work. Somehow, Executioner had gotten the house cleaned up. He was insisting he'd get the repairs done as soon as possible then it could go on the market.

I now had the club's seven businesses, plus six others, and two more had asked for my help. Ex said I couldn't do more until I let go of the store completely. We'd argued for the past two days. In fact, we were still at odds over it. So, while he was working at the dealership, I'd taken one of the guys and did my rounds to my various clients' businesses.

When I met with Ben from the real estate office, he was thrilled with what I'd done. I pointed out to him that they had a lot of places on the books that they had bought but never sold. Most showed they were being rented out monthly—some as houses and others as acreage for cattle grazing or crops. That seemed to be making them a lot of cash, but I thought he'd told me they mainly sold and didn't do property management. So, when we met, I asked him.

"Skye, I'd have to check into these to be honest. You're right, we're mainly a real estate agency. We do very little property management. Dad always said it was too much of a pain and the liability of having to fix things when renters tore stuff up wasn't worth it. But my brother, Jonathan, has been overseeing that small chunk of the business and the books. I hired you to give him a break. I need his help on the other side and if he doesn't have to do our books, he can easily help."

"Maybe I can ask him."

"No, let me find out. I haven't told him I hired you yet. He hates change. It's better to ease him into it. Give me a couple of weeks and I'll get back to you."

"Okay, let me know. In the meantime, if something comes up, just give me a call."

"I will. By the way, I don't mean to pry, but I can't help but see one of the Ares' Infidels came with you today. May I ask why?" He shot an uneasy look out the window. Dash was leaning up against his bike next to my car. He was scanning the whole area.

"It's nothing, Ben. My boyfriend is just a little over-protective. He doesn't want me to go anywhere alone."

"Your boyfriend? Who, one of the Infidels?"

"Yes, do you know Executioner?" His eyes grew round when I said Ex's name. Of course, even if he didn't know him, the name was enough to scare the hell out of people.

"E-Executioner is your boyfriend? The giant one with the long dark hair?" He gulped. I held onto my laugh.

"Yeah, that's him. He's just a little more nervous with the stuff happening around town to some businesses and with me being pregnant."

"You're pregnant? Well, congratulations, Skye, that's great news. I had no idea you were seeing anyone. And I don't blame him. I heard what happened to your mom's store. It's terrible that stuff like that is happening in our town." We chatted a few minutes more, then he looked at his watch. "I hate to cut this short, but I have a three o'clock appointment. Let me know if you have any questions. I'll send over the updated financials for the week on Sunday or Monday."

He walked me to the door. As I told him, "Have a good weekend," I saw a man stand up in the waiting area. That must be his appointment. Ben smiled and waved at me. As soon as I was outside, Dash was over to me. "Dash, I want to take a quick run. It's outside of town on the other side of the highway. There are some rental properties over there I'd like to take a look at."

Dash frowned. He hated the idea, but something was telling me I needed to go see some of those properties Ben and his brother were renting out. Maybe if I did, I could recommend which ones they might want to consider offloading after I ran the comps and did some checking. "I don't know, Skye. I don't think Executioner would like that. Around town is one thing, but out there, I don't think he'll like that."

I thought about it. How could I get out there and still have enough protection to suit my man? A damn Marine battalion probably wouldn't be enough for him! I loved him, but he was super protective. "Give me a minute, will you?"

"Sure, but will you sit in the car? I hate you out in the open like this." He was still looking around. I gave him a break and got in the car without arguing. As he stood beside my car, I called Ex. He answered before the second ring.

"What's wrong, baby?" I could hear the anxious tone in his voice. I realized we texted during the day but didn't call.

"Baby, nothing is wrong. Sorry I scared you. I wanted to know if you might be able to get away early and come with us? I want to check out some rental properties. The Bentley's have several outside of town all grouped together. I want to check them out. Dash isn't comfortable it being just the two of us."

"Where outside of town?"

"On the other side of the highway, back behind that truck stop and strip mall area over there."

"Dash is right, you're not going over that way with just him. Where are you right now?"

"Outside Bentley's Real Estate office. We can come and meet you at the dealership." It wasn't more than fourteen or so blocks over to the Harley dealership on Soleil Avenue and First Street.

"No, we'd just backtrack. I'll meet you. Why don't you have Dash take you to Jitters? It's close and you can get yourself one of those iced teas you like. You haven't had caffeine today, have you?" I rolled my eyes. He'd been on this kick to make sure I drank more water and had less caffeine after he read somewhere it wasn't good for me.

"As a matter of fact, I haven't. We'll meet you there. Do you want me to grab you something?"

"Naw, baby. See you in a few. Love you."

"Love you, too. Bye." I couldn't help but smile as we hung up. I still couldn't believe it when he'd tell me he loved me, which he did several times a day. It was like now that he'd said it, he wanted to make sure I knew he meant it. I rolled down my window.

"Ex said to go to Jitters and he'll meet us there. His highness has said I can have some caffeine." Dash snickered. He knew of Ex's edict, and he was supposed to make sure I behaved. I think he told all the guys to watch me because more than one had cautioned me if I went to drink more, and they saw it.

While he got on his bike, I rolled up my window, snapped my seatbelt and got situated. We pulled out and went a few blocks down and over to Jitters. They were busy as usual. We decided to go inside and wait. By the time we got through the line, and I had to wait for the barista to stop flirting with Dash, we'd barely sat down with our drinks when Executioner came striding through the door. He got even more attention than Dash. I think the height and the hair did it. I saw Miss Slutty Barista eating him up with her eyes.

When he got to our table, I stood up and made sure I laid my claim down. I kissed the hell out of him. He lifted me off my feet and kissed me back. Dash cleared his throat. "Hey, you two, we're in public. There are kids in here you're going to scar for life if you keep it up." We both moved apart, so we could laugh and look at him. He was grinning at us.

"I had to. Your girlfriend, the slut barista, was eye fucking my man." Dash laughed and Ex wrinkled his brows down. "Never mind. Let me finish this really quick and hit the bathroom and then we can go." I sat down. Ex took the seat next to me. "How was the dealership today?"

"Good. Sold two bikes and did some work on a few more that should be picked up in a few days. Lots of foot traffic in and out of the store, too. Did you get your visits done?"

"No, but I can do those later. I really want to see these places. Ben told me they never used to do many rental properties or as he calls it, property management. He was surprised they had that much. Jonathan handles that I guess. I want to see them and do some research. Maybe I can help them decide which to keep and which to sell. I like being able to make things more profitable."

"Damn, what did I do to deserve such a smart woman? Sexy, beautiful, and smart, that's what you need to look for, Dash. Add in loyalty and you have the whole package."

Dash winked at me. I shook my head. I wasn't going to touch that. When I was done drinking and had hit the bathroom, we got on the road. When we got outside of town, I admired the scenery and the amount of land. We didn't pass a whole lot of cars. Not like we saw on the other side of town where the compound was. I looked at my phone. I'd programmed in the various addresses and the route so we could go from one to the other.

When we passed the first place, I saw it was a huge area that stretched for miles. It was five hundred acres in total. No house, just land according to the records. I didn't see any fences, cattle, or even planted fields. At this time of year, they should be well underway if they were growing crops.

The next one was a few miles down the road. It had a house on it, but the yard was overgrown with grass and weeds. I saw nothing that would make me think anyone lived there. We went by a total of six places. Two were large parcels of land and the rest houses. All of them looked the same. It didn't make any sense. At the last one, I stopped, and Ex came over to the car. "What's up, babe?"

"This makes no sense, Slade. None of these looks like they're leased or used. I need to go home and sit down at my computer. Maybe I made a mistake, and these are the ones they don't lease." Though I was positive I had them right.

"Let's do that. It's getting late and you've been working all day. Time to get some dinner and put your feet up." He gave me a kiss and went back to his bike. The whole drive back I racked my brain on an explanation for them looking like that, and if they were the ones being rented.

When we got to the compound and to his trailer, I opened the door to find Sara and the boys inside. I could smell dinner cooking. I looked at the clock. Damn, it was after six o'clock. I hurried into the kitchen. "Sara, what're you doing? I can do this."

"Sit your ass down and relax. You've been up all day and I know you went to look at properties. Ex told me before he left the dealership. I knew you'd be tired and so would Jackie. I'm cooking tonight. Don't argue with me." She gave me a swat on the butt.

Lord, I had her bossing me now. I went to the bedroom to change. Ex followed me. As I stripped off my work clothes, I asked him, "Do you have the whole club watching me and making sure I don't overdo it, as you say?"

"Yep. You're used to doing too much, Skye. You need to slow down and take care of you and the baby."

"So, after this baby is born, you'll stop it."

"Hell, no. You're not going to work yourself to death ever again," he growled. I went over to him and wrapped my arms around his neck. When he cupped my ass in his hands, I jumped up and wrapped my legs around him.

"I guess the upside to you doing that, is I'll have more energy for this." I kissed him while I rubbed my pussy against his growing erection. I could feel it through his jeans and my panties. He groaned and pushed harder against me. His zipper raked over my clit and made me shudder. He slid his finger under the edge of my panties and teased my slick folds.

"Behave, or I don't care if your brothers and Sara are in the other room. I'll have you naked and my cock buried in you in no time. I'll pound this pussy until we both scream."

I moaned. "God, yes. I want that. Let's hurry up and get rid of them. I don't know how long I can wait." He teased me for a few more seconds then let me down. My legs were shaking. I changed my panties and got dressed in my tank and shorts. He washed his hands after he licked his finger clean.

It wasn't long before Mom was home, and she came

in the door. I guess Sara had texted her to come to our place. We all sat down to dinner together. We insisted Sara stay. I loved spending time with my family, but I was counting the minutes until they left tonight, which unfortunately, wasn't soon enough. It was Friday, family game night. Mom got to choose this time.

Knowing we'd have to wait, I made a suggestion, "What do you think of going to the clubhouse and seeing who else might want to join us? We might have to take turns playing, but some of the others might like to join. Or is that too silly for bikers?" I asked Executioner with a smirk.

"I play, don't I? I think it's a good idea. Some will probably like it. We'll go now and leave before it gets too late." I knew he was referring to when the bunnies would be over hooking up with the guys. My brothers knew about sex, but I didn't want them to see that. Tan and Ty jumped up, excited as hell. I yelled at them. "Grab the games from the house and bring a few video games too. I know some of the guys love to play those. I've seen them." They ran off to Sara's to get them.

"I love to see how much you all do things together. Families don't do this kind of thing anymore. I remember when James and I would play games with Sin. They need to see this. A lot of them didn't have the best family lives."

"We may not have had a lot, but this was something we could all do that really didn't cost much other than the cost of the board game," Mom told her as we walked over together. Inside, the guys were already there and starting to wind down from the week. The big screen was on, and Wrecker and Pitbull were playing some war game. Boomer and Saint were playing a game of pool.

Phantom and Rampage were at the dart board. Torpedo and Talon were sitting at the bar talking to Blake, who was serving. I didn't see Dash and of course Brennan and Omen weren't hanging here. Sin was coming out of the kitchen with Lyric. Sara gave a whistle.

"Tanner and Tyson are bringing over some games, who wants in on family game night?" They all looked at us, then they were all talking at once. When the boys got back, everyone started to divide up. I held back my laugh to see a bunch of bikers so eager to play games. In the end, we had a game of *Yahtzee* and *Monopoly* going as well as two-player video games.

I lost track of time. At several points, I was laughing so hard at their antics, I had tears in my eyes. Executioner was as bad as the others. It was true, men were just big boys at heart. I got up and told him I'd be back, I had to go to the bathroom. I drank too much water. He'd been pushing it on me all evening. When I came back, it was to see that the bunnies had come in while I was in the bathroom. The games were breaking up, which looking at the clock, I was stunned to see it was after ten.

Mom had Tanner and Tyson putting away games. I went to help them. That's when shit got ugly. As I crossed the floor, one of the bunnies, I think Lyric said her name was Vonnie, opened her mouth. She had a sour look on her face. "What in the hell is this? Since when is this a daycare for brats? If they're not old enough to drink and fuck they shouldn't be in here." I saw red. I changed course and went straight for her.

The guys were yelling at her to shut her damn mouth. I saw Lyric come out of the kitchen and head in her direction. None of us saw my mom move. Next thing I knew, she was in Vonnie's face. "What did you just say?" she snapped at her.

"I said you should keep your brats out of here. This is a clubhouse not a daycare. I don't know why you're staying here anyway. Your daughter might be fucking Executioner, but who're you fucking? Or are your boys here to learn how to be men?" she asked nastily. Mom shouted at my brothers to go outside, and they reluctantly did. Their eyes were huge as they went. As soon as the door closed, my mom lost it. She hauled back her fist and punched Vonnie in the mouth.

You could hear the punch and the gasp from everyone in the room. Vonnie screamed and clutched her mouth for a moment, then she charged my mom. Only she didn't get to her because I stepped between them and tripped her. When she hit the floor and rolled onto her back to glare at me, I pressed my foot down on her throat. She was beating at my leg and gasping for air.

"Talk shit like that again or touch my mom, bitch, and I'll kill you. Don't ever say that disgusting shit around my brothers again either. Who the hell says stuff like that?" Executioner pulled me away from her. Vonnie got to her feet slowly. She looked around.

"Are you going to let her talk to me that way? Or threaten me?"

"Vonnie, you're done. We've had enough of your bullshit. You did it to Lyric and now this. And in case you forgot in two minutes, you started it! Jackie, Skye, and the boys have more right to be here than you. They're family. Skye is Ex's old lady. Jackie is her mom. Those boys are her brothers, and that makes them family. Get your shit and I want you gone by morning," Sin told her. She looked stunned.

"You can't mean that, Sin! You can't."

"Oh, yes I do."

She stomped to the door when she saw none of the guys were going to defend her. The other three bunnies —Shy, Tabby Cat, and Barbie were all standing there looking scared and stunned. Vonnie looked at me, Mom, and Lyric. "You bitches wait. They'll get tired of you, and they'll beg me to come back. No way they can want you for long. These bullshit changes will be forgotten." Then she looked at her fellow bunnies. "You should come with me. That'll show 'em. They won't have anyone to cook, clean or fuck 'em. They'll be begging in a week."

Lyric burst out laughing. "Oh my God, I was right. She does think her pussy is golden. Sorry, Vonnie, but all the guys assured me it's not. I know that Sin and Executioner won't be looking for you, and I highly doubt the rest will have a second of trouble finding someone to screw for fun. Good riddance." Vonnie screamed and slammed out the door. I took after her. Executioner tried to grab me, but he missed. I remembered my brothers were outside!

As I pushed out the door, she was standing out there mouthing off to them, saying, "Your sister is a slut and your mom's a cunt." I grabbed her by the hair and swung her into the side of the clubhouse. She hit face first, then I dragged her face down the brick wall and threw her to the ground. I would have kicked the hell out of her, but I was picked up. I recognized Ex's arms.

"Calm down, Baby Girl. She's had enough, and you don't need to be getting so upset and fighting in your condition. Think of the baby," he whispered to me. I was breathing like I'd run a marathon. I still had rage coursing through me. Saint sneered and looked at Dash and Blake.

"Help her to her apartment. Make sure she's alright. If not, let me know. Hell, help her pack, because she needs to be gone by noon. I'm sick of this shit." Vonnie moaned and cried as they helped her up and around the corner.

"This was one helluva family game night. Same time next week?" Talon piped up. That broke the tension and we all started to laugh. After making sure I was okay, Mom took the boys back to Sara's. Executioner was trying to insist I be checked out. He wanted to call Paula, Hook's woman. I guess she was some kind of doctor. It took some convincing to get him to not call. Damn, not the way I'd been hoping for our night to end. What happened to sex and then a nice nap? We said goodnight and he insisted on carrying me home. Maybe I could convince him I needed him to make love to me so I could calm down. It was worth a try.

Executioner: Chapter 18

After all the excitement with Vonnie, Skye and I didn't think about the real estate properties until late Sunday night. When I'd taken her back to the trailer Friday night after the fight, I'd made love to her thoroughly. The rest of the weekend we rested and took things easy.

However, she was busy working on it today. The only way I got her to stop was because we had the baby appointment in the afternoon. We were going to have them do the chromosomal test and to make sure she was doing okay otherwise. I was nervous as hell. Not that we'd find something wrong with the baby or her. I was nervous that the doc would come back and tell us it was all a mistake, and she wasn't pregnant.

I had no idea why the thought hurt so much. I mean, I wasn't expecting to have a kid any time soon or maybe ever before Skye. If we'd gotten together and waited to have one, I'd have been okay about it, but to be told she was and then to find out she wasn't was awful to think about. As soon as I heard that I was going to be a father, I'd started to dream about all the things I'd do with my kids. Yeah, kids, because I hoped like hell, we'd end up with more than one over the coming years. It made me realize I wanted to be a dad right now, but only with her as the mother.

Our meeting wasn't conventional. Our start was one of the worst ever, but it was ours. I knew as soon as I opened my eyes the next day, she was meant to be mine, which had made not knowing who she was or where she was, that much more painful. I'd wondered if I'd lost my mind. I was frantic to find her, but kept it locked down and hidden from my brothers.

Skye shook me from those memories when she took my hand. We were in the waiting room at the doctor's office. We'd signed in and she'd filled out all the papers they wanted. I'd answered the questions for my side of the family as best as I could. Some things I just didn't know. She gave me a concerned look.

"Are you alright, honey?"

I kissed her hand. "I'm fine. Just thinking about the night we met and how damn happy I was when I found you that day at the shop."

"Happy? You seemed a little pissed at me."

"No, it was relief coupled with being upset you didn't seem to want anything to do with me."

"Baby, you know why I acted that way. I was so messed up about what my dad did and said."

"I know. Which I hate. But I'll never do that to you or our kids. I love you so damn much, Skye." I gave her a kiss. I made sure not to let it get too heated, since we were in the doctor's office. Hearing a woman call out her name was what made us stop. Looking up, we saw a woman in white standing there with a paper in her hand. We both got up. The nurse—I assumed she was one—looked at me stunned. We followed her to the back to get Skye weighed, her vitals checked, and then into a paper gown. Skye was fidgeting as we waited for the doctor.

"Baby Girl, what's bothering you? You're fidgeting."

"I'm scared, Slade. What if she says I'm not pregnant after all?" Hearing my worry come out of her mouth stunned me.

I tried to reassure her. "They won't. You said they did a blood test last time to confirm you were. You've been nauseated and sick. And baby, those breasts have gotten bigger already." I wiggled my eyebrows at her, and she giggled. I loved her breasts and there was more to them, which made me even happier. Seeing the changes in her body only made me want her more not less.

A soft knock on the door had us sitting up straighter. The door opened and in came a slightly gray-haired woman. She looked like she was in her early fifties. She smiled at us. "Hello, Skye, good to see you again. And this is..."

"I'm her man, Executioner." Doc's eyes got big when I stood to shake her hand. She took in my rag and name on the front. She barely shook my hand before she drew her hand back.

"I see. Executioner, I'm Ms. Trellis, one of the midwives. I'll hopefully be the one to deliver this baby. Why don't we listen and see what we can hear? But first, I see here it says you want to have the chromosomal test done. May I ask why? Is there a history of Down Syndrome or something in your lifestyle that makes you think the baby may have a birth defect?" Before we could answer her, she continued, "You do know that if you're drinking and doing drugs, that will increase the risk not only for defects, but for fetal alcohol syndrome and a whole host of other things. That goes for both of you." She gave us a disgusted look. Her demeanor and insinuation pissed me off. I stiffened.

"Why in the hell would you think we'd be drinking or doing drugs?"

"W-well, I mean you're a—"

I cut her off, "A biker? Is that what you mean? What

in the hell does that have to do with anything?"

She was getting over being tongue tied. She sneered. "Well, come on, everyone knows bikers and the women they knock up aren't exactly model parents." I came tearing up off my chair. She hastily backed toward the door. Who in the hell did this bitch think she was?

"I want to speak to your fucking boss." She stood there frozen. "Fucking right now!" I shouted. She ran out of the room. Skye caught a hold of my arm.

"Slade, honey, calm down."

"I won't calm down. She fucking just insinuated we're both a couple of—" The door swung open and in came a man. He looked like he was in his sixties. His hair was snow white. He was frowning.

"What seems to be the trouble here? I heard you yelling. I won't have my staff yelled at."

"Maybe you should worry more about what your staff says to your patients! Come on, Skye, we'll find another doctor. I don't want anyone here touching you or our baby." She started to get to her feet.

The man stopped us. "Hold on. Sorry, let's start over. I'm Doctor White. Why were you yelling?" I ignored him as I picked up her clothes. She was taking them and looking around us for a place to change. "Excuse me, please wait. I need to know what happened."

I whipped around. "I'll tell you what happened. That bitch of a midwife came in here and started spouting shit about why we wanted a chromosomal test run. She more or less insinuated since I'm a biker and this must be my biker slut, we drank and did drugs before and even after we found out she's pregnant. She's lucky I don't hit women!" I was breathing hard by now. I was ready to show him why they called me Executioner. His face went white.

"Me and my club know a whole lot of people in this town. We own numerous businesses. I can promise you that when I get done, no one will come here," I threatened.

Skye grabbed my arm. "Honey, stop. Calm down please," she begged me.

"I'm not having anyone disrespect you, Skye. And I won't let them take care of you or our baby either. I didn't serve my damn country for years to put up with shit like this."

"Sir, I can't tell you how sorry I am. I had no idea. I can promise you., Nurse Trellis will not be working here after today. I won't stand for anyone doing that to a patient. Will you and your wife please have a seat and give me a minute? Please." I let Skye tug me back down on the chair. He hurried from the room. I pulled out my phone and started to text.

"Slade, are you alright?" I finished my text quickly and then I got up to stand next to her. I took her in my arms.

"I'm pissed, baby. No one is going to act like that toward you. You're worth a hundred of her and she thinks she can look down her nose at you. All because you're with me."

"She's a prejudiced bitch, Slade. People like her have no place in the medical profession. Hell, anywhere, but we can't leave every place we run into one. This is the best doctor in town for pregnancy and women's health."

"Shit! Okay, let's see what he has to say. But if we have to, I'll take you to Fort Worth to be seen." The door opened and in came Dr. White. Behind him was Nurse Trellis. She looked scared. He tugged her inside. I bared my teeth and growled at her. I think she might have pissed herself. I might not hit women but scaring her would be a privilege.

"I wanted to make sure you saw this. I asked her if she said what you said she did. She didn't deny it. Ms. Trellis, do you mind telling me why you'd say such a thing to a patient?"

She drew herself up. "They're just a dirty biker and some woman he got pregnant. He probably has kids running all over Texas. They shouldn't be allowed to have kids," she spat out. His face turned beet red. I was afraid he was going to have a stroke.

"Well, I'm glad you told me how you really feel. Get your things and go. I won't have someone like you working here. You have five minutes. If you're not gone, I'll call the cops," he told her sternly. As she sputtered, there was a knock at the door. He opened it and there stood another woman and my brothers, Drake and Wrecker. I smiled. I wasn't above proving a point.

"Excuse me, Dr. White, these two gentlemen are Detective Marshall and Deputy Police Chief Dickerson. They need to speak to you."

"Did you call them?" he asked both women. They shook their heads, but I saw a smirk on the bitch's face. She thought I was going out of here in cuffs. The joke was about to be on her.

"I did," I said. They all looked at me with their mouths hanging open. Wrecker and Cuffs stepped into the room.

"Hey, Skye, Ex, what's the problem? You said you needed us down here for some reason. What's the problem, brother?" Wrecker asked. Skye hid her face in the back of my rag. I could feel her shaking. She was trying not to laugh out loud.

"Well, I thought I might need you to help keep me from strangling this one." I pointed at the nurse. "But it seems she's leaving and if she doesn't, the good doctor was going to call you to help her leave. So, I guess you didn't waste a trip after all."

"Sir, do you want us to escort this woman off the premises?" Cuffs asked, all business like.

"I-I don't know. I mean if she leaves, then no," Dr. White stammered.

She hissed. "Why me? They're the ones causing trouble. And what do you mean coming in here and calling him brother?"

"He's our club brother. You see, we're all in the same MC together. He and his woman were coming here today to get some tests run on the baby. You must have done something damn serious for him to want to strangle you. I'd leave if I were you," Wrecker told her with a smile. She gave all of us a shocked look then hurried out of the room.

"I'll just go make sure she leaves," Cuffs volunteered. He left the room. Wrecker handed his business card to the doctor.

"Call me if you have any more trouble with her. See you two back at the club tonight." He walked off without another word.

Suffice to say after that, the doctor couldn't do enough for us. He was professional as hell, gave us his number and promised he'd be the only one to see Skye. When we left, he promised he'd make sure to put a rush on the blood results. When we got in the truck, she was shaking with laughter.

"What's so funny?"

"My big badass biker scared the hell out of the doctor and all his staff. I love you, Slade."

"I love you too, Skye. I'll do it anytime you need me to." I winked at her. I put the truck in drive and headed back to the compound.

As we cruised along, she added, "I thought it was so sweet of the guys to do that. And the way Drake, I mean Cuffs, was acting all super professional. I had no idea he had it in him." Her smile had me thinking back to when we'd first reconnected and he'd been the one to text her that Tanner had been beaten up.

"Speaking of Cuffs, I have a question for you. Why in the hell did he have your phone number?" She gave me a puzzled look. "Back when he texted you that Tanner got beat up that day. Why in the hell did he have your phone number? Did he ask for it and you gave it to him?"

"Yes, he did, and I gave it to him."

My hands gripped the steering wheel in a death grip. "I'm going to kill him," I snarled.

"Why in the world would you do that?" she asked in alarm.

"He was putting the moves on you. He knew that I wanted you."

"Oh God, no, Slade! He asked for it in case he ever needed to notify me about something with Tanner. He'd ended up being his guard a time or two before that. He wasn't making any kind of move on me! None of your brothers or prospects have ever done anything even re-motely inappropriate or acted like they were interested in me." Her explanation made me start to relax. I blew out a relieved breath.

"Thank God, I'd hate to have to kill a brother." She snorted and shook her head at me. She needed to know that when it came to her, I wasn't far out of the cave. Anyone even acted like they wanted to take her away from me, and I'd go into Executioner mode. The remainder of the drive was made in a relaxed silence. I couldn't wait until we got the results. I wanted to go baby shopping.

◄II► ◄II► ◄II► ◄II►

The week went by fast. Skye spent time digging more into the real estate rentals for the Bentley's. She kept telling me it didn't make sense to her. Pop's construction guys started working on our house. They'd sourced all the materials and said they'd have it up in no time. As soon as it was done, they'd start on Jackie's, unless another crew was freed up, then they'd work on both at the same time.

While this was happening, we prepared for the first of June. We were hoping we'd get our hands on the extortionists. More places around town had been vandalized and houses broken into. It was no coincidence they all belonged to the owners of the businesses that had refused to pay or stopped paying them, though none, according to Cuffs and Wrecker, had messages or cum left behind.

It was taking forever to wait on DNA results from the cum. The fingerprints ended up being the families and mine. They'd been smart enough to wear gloves. I was anxious to put this behind us. I had things to get done. I was at the clubhouse while Skye took a nap. I was too restless to sleep with her. Phantom came up the hall. "Hey, Ex, you got a minute?"

"Sure."

"Come to my trailer with me."

I followed him, wondering what it was he'd found. Inside, he went to the bedroom he used as his office. He had me sit in a chair next to him, so I could see the screen on his computer. He pulled up a document. I looked at it without really understanding what I was seeing.

"What is this, Phantom? Does it have something to do with the extortionists?"

"No, unfortunately, not them. They're being crafty on what they're doing. If I had a name or something that would be different. I sure hope Brennan or Omen catch them at the pickup in a couple of weeks. This is about the search you asked me to do on Skye's dad."

"You found him?" I asked excitedly. I wanted so badly to get my hands on that dickhead. He shook his head.

"Not yet, but I've been tracing him and where he went and did after he left them high and dry ten years ago. The bastard was into some shit before he left, I think. I can't seem to find evidence to prove it though. After he left, he'd been moving all around, mainly Texas. He gets involved in stuff, stays and does his thing, and then moves on. He's been involved in con-artist scams, dealing, muscle for hire, you name it."

"Jesus Christ, he is a bigger piece of shit than I thought. Any idea where he might be now or what he's into? I want him gone, Phantom. Jackie needs to be free of him and the whole family needs to have closure, even if we don't tell them what happened to him. He mentally and even a few times physically abused my woman, and for that, he's a dead man. No parent should ever do that to their kids."

"I know and I agree. He's seemed to have gone off the grid somewhat, which is strange because until a year ago, he was pretty sloppy about leaving a trail. It makes me think he might now be involved with people who know how to be more covert. I'm not done digging, but I wanted to let you know what I found so far. It may take longer than I anticipated to run him to ground."

"Thanks, Brother, I appreciate you doing this for me. I know you're busy as hell just trying to find the people taking women and now extorting money. You and Preacher must be tired."

"I don't sleep much anyway, you know that. It keeps me busy. He's the same, though he does come up with ideas I would have never thought of. We're also tying in the monitoring systems and cameras for all our businesses and homes with those the Time Served guys have. That way we can help each other monitor them."

"Wow, I had no idea you could even do that. That's amazing. Hey, Derek Fulton is someone that can be put on the back burner if you need to do something else. I'm anxious to find him, but in the whole scheme of things, he's not important. Not like finding those women and ending the extortion around here. Not to mention the drug dealing we know was happening at the high school. Speaking of that, anything new on Officer Hannigan?"

"Yeah, I'll be updating everyone later in church, which looks like it will be in two hours. I'll tell you all about Officer Hannigan's world now." He sneered as he said it. We hated to let her walk around free, but we were following her to help Boss find out who was behind the drugs in Tenillo. Hannigan was just small potatoes compared to the big boss or bosses. That's who we wanted. I got up and clapped him on the shoulder.

"Again, thanks and I'll see you in a couple of hours. I

need to go see if Skye is awake and make sure she eats dinner."

"You're totally digging this father thing. Aren't you scared? I don't know if I'd be able to have a kid. I'm scared I might fuck them up or be a shit dad," he confessed. I could see that the idea really bothered him. All of us had baggage we carried around. Some we knew about each other, and some was all kept to ourselves. I tried to reassure him.

"I am excited and scared. I think every person wonders what if they do something wrong, but the biggest thing is if you love them, protect them and teach them right from wrong, the rest will turn out fine. Maybe not perfect, but not a serial killer or shit."

He chuckled. "Maybe. At this point, it's not anything I have to worry about. I'm not looking to settle down."

"That's when it happens, when you least expect it. Sin didn't expect Lyric and I sure as hell didn't expect to meet Skye and fall for her instantly. When you find the right one, it just happens. Make sure if you feel that way about someone, don't ignore it or walk away. You'll regret it for the rest of your life," I warned him. I was thinking of what it would be like if I'd never found Skye.

"I won't," he promised me gravely. I left him to his work and maybe to his thoughts. I went next door to my place. Skye was just starting to wake up from her nap. We had a relaxing time, fixing dinner together. After I made sure she ate, we relaxed, watching television until it was time to go to the clubhouse for church. She wanted to visit with her mom, so I took her over to Sara's before I went to church.

Executioner: Chapter 19

When Sin called the meeting to order, I could tell everyone was a little antsy. Sin dove right into the biggest thing weighing on all our minds. "Okay, let's talk about these two guys and the whole extortion ring. Omen and Brennan reported to me earlier today. They haven't seen any suspicious characters around either place, but Seth and Abe are aware of who they are and know to tell them if any of those who are in on the ring come in there.

"We have another week until the first of the month. According to everyone we've talked to, they come in between the first and third of the month. We're going to have to be prepared to drop everything and respond to texts or calls from our two guys. Boss has a few of his guys at the ready too. We need to contain these guys as quickly and quietly as possible. Then we'll bring them to the Gallows or the wellhouse out at Boss' place, where we can have a nice chat with them." All of us gave evil chuckles. Yeah, they wouldn't like the chat we had in mind. It was the kind that involved lots of pain and an unmarked grave.

"Wrecker, Cuffs, anything new on those missing women or the petty vandalism happening to vehicles all over town. Jesus, if I find out it's a bunch of punk-ass kids doing the vandalizing, I'm gonna have to beat their asses. Like their parents should have," Sin growled.

"I'm right there with ya, Pres. Right now, there doesn't seem to be a pattern to who or when they hit vehicles. They don't steal them or strip them for parts, which makes me think it's not an illegal parts ring. The cars tend to be new or newer models. They rip the inner doors off and trash the insides. The only thing in common is they've been bought from Fairchild's Motors, but so have most of the cars in town. He's the only dealership here and he's got the best prices. Other than that, we have zilch," Wrecker said with a shake of his head.

"And what about the missing women?" Saint asked.

"Not a fucking thing. It's like they disappear into thin air. It's up to thirteen now from Tenillo. A few left notes that they were leaving, but their families and friends swear they wouldn't do that. The rest we find their car and purses abandoned and they're gone. But we found out something else this week." Cuffs' tone had us all sitting up more alert.

"We expanded to see if anyone else was having issues like us. Preacher and Phantom did some fancy computer program and it's bad. Since we're all in different counties and jurisdictions, no one had put it together. They did. We're not just looking for thirteen women anymore. It's more like fifty across the whole surrounding area. It's been going on as far as we can tell for two years." A wave of disbelief and swear words rang out around the room. What the fuck? My brothers looked as stunned and angry as I was.

"You have to be kidding me! And no one knew it? Jesus Christ, we have to find them. You know what this means?" Pitbull snarled.

"Yeah, it means we most likely are dealing with a human trafficking ring. And if that's not it, then they're being taken and probably used as prostitutes elsewhere. This is what typically happens in cases like this," Wrecker replied.

"Damn, I was hoping we might get our hands on someone soon. There's some sick fucker out there needing to be cleansed off the face of the earth," Boomer growled. If I knew him, he'd do it using something very loud and deadly. He did like his explosives and devices, hence his name Boomer.

"Any other good news to share?" Talon asked with a sarcastic bite to his words.

"Well, there was some news that I think we can take as a positive. Not totally resolved, but a step in the right direction. It involves Officer Hannigan." Everyone got quiet. We'd been following her for weeks.

"She's still doing her too-frequent trips to the gym and the laundromat. Still no sighting of hand-offs of anything. However, Boss did replace her at the school with a new officer. I don't know his name, but he was brought back on the force. Something about him and the old chief not seeing eye to eye on how they should handle people. He hated them being given a smack on the wrist or just let go. That should end the dealing at Alamos High School. Doesn't mean there isn't stuff going on at the other high schools. We're going to have to find out at some point, but he's taking it a step at a time. We have way too many fires to do it all now," Sin explained.

"Well, it's better than nothing. Hopefully we'll have the extortion ring taken down in a matter of a week or two. I don't know about all of you, but the thought of this all going on here has me stumped. Sure, there's stuff like this happening all over the country, but to have so many all concentrated here. Why? Tenillo is nothing special. We're a decent-sized town, close to Wichita Falls, but that's it. What in the hell is attracting these fuckers to set up shop here?" Torpedo chimed in to ask.

We looked at each other and shrugged. We had no idea. Our town was around a hundred thousand in population. We had decent businesses but no big industry, still a lot of individually owned businesses. Some areas of town were better than others, but that wasn't unusual. It left us with a lot to think about. I was only half listening when Talon gave the financial report for April. As treasurer, he kept on top of that. That is until I heard him say Skye's name.

"Skye is doing a fantastic job. Never had shit come in so detailed and orderly. Saved me a lot of time sorting through it. She's got a great system going and it shows in the book. Executioner, never piss that woman off. She's worth her weight in gold. We don't want to lose her," he told me with a grin on his face.

"I don't plan to, so no worries. She loves it and now she's looking at ways to improve shit with her other clients. She's working on something right now for Bentley Real Estate. Says they could make better margins if they offloaded some properties or something. I don't know what she's always talking about when she gets going."

"Welcome to the club. Lyric can be the same way. Alright, I don't have anything else unless one of you does?" He waited a moment, no one spoke or raised their hand. "Good. Get out of here and start enjoying the weekend!" Sin shouted as he banged his hammer on the table. It had been a joke when we formed the club. Since we were called Ares Infidels, Pitbull and Boomer thought it would be funny to give Sin a big hammer like Ares would use. Sin had taken one look at it and started using it to bring meetings to order and to end them. That along with the club's emblem burned into the table had been our way of formalizing the club.

When we got to the common room, I saw that Skye, Sara, Jackie, and Lyric had come over to the clubhouse. Tyson and Tanner were involved in a video game on the big screen. The women were sitting at one of the tables talking. They had a book on the table. As I got closer, I saw it had wedding stuff in it. They must be talking about Sin and Lyric's wedding. He'd asked her to marry him over a month ago. They had the big day planned for July Fourth. Which when I thought about it, was only six weeks away. Damn, time was flying.

I leaned down and kissed the back of Skye's neck. She had her hair up in a messy knot on the top of her head. I nibbled on her soft skin. The scent of her had me thinking of other things. I was still amazed that simply looking at her, hearing her voice, or smelling her could make me forget everything and everyone else. She shivered and turned her head, catching my mouth with hers. She gave me a sweet but tantalizing kiss.

She drew back and smiled. "Is there something I can do for you, honey?" she asked softly as the others watched. Or I should say Jackie and Sara watched. Lyric was busy being kissed by Sin.

"Yeah, you could come back to the trailer with me and spend the next twelve or more hours in bed with me."

"Really? You need a nap that long?" She teased me. She knew damn well I wasn't talking about taking a nap. I needed my baby girl, and that need was growing by the second. I hauled her gently up out of the chair and into my arms. My hands grasped her ass and I held her flush to me. There was no way she could miss the erection I was sporting.

"I don't plan on napping. I plan on taking my woman over and over until she needs a nap. Sound like something you might want to do?" I teased her back as I rubbed my hard cock back and forth over her stomach. She gave a quiet moan and her eyes drifted half closed.

"I could be persuaded to do that. Do you want to go now or after you visit for a while?"

"Sorry, but your visit is over. Say goodbye to the ladies," I told her as I lifted her higher. She had to put her arms and legs around me. Just what I wanted. The others were all laughing, including her mom. She called out her goodbyes as I carried her to the door. I threw up a hand to them. I didn't have the energy to waste on talking. At least not to anyone other than my woman.

As soon as I got her in my place and the door was closed and locked, I let loose. This overwhelming feeling to be inside of her had grown from want to need. I didn't even take her to our room. I laid her out on the kitchen table. She gave me a surprised look. I tore off her shoes and leggings along with her panties in one sweep. Her upper body was still clothed, but her whole lower half was bare to me. I panted as I saw her pussy all pink and wet with her cream. She'd gotten as turned on as me. Good, because I wasn't in the mood to play around much this first time.

As she laid there watching me, I sat down in one of the kitchen chairs which put her pussy at the perfect height. I pushed her legs further apart and licked her from her ass to her clit then back down. She moaned and more cream spilled from her pussy. I zeroed in on her clit and sucked it into my mouth, so I could use my teeth. She grabbed the edge of the table. As I teased that hard nub, I thrust two fingers in and out of her. She was so damn hot. I thrust a few times, then took one of my cum-covered fingers and slipped it into her ass. She hissed but bore down on my finger.

Then I set about making her come. My mouth and fingers fucked her in a fury. She was rolling her head from side to side, moaning. I lifted long enough to command her, "Push up your top and take your breasts out of your bra. I want to see you play with those hard nipples." She quickly though clumsily did it. I was right, they were hard.

As she played with them, I watched as I went back to eating her pussy and finger fucking her. Her eyes were on mine. She got into it more, then started to really tug and twist them. This was causing her pussy to contract. I sped up my tongue, fluttering and thrusting until she tipped over the edge and came, sobbing. She clamped down hard on my fingers and her cream gushed out of her. I lapped it up and didn't stop my thrusting fingers until she stopped coming.

As soon as she did, I was up and tearing open my jeans. I shoved them down far enough to free my cock and then I slammed into her. She was so swollen from her orgasm, she cried out and shook. I didn't stop. I buried myself and then pulled out. This was about me getting us both to come. I needed to spill my seed inside of her. My balls felt like they were going to burst if I didn't.

I held her legs up against my chest so I could go deeper. She was pushing back at me and panting. I wrapped my arms around her legs and lifted her ass off the table. I slid in a little more. My balls were now brushing against her ass. I rode her hard.

My thrusts had my balls slapping against her ass and I wanted to howl with how fucking good it felt. She was twisting her nipples again and her pussy was contracting around me. I went a little faster. "Lift up that breast and suck on your nipple. Suck hard," I told her. I'd never asked her to do that. She hesitated for a second then lifted her head and breast. She was able to get it to her mouth like I thought. As her pink tongue came out to flick the nub, I shuddered. I was going to fucking come soon. As I watched, she sucked it into her mouth and slid her other hand down between her legs. I felt it touch my cock as she played with herself. It was too much.

I opened her legs and brought them down and wrapped them around my hips. I leaned down and took her breast into my mouth, so I could play with them. I used one of my hands to rub her clit. She tensed and it was a matter of a few thrusts and sucks along with rubs on her clit and she came. She screamed and bucked her hips into my stomach, driving my cock even deeper. I groaned and then threw back my head to yell her name, "Skye," as I came, filling her just like I had wanted.

It took several minutes before I was able to lift off her and pull out of her. She was still jerking with small orgasms. I fell back on the chair. It took two tries before I could bend down to take off my boots and socks then my jeans. Once I was done and had my shirt off, I stood and picked her up. She was almost boneless. "Come on, Baby Girl, let's take a shower and then we can go for round two."

She gave me a dazed though sated look and smiled. Yeah, she was up to the challenge. Tonight, I was going to love her until she passed out, and I couldn't come anymore. What a way to start the weekend!

Executioner: Chapter 20

The weekend was over too soon for me. I hated to see Monday come and I had to let her go. Even those few hours when we were both at work, I hated. Not only did I want to keep her by my side, because I loved being with her, but I was also getting this sense of dread in my stomach. I had no idea why, but it was worrying the hell out of me.

I was sitting at my desk, thinking of calling it a day and going over to the flower shop. She'd gone there today to work on the books. I'd go and see if they needed me for any kind of manual labor, anything to get me near her. My phone rang. I looked at it and saw it was Omen. I wondered if something had happened at the strip club, though they weren't open right now. He was the one covering Bubbles.

"Hey, buddy, what's up? Everything alright over there?"

"It's quiet over here. That's not why I'm calling. Ex, my fucking gut is rolling, and I've got that feeling. You know which one I'm talking about," he said all serious and worried. I swore. I knew exactly which one he was referring to. The one that earned him his call sign, Omen.

"Jesus, Omen, I don't need to hear this."

"Is yours acting up, *mon ami*?"

I didn't say anything for a moment or two, then I sighed. "It's been acting up all morning and it's getting worse. I was just about to call it a day and go to the flower shop. Skye's there with Jackie today. I don't know what it means, but something is coming. Damnit, you know that shit is stronger when you're around. I think you're bad luck."

"Not bad luck, my mojo just enhances what you have. Are you sure there's no Cajun seer in your blood?"

"I'm sure."

"Then it has to be a shaman. I'm gonna tell Sin that something is coming. He doesn't know me like you do. You'll need to convince him my gut is never wrong. Something bad is about to happen and soon. I just wish I knew what and where." Dread crawled through me as we said our goodbyes. I had to get to Skye. If something happened to her or our baby, it would be the end of me.

I hurried out of my office and through the front. Sara was working there as usual. She saw me and came racing over to me. "What's wrong, Executioner?" I saw a little panic in her eyes.

"Nothing's wrong, Sara. I just need to get over to Skye. Something doesn't feel right, and Omen is feeling it too. I want you to make sure you don't leave here alone. In fact, I'm going to have Dash and Blake come over here and stay."

"Do you really think that's necessary? I mean, no one would mess with one of the Infidels' businesses, surely."

"We hope not, but we don't know. Let me get them here then I'll go." I hated to delay, but I couldn't leave Sin's mom here without protection. I called the guys and then I called Sin. I went to stand in the back, so none of the customers could hear me.

"Sin, I'm having Dash and Blake come over to stay with your mom. I need to go to the flower shop."

"Why does she need them?" he barked. Anything that messed with his mom or Lyric made him crazy.

"I don't know that she does. Listen, my gut is going nuts. Something is going to happen. Omen called me and his mojo, as he calls it, is doing it too. You might not think that's real, but I'll tell you, his gut feelings have never been wrong. Mine rarely. Some kind of shit is coming. I don't want to leave Sara here alone just in case it happens here. It's just a precaution."

"Okay, get them there. I'm going to make sure Lyric is covered at the high school. Then get your ass over to your woman. Isn't Torpedo with them today?"

"He is. And I know he's capable, but I still need to be there. You know how it is."

"Hell yeah, I do. Call him and make sure he's on alert. I'll tell the others. Let me know if you see anything or if Omen's mojo tells him more."

"Will do. Later." I hung up. As I waited for the prospects to get here, I texted Torpedo and told him what was up, and then texted Skye telling her not to leave the store. She asked why, and I told her I'd explain when I saw her. I was pacing when Blake and Dash came rushing into the store. They came right over to me, and I gave them the run down. They assured me they wouldn't let Sara out of their sights. With that settled, I ran out to my bike.

When I got closer to Blossoms, my gut got even tighter. I didn't see anything, but I knew something had happened. Instead of stopping out front like I usually would, I kept going. I tried to look at the store from my peripheral vision, but I couldn't see inside. I went down the street and parked on Sixth Street. I then took the back street that ran behind the store in those few blocks. As I came up to the back door of Blossoms, I saw it was cracked open. No way they'd leave it like that. They were way too security conscious.

I didn't hesitate. I knew someone was in there and they were in danger. I had no idea where Torpedo was. I took out my phone and hit the speed dial. Sin answered, and I said, "There's trouble at Blossoms. Don't know what yet. Come in silent. I'm going in the back. The door is open, Sin. No sign of Torpedo."

I heard him swear. "Go but be careful. We'll be there soon. I'll call Boss. Watch your six." He hung up. I knew he'd send the cavalry. I eased up and barely pushed the door to see if anyone would react. Nothing. Then I slowly eased it open an inch at a time. It was killing me to go slow, but I knew I had to. It wouldn't do anyone any good if I got killed.

When no one shot at the door, I quickly stuck my head around the corner and then pulled back. The room looked to be empty. As I crouched and went in with my gun out, I thought of who would be closest. Out of my club, it would be Pitbull if he was at the Hangout and Brennan at the Grain and Kernel. None of Boss's guys unless they were out and about. Maybe Wrecker and Cuffs if they were on patrol or something.

A call of a mockingbird came from out back. I called back. In the door came Omen. He slithered up to me. "See anything?" he whispered. I shook my head.

"No. What the hell are you doing here? No way you had time to get here after Sin sent out the alert."

"I was almost here when I got the text. My fucking gut went apeshit, and I knew you'd need me."

"Damn, you're freaky as hell, but I'm glad you're on our side. Listen, when we go through that door, it leads to a small hall where there's an office and a small storage room and a bathroom. We have to clear those before we go through the door to the front. I have no idea what we'll find, but it's too quiet. I'll take right, you go left." He nodded.

We went through the door. It was like old times. We moved in sync. We used old hand signals to silently communicate. I cleared the storage room and the bathroom. He did the office. They were all empty.

As we eased up to the open door to the front, I heard footsteps pacing and then an angry male voice talking. "You bitches think you can screw us? I'll show you. Because of you and your refusal to pay, other store owners think they can do the same. Well, that's not going to happen. They need to see what will happen to them if they stop. You're going to become an example." He snickered. My blood began to boil.

"The only one who's going to be an example is you. My God, you just harmed an Ares Infidel. And I'm an old lady to one of their members. They're going to be pissed as it is, but if you hurt us, you're screwed," Skye told him. I could hear a faint quiver in her voice, but she sounded like she was holding it together.

"Fuck them, they don't scare us!" he yelled. I signaled for Omen to go left as we crawled out of the back. We were hidden by the counter. From the sound of it, they were out in front of it and to the right, over near some of the glass refrigeration units. I used my elbow and the tips of my toes to drag me closer to the end of the counter.

"Why are you watching the windows?" I heard Jackie ask him.

"I'm waiting for someone. We're going to be taking a little trip, ladies. And we're going to have a little fun." He laughed.

"We're not going anywhere with you. Now, let us check on his wound," she said forcefully. Shit, how bad was Torpedo hurt?

"Shut up, bitch! You're not the boss here!" he yelled, then I heard the smack of flesh against flesh. Jackie gave a tiny cry of alarm. Had he hit her? I glanced back at Omen. He had on his death face. People said I had the death glare, but he was just as bad or worse. We had to get them away from this guy. He seemed to be slowly escalating. The pacing was faster, and his breathing was loud.

"Keep your hands off my mother, you bastard! I'm checking him out whether you like it or not. His head is bleeding all over the place. If you kill me, then you don't have a bargaining chip with the Infidels. Keeping us alive is your only hope to survive. Now, see that first aid kit on the wall, I'm grabbing it." I looked up. I knew which one she meant. It was on the wall above me. I prayed she wouldn't give away that we were here.

When Skye came around the end of the counter, her steps barely stuttered. She had her back to whoever was out there. She flicked her eyes down and then back up. I saw the relief there. She took down the kit. As she turned to go back, her left hand was down by her hip. She held up one finger and then pointed to the left. Somehow, I knew she meant he was to the left of her, and they were clear. I had no idea how I knew it. I just did.

I gave her to the count of thirty then I signaled Omen. While I did, I heard Skye tell Jackie, "Come here, Mom, I need your help to wrap his head." Light footsteps went off to the right. I held up my fingers and counted off to three. When that third finger went up, we both exploded out from behind the counter with our guns up and at the ready.

He had his back to us looking out the front. He whipped around and fired a wild shot. It hit the wall ten feet from me. While he was busy trying to shoot me, Omen charged him and tackled his ass. They went down hard, then Omen punched the hell out of him. I ran over to Skye, Jackie, and Torpedo.

I took a moment to pull Skye into my arms and kiss her. A quick glance showed me she was alright. Then I looked over Jackie. Other than a red cheek, she seemed to be fine. I then checked out my brother. Torpedo was lying on the floor. His hands were tied behind his back, and he had a big gash in his head that was bleeding all over the place. I had no idea how serious it was. He was moving though, so I took that as a positive.

As I hunkered down to check him, Omen stopped beating the guy's ass and zip tied his arms and legs behind him. He was trussed up like a calf. Then he hurried over to us. Together we got Torpedo untied and on his back. A whistle came from the back a moment or two before my brothers came in. They were armed and looking like they were ready to kill. That look got worse when they saw Torpedo.

Right behind them was Boss, Hook, and Captain. Hook came running over. He was a veterinarian, but in this instance that was as good as a doctor. He kneeled next to Torpedo and started to check him out. Boss and Sin looked at the guy on the ground then came over to us.

"What in the hell happened?" Boss asked.

"I don't know. We just got his ass subdued. The women can tell us, but first we need to figure out if Torpedo needs to go to the hospital."

"Of course, Wrecker. Make sure the front door is locked and the closed sign is up. Pull those blinds too. We don't want any nosy bystanders seeing this." The whole time he spoke, the guy on the floor was hollering and swearing at us.

"You sons of bitches are gonna pay! You touch me and my friends will end all of you!" he yelled.

"You think? I'm gonna tell you what's going to happen. You're taking a ride with us, and we're gonna do whatever we want until you tell us what we want to know," Captain told him with a grin. Then he stuffed a rag in his mouth. He looked up at us. "It was too damn loud in here. Can't hear myself think." As he stood up, he kicked the guy in the ribs.

I turned back to Hook. With help from Skye and Jackie, he had Torpedo's head wrapped. My brother seemed to be awake now and a little confused. I would bet money he had a concussion. I wondered how this little bastard got the drop on him. I didn't want to ask him, so I pulled Skye aside. She came with me to stand with the others. "Baby Girl, are you sure you're alright?" I had to make sure before anything else. She and the baby were my priority.

"I'm fine and so is the baby. He never touched me, though he did hit Mom when she made him mad. Did you guys hear that?" I nodded. Omen was next to me. His eyes were blazing when he nodded.

"He hit Jackie?" Captain asked with a growl in his voice. When she nodded, he went over and slammed his fist in the guy's face, then he came back like nothing happened.

"Baby, tell us what happened. How in the hell did he

get in here?"

She leaned against me. I held her close. "He came in with a couple of women. Or I should say he came in making it look like he was with them. He was looking around while they were at the counter. I assumed he was waiting for them to get done so they could leave. Only when they did, he stayed. He'd wandered around until he was close to Torpedo. It was my fault Torpedo got hit. I distracted him."

"How did you distract him?"

"As they left, I'd been working on some roses. I accidentally got stabbed by a thorn. I thought I'd gotten them all. I cried out, and he came hurrying over to check on me. When he did, he had his back to that man. All of a sudden that guy had a gun and he slammed it into Torpedo's head. When he grabbed his head and bent over a little, that bastard hit him with one of those heavy glass vases." She pointed to one on a shelf.

"He fell. When I tried to help him, that goon held the gun on me and made Mom tie Torpedo's hands. We didn't have time to call anyone. He was saying a bunch of stuff about making an example of us to other business owners. They must be threatening not to pay anymore. He was waiting on someone, Ex. Someone who would help him get us out of here."

Hearing this, Boss jumped into action. "Wrecker and Cuffs, go out the back. One of you set up there and the other across the street in front. Sin, I want your other guys out of sight. Captain, go with them. Maybe we'll get lucky and catch the other one." They hurried outside. I turned to Skye.

"Why didn't you recognize him? Isn't he one of the other two who ran you off the road that time?" I was confused about that part. She shook her head.

"No, he isn't. There must be more than those three. I think he was waiting on one of them to come help. God, Ex, how many are there?" she asked with a look of fright on her face. I couldn't stand it. I picked her up and sat down on the chair behind the counter. I cuddled her on my lap. The guys walked off to take different spots around the room. I saw that Omen was talking quietly to Jackie. Hook had remained with Torpedo.

I raised my voice and asked him, "Hook, do we need to call an ambulance?" I was worried we weren't paying enough attention to my brother. It was hard when your woman was involved to not focus only on her.

"Naw, I texted Paula. She's going to come check him over. She'll know for sure if he needs to go. He seems to know who he is and where."

"Paula, you told her to come? God help us, just keep her away from this asshole. No telling what she might do to him," Captain said with a chuckle. He was right, Paula was a firecracker and unpredictable.

"She can't be seen coming in here, Hook," Boss growled.

"She knows to come in the back. Don't worry, she can be sneaky as hell. Remember how she was raised, Boss." Boss seemed to think for a moment then nodded.

"I'm doing fine, guys, just one helluva headache. And a damn urge to get up and kick the shit out of him. Can't believe he got me. I'll never live this shit down," Torpedo grumbled. We all laughed in relief. If he could worry about that, he was okay.

"Baby, I need to get you home. I don't want you here. It's dangerous and all this stress isn't good for you."

"Slade, I'm fine. It was scary. I just hope you can find

the others and get them all. This is ridiculous that we have to put up with them."

"We'll get them. If not today, soon. Let me see if we can get you and your mom out of here without being seen. We need to keep the store closed. I'm sorry."

"I understand. Let's see if Mom is ready to go." She looked over to see Jackie was now standing talking to Captain. Omen was nearby, and he seemed to be paying a lot of attention to the two of them. He had a frown on his face. God help me, was he interested in Jackie after all? I'd warned him, but it didn't seem to be deterring him. Fuck, I couldn't deal with that right now. But when this was over, we'd be having a damn talk. He wasn't going to play loose and fast with my woman's mom.

I took Skye over to Boss and Sin. "Guys, I need to get them out of here. Is there any way we can sneak them out? And what about this one? I assume he's going to our compound."

"We were just talking about that. What if we take them out in Paula's car? She should be here any minute. We'll set out a watch and load Torpedo, Skye, and Jackie in the back where they won't be seen," Boss told me.

"Sounds like a plan." I had Skye and Jackie sit. Torpedo was propped up in a chair. It was maybe five minutes later when Paula came in from the back. She had a bag with her. She went straight over to Torpedo and Hook. Hook gave her a kiss and then whispered to her. She got down to business.

"We have to stop meeting like this. But at least this time, no one was shot. You need to learn to be stealthier, like a ninja. I can help you with that, big guy," she teased Torpedo. He grinned at her. She was reminding all of us of the trouble we got into a couple of months ago when we were out hunting low-life drug dealers. We'd had fun, but Boss and Sin had found out and made us stop. It was after Preacher, Hook, and Chef got shot. Not seriously, but enough that Paula had to dig out bullets. I think she enjoyed taking the one out of her man, Hook's, ass.

Ten minutes later after assessing him she said, "He's fine. The ER isn't necessary. Thanks to that hard head of his, he only has a mild concussion. Just watch him and if anything changes, call me. Get some rest, Torpedo." She patted him on the arm.

"Thanks, Paula. I hate that they dragged you out for this."

"I needed a break from my jewelry making, anyway. Okay, how do you want to do this? Hook explained you want me to take these three with me."

Sin and Boss had Talon and Phantom take point down the street in the back alley. When they gave the all-clear, we hurried them to her SUV parked a block over. She really did know how to keep a low profile. We got them in the back. Before they left, I gave Skye a kiss and then kissed her stomach. I watched as they pulled away.

As they turned out of sight, I told Sin, "Let's get this show on the road. Any word from the guys? Anyone suspicious seen out front?"

"Not yet, but there's still time. Let's get back inside before we're noticed."

Back in the shop, I kept watching the front door. We'd unlocked it though we kept the closed sign displayed. Omen was chilling by the front window. The others seemed alert but relaxed. I was about to suggest we call it quits when Sin's phone buzzed. He pulled it out of his pocket and looked at it. He cocked his head and looked at his phone a little funny, like he couldn't believe what he was reading. "Seems like we have Brennan outside. Says he needs to come inside. He's got something we need to know." He texted him back.

A few minutes later, Boomer brought him in through the back of the store. Only he wasn't alone. He had a man in front of him all tied up. He had his mouth taped with duct tape. We all looked at Brennan for an explanation.

"This bastard thought he'd show up at the feed store and demand his monthly payment early. Luckily, Seth recognized him before he got to him and signaled me. He hasn't said a whole lot, but I knew what was happening over here. Thought you'd like a matching set." He shoved the guy down beside the one we'd caught. They were both looking at us with glares on their faces.

"Damn it, they're collecting early. I wonder where the other one is?" Boss asked with a contemplative look on his face. He and Sin walked away and talked to each other in the corner for a few minutes. Finally, they came back to the rest of us.

"Let's pack it up and get these two back to the Gallows. We can make them comfortable there. I think they'll be much more talkative once they're in a nicer place." We all laughed at Sin's remark. The Gallows wasn't anyone's idea of nice. I made sure the store was locked up and everything turned off, then I set the alarm and we got out of there. We had the vehicle Brennan had brought goon number two in. That's what we used to take them to our compound. We had them lay down in the back. Amazing what a gun to your head will do. Now the real work begins.

Skye: Chapter 21

This had been one helluva day. It wasn't until we got home and at the trailer that the whole thing hit me. We could have died today. All because someone wanted what we barely had. They didn't want to work for their money. They wanted to take it from others. Thinking of how it could have turned out, I ended up throwing up. Mom was hovering around and debating if she should call Executioner.

"No, Mom, I'm fine. Just a little sick. That's to be expected. I'm going to lie down for a while. How about you? How's your face?" I touched her cheek. It had a faint bruise.

"It's nothing, honey. I'm worried about you and the baby. Maybe we should have you checked out. Damn, we should have had Paula do it before she left. I wonder if she's still close by?" She fumbled in her purse. I grabbed her arm.

"I don't need Paula. You're overreacting. Come talk to me." She reluctantly followed me to our bedroom. I laid down and she sat on the side of the bed. "I want to ask you something, Mom?"

"What?"

"What's up with you and Omen?"

Her face flushed and she looked away and then back at me. "There's nothing up. He was checking that I was alright. Like the others did."

"No, the others asked if you were okay, they didn't hover and give poor Captain dirty looks. Is there something going on between you and Captain?"

"Captain is just nice. I like to talk to him, end of story. Why're you asking me these questions? Skye, I'm not looking for a man. Besides, even if I did want a man, who wants to be with a middle-aged woman who's married to some man no one knows where he is? I have stretch marks, cellulite and my belly hasn't been flat and tight in years."

"You act like you're old. You're not. You're in your prime. Mom, you're a beautiful woman. Plenty of men would and do want you. You're being ridiculous. Your body doesn't look like you just described. As for Dad, that's something we can deal with if you want. Don't let him keep you from finding happiness."

She sighed and laid down beside me. "Skye, I don't know if I could ever let a man in again. Your dad hurt me terribly. I don't want to ever go through something like that again. It's better if I stay the way I am. Besides, I'm not alone. I have you and your brothers, and now the whole Infidels' club to fill my life. Now, enough talk. You're supposed to be taking a nap." She laid there rubbing my back like she did when I was a kid. It soon lulled me to sleep.

I woke up some time later to find Executioner kneeling beside the bed. I smiled at him. "Hi, baby, what're you doing kneeling there like that?"

"I was watching you sleep and trying to decide if you should go to the hospital."

"Hospital? Why would I go there?"

"Your mom told me you vomited when you got back, and you wouldn't let her call Paula to come back and check you out." I sat up and tugged on his hand until he got up and sat beside me. I laid my head on his chest and rubbed his arm.

"Yes, I vomited. It was rather stressful today. But the baby is fine. I'm not having any pain. I'm no longer nauseous and I don't feel funny or weird. You're both worry warts. What happened after I left?"

He shrugged. "Not much. Not anything I can really talk about. I'm going to have to go out for a bit. I won't be far. Text if you need me. I hate to leave you, but this needs to be taken care of."

"You mean you have someone to torture. Don't think I don't know what you guys are doing, but you can pretend I don't. I'll see you when you get back." I gave him a kiss. He devoured my mouth and when he broke off the kiss, I was ready to remove our clothes and show him how good I was. He groaned and slowly got off the bed. I could see the bulge in his jeans. I giggled, and he growled at me.

"Eat something while I'm gone. Love you, babe."

"Love you, too. Should I say, have fun?" He laughed as he left the room. Mom popped in right after he did.

"If you're feeling up to it, Sara's here. Why don't we relax, you took a nap? We can watch a movie and fix something to eat. Have girl time."

"Give me a minute to freshen up and I'll be out. Where are the boys?"

"They're at the clubhouse. Dash and Tanner are in a gaming match of some kind." She shook her head as she left. I didn't understand the attraction to the games either. It seemed to mainly be a guy thing. Well, I guess it was girl time. But what I wouldn't give to know what was going on out in that building they called the Gallows.

◄‖► ◄‖► ◄‖► ◄‖►

Executioner:

As I entered the Gallows, I put on my death face. It was time to get answers. I was called Executioner for a reason. I'd earned that name in Marine Force Recon. Right or wrong, I'd found I had an ability when it came to getting people to talk. It had come in handy when we had to question insurgents and other enemies.

When we'd built the compound and I found this old slaughter house on the property, I told the guys we needed to fix it up. That it would come in handy one day. They'd thought I was nuts, but they did it to humor me. This would be the second time in a matter of a couple of months it had been used.

Before we came, I'd talked to Sin. I told him I wanted to do the questioning and torture and no one else, other than Omen. He had another ability we'd discovered over the years. He knew when someone was lying or keeping something back. Even the most consummate liars couldn't fool him. We'd worked together several times. Sin had agreed with the plan. Usually, a prospect would watch but not participate in something like this.

As the club's enforcer, I was responsible to protect the club. And torturing or even killing was part of that when necessary. Like this time, these guys wouldn't be walking away. Was it wrong to take the law into your own hands? Maybe, but justice wasn't always served any other way. The law could only do so much, no matter how much they may want to do more. People like this didn't stay behind bars forever.

When I got inside, I found Boss and his guys were

there already. They were standing with their arms crossed, looking at the two prisoners. Both of them were trying to look tough and unaffected, but I could tell by their elevated breathing and the sweat on their faces that they were scared. I walked up to the cell they were in. I looked them up and down before I spoke.

"Do you know who I am?"

"Yeah, some dumbass biker," the one from the flower shop spat out. I'd dub him Stupid One.

"True, I'm a biker, but I'm not a dumbass. You two are the dumbasses, for doing this shit in our town. Let me educate you. My name is Executioner. I'm the enforcer for this club. I'm responsible for protecting it. A job I take very seriously."

"Ooh, are we supposed to be afraid?" Stupid Two sneered.

"You should be. I didn't get this name from the club. I got it when I was in the Marines. And compared to the guys I've tortured and killed for my country, you're barely worth my effort. You're going to tell us everything we want to know. And my buddy, Omen, is going to make sure you leave nothing out. So, why don't we get this party started? Which one of you wants to play first?" I gave them a smile. One I'd been told was evil. Both of them visibly shrank back. It seemed like their bravado had abandoned them.

Stupid Two cast a much more nervous look around and then at his buddy. Bingo, he was the first one. I opened the cell door and grabbed him. He tried to get away, but I dragged him out and over to a wall where I'd installed chains with manacles on them. I cuffed him to the wall by his ankles and wrists. When he was secure, I stepped back.

"Okay, let's start at the beginning. You and your friends started this little extortion ring. I want to know who came up with the idea? How many are there? What are all your names? Where are the others? I know there's at least one more of you out there. Your friend Marcos was taken care of a few months ago, wasn't he?" His eyes got round. They had no idea what had happened to him. He'd made the mistake of attacking Boss' woman, Jenn. After we were done with him, there hadn't been much left of him.

He clamped his lips tight. Like that would stop me. I went over to the cabinet against the far wall and picked up a dental cheek retractor. It was what the dentist placed in your mouth to prevent you from closing it. He tried to shake his head, but Omen applied pressure to his jaw joints until it hurt so much, he opened up. I shoved it in. Then I took out the other two things I'd slipped in my pocket. It was a medical clamp pliers. Like what they use to pierce your tongue. Only the needle I was going to use was way bigger than what was used in regular piercing. I'd gotten this idea when I watched Phantom pierce someone's tongue.

He whimpered as I grabbed his tongue with the pliers and pulled it out. Then I held up the huge-ass darning needle I'd found. "I'm going to loosen up your tongue since it seems like you were having trouble answering me. A couple of holes should help, though I hear it hurts like hell." He tried to talk. I ignored him, and Omen held his head as I shoved the needle through his tongue. I didn't do the standard vertical hole. I did a horizontal one that took time to push it through the entire width of his tongue. He was screaming as much as he could, and tears ran down his face. Cruel, yes, but this was to protect my family and others.

When it was all the way through, I left it there for a minute then I ripped it out as fast as I could. He sagged, and the chains were the only thing holding him up. I took the dental guard out. Blood ran down his chin. "I'll ask you again, who's idea was this?"

He sniffed as he looked at me with bleary eyes. "It was Marcos' idea. He said we could make a shit load of cash. And he was right. We did until you came along and started to tell people to stop paying us," he said, having a hard time talking. He did try to glare at me.

"How did he find you? Were you friends?"

"We knew each other. I wouldn't say friends."

"Who did Marcos report to?"

"No one, he was the boss."

"He wasn't smart enough to set this whole thing up. There had to be someone above him." He looked confused. "Okay, we'll come back to that one. What's your name?"

He hesitated. I picked up the darning needle. He started to babble, "It's Donnie."

"Donnie, how many are there besides you and your buddy over there."

He glanced at his buddy. "Just me, Marcos, Gene," he nodded toward his buddy, "and Pedro."

"Shut the fuck up, Donnie. Don't tell them shit," Gene yelled from his cell.

"Where's Pedro?"

"I don't know. He should have been with Gene."

"Goddamn it, shut up, Donnie. I'm gonna kill you," Gene yelled as he glared at Donnie. I left Donnie and walked over to Gene.

"Seems like you have a lot to say, Gene. Why don't we

give poor Donnie a break? Honestly, he's no fun. He gave all that up after I barely even did anything. What a fucking disappointment. I think you'll give me more fun." Omen had followed me over. He opened the door and yanked the struggling Gene out. The others remained silent sentries.

We wrestled him over to the table we had in the center of the building. It had been used for butchering livestock, deer, and other game years ago. We got him on it and secured his ankles and wrists with the restraints attached to it. He kept yanking on his wrists like he thought he could get loose. I leaned down and peered into his eyes.

"So, Gene, tell me about Marcos and Pedro. Who did Marcos report to? And where is dear ole Pedro?"

"Fuck you, I'm not telling you anything. Pedro is going to kill you and those two cunts from the flower shop. He'll make sure they suffer before he kills them. He said he liked the idea of a mother-daughter combo," he said with glee. It was all I could do not to slit his fucking throat right there, but I knew he was trying to piss me off. He thought he could get me to kill him before he would talk. I heard the swift intake of breath from Omen at his remarks. I gave a low growl at the back of my throat.

"Well, I hate to burst your bubble, but no one is going to touch my woman or her mom. Again, tell me about the real boss and Pedro." He shook his head. With Omen's help, we cut off his clothes and proceeded to cut him repeatedly. I had to hand it to him, he was keeping his mouth shut.

As he laid there, I got tired of this. I wanted to go back home to my woman. It was time to up the fucking pressure and pain. I looked over at Omen. "Get me that blowtorch. I have the urge to cook." He grinned as he went to fetch it. Gene's eyes widened and he started to struggle again. So, he wasn't afraid of the knife and pain seemed not to affect him much, but the idea of fire had him worried.

When Omen handed it to me, I fired it up. Gene watched as I looked at him from head to toe. "Hmm, where to begin? Eenie, meenie, miney, mo." I moved my hand with the burning torch over his body. "Catch a tiger by the..." I stopped over my target. He screamed when he saw where I'd stopped. My hand and the torch were hovering right above his limp cock.

"Not much to work with, might not be worth the effort, but so be it. Your cock it is. Omen, I want to be sure to get all of it. Grab those pliers we used on Donnie's tongue. Hold that little thing up for me." The other guys all started to laugh and point.

Gene's face went from stark white to red as he heard their remarks about having a tiny cock. "Hell, Ex, you're doing him a favor by burning that itty bitty thing off. I bet he's never fucked a woman in his life," Omen sneered as he came back with the clamp. He'd donned gloves and didn't wait. He clamped onto Gene's cock and lifted it, making sure to stretch and pull hard. Gene cried out.

Watching his face, I slowly lowered the torch. He was shaking but still not talking. I guess he thought I wasn't serious. Suddenly, I swept it down and across his cock. It was a quick pass, but enough to burn like hell. He screamed. He didn't last long after that. Another swipe and he was telling me everything.

"Marcos would call some guy. He had a phone he

used. Not his every day one. He only used it when he called the boss. I only ever heard him refer to him as Mr. C. He was the one who Marcos made drops to. He got the biggest cut. He was also the one who told Marcos who to target and who to avoid."

"How is he getting the money now that Marcos is gone?"

"He has me drop it at a different park each time. I get a text from Pedro telling me when and where. I never see or talk to the boss. I just do what Pedro tells me to do."

"What about your friend, Pedro? Tell me where we can find him." I could tell he was fast approaching his limit. No stamina in these guys, though he'd held out better than Donnie. I looked over. Donnie was hanging, passed out in his chains. Gene shook his head.

"I don't know where he is. He was supposed to meet me at the feed store, then we were to go over to the flower shop and help Donnie with the women. Pedro said we could use them to get you to back off."

"You don't know where he lives? I don't believe it. Which business is next on your list?"

"I don't, I swear. He always just meets us. He's the one who knows who we are seeing on which day. I don't decide."

"Omen, tell me if he's telling the truth. Is he telling the truth about not knowing the next target and where Pedro is?" Omen came over and leaned down to look at Gene. Omen had one other uncanny ability that used to freak the shit out of guys, even those in our squad. He could stare at someone, and it was like he got in their heads and would know if they lied, and he made them tell the truth.

As he stared at Gene, he began to shake and tried to turn his head. Omen held him still. "Ahh, I see it. You're lying. You do know when, where to hit, and even where we can find Pedro. Tell me." He continued to stare into Gene's eyes. Suddenly, Gene screamed and started to sob.

"He's going to be at the park over off Bonham Drive at midnight. That is our backup plan if something goes wrong or we get separated. We wait until then and meet. Tomorrow, we're supposed to hit the strip club."

"What does Pedro look like?" I thought I knew but I had to be sure. Neither of these guys had a tattoo on his cheek.

"He's about five foot nine and has dark hair and eyes. He has a tattoo on his right cheek of a tear."

"Tell me, were you one of the ones who ran my woman off the road and then threatened them if they didn't pay?" He slowly nodded. "And the one who touched her. Who was that?"

He swallowed and then whispered, "It was Pedro. He wants her something bad."

"And the cum on the sheets at her house?"

"That was him, too. God, listen, if you let us go, we'll never come around this town again. We'll go somewhere far away." He was pleading. I shook my head and gave him a sad look.

"You should have never come to our town to begin with. Omen, is he done?"

He looked into his eyes for a moment then nodded. I didn't wait. I stabbed my knife into his throat, and he gasped as he drowned in his own blood. Donnie had woken up and was screaming and begging. Omen took out his knife and stabbed him in the heart. They were both dead in a matter of minutes. Dash, Blake, Omen, and Brennan were directed to clean up the mess. Dash and Blake knew the drill. They'd teach our newest prospects what it was.

I walked out and got on my bike. I was going to the clubhouse to clean up. I knew we'd have church to discuss this and then I was going home to hold my woman. I needed to feel her safe in my arms.

Skye: Chapter 22

I tried to sleep while Executioner was gone doing whatever they were doing to the two guys they'd caught. I knew whatever it was, they weren't going to walk away afterward. I knew that I should feel outraged about that. I mean, they were going to torture and kill two people, But I couldn't do it. They were hurting people for financial gain and if they had to harm or kill to do it, they would. They made it plain they were going to at least rape me. People like that either got off or got out of prison way too early. I didn't want them ever to be able to come near me and my family again.

I finally gave up and went out to the living room. Mom was sitting there, staring out the window, lost in thought. She looked up when I came into the room. "Honey, you should be sleeping."

"I can't. Not when I know Ex and the others are questioning those men. I want to know what they find out."

"I know, I do too, though I'm not sure how much we'll be told. Omen said that club business is not told to those outside the members usually."

"Omen said that, did he? Anything else Omen said?" I asked with a teasing tone. She rolled her eyes.

"I'm not going there with you. He's just being nice. He's a good friend of Ex's and I'm your mom. He's going to be nice. Now, what do you think of the club's stance on keeping their women in the dark? Are you going to be able to live with that?"

"I've been thinking about it. Lyric told me that it's their way of keeping us safe. That if it ever came back on anyone, they don't want it to be on us. While I love that they're that protective, it's going to be something I have to work on." I stood up to pace. "I don't want to think about what's going on. Let's talk about something else."

"How're your new accounts going? Anything exciting? I know they have to be loving your work. You always do such an outstanding job. I never liked numbers like you do. It must have come from your grandpa, he loved them. Maybe that's why he was in banking the whole time I was growing up and stayed in it."

I liked the idea I'd gotten something from one of my mom's parents. "They're going wonderfully. In fact, I'm working on something for the Bentley account. They seem to have a lot of rental properties and Ben didn't realize it since Jonathan handles those. I'm doing some research to see if they'd be more financially sound if they sold some of them. Honestly, I have no idea how they're able to rent them. I went by several of them a few days ago. Some are large parcels of land for raising crops or cattle and others are actual homes. Mom, they looked abandoned, though I double checked and every one of them shows as paying a monthly rental. No cattle, no crops and the houses had overgrown lawns that looked like they hadn't been mowed in forever. I'm going to talk to Ben about those. I'm missing something here."

Mom frowned. She might not like numbers, but she was far from stupid. Mom had a keen mind. If she didn't, Blossoms would have gone under a long time ago. The only reason we'd struggled like we had, is Dad wiped out the savings before he left. Then there had been a financial crisis that affected most businesses. She'd fought to keep a roof over our heads.

"Do you know the names of the renters? Maybe you should talk to them? Present it to them in a way that you're just trying to get familiar with Bentley's portfolio, so you can do the best job. I don't think many people would object. They have to be getting something out of it, or why would they rent those properties?"

I sat there thinking and then I thought about the location. That part of the county was more rural than others. The road we'd been on was the main farm-to-market road out there. We hadn't seen but a couple of cars the whole time we'd been driving along it. The houses looked abandoned, but someone was paying supposedly a couple of grand a month to rent it, and the farms were going for much higher. The Bentley's had bought most of them in auctions where the family had defaulted on their loans and they were repossessed. Others were ones where the owner died and the family either sold it, or they had no family and it went to the state and they sold it. They got them well below their market value.

As I was contemplating all this, my mind wandered to all the crazy stuff going on in Tenillo. Besides the extortion ring, I'd overheard some talk about cars being vandalized. We knew about the drugs at Tanner and Tyson's school, and I knew there had to be more around town. Plus, there were a number of women who'd gone missing. What in the world was going on? Then a horrible thought popped into my head. Maybe it was because I'd watched several episodes of a crime show with Lyric and her friend, Kerrigan, last weekend.

I turned around and looked at Mom. I knew my eyes were wide and my mouth was hanging open. "What's wrong, Skye?" she asked as she jumped to her feet. I grabbed her arms.

"Mom, what if the reason those places are so over-grown and look like they're not being lived in, is because they're not? What if they're being used for other things?"

"Like what?"

"What if they're doing illegal stuff out of them? You could grow things on those farms and do other stuff in those houses."

"What kind of stuff, you mean drugs?" I heard the alarm in her voice. She didn't know about what happened with Linc at the school. Tanner and I had kept that from her. But she knew he'd gotten beaten up going to school and she wasn't naïve enough to think that kind of thing didn't go on in Tenillo.

"I don't know what I mean. It's possible they could be, right? And if Ben and Jonathan don't go out there, they'd have no idea the properties aren't being used like they think. They get paid every month, no problem."

"Skye, I think you're getting a little off track. Why in the world would you think that? I mean, there could be other reasons we have no idea about. I think you should talk to Ex and see what he thinks. I wouldn't go telling Ben that you think his properties are being used for il-legal stuff."

"I wouldn't do that, Mom. But I will talk to Ex and see what he thinks. However, I'll wait until this whole ex-tortion thing gets settled. He has enough on his mind as it is. This is probably my wild imagination anyway. Ker-rigan and Lyric are a bad influence with those crime and detective shows they love. They sucked me into watch-ing them the other day with them."

"Oh my, those two are hilarious. I do enjoy some of

the things they come up with. And Jenn, Paula, and Brea, I haven't laughed that much in years. They're a fun bunch." She laughed.

"Yeah, they are. It's wild that we had never connected with them. Once this craziness is over, we're all going to go for manicures and pedicures. Jenn and Paula know of a place. They said it was where they met. They laughed really hard when they said it, so I can only guess what happened."

After that, we started to talk about the shop and then decided we might want to cook dinner. It was after six already. I had no idea how much longer he'd be gone, but the boys would be starving. We headed into the kitchen. As we cooked, we talked about what we were cooking tomorrow night for all the guys. Lyric had recently started to cook with Sara a couple of nights a week in the clubhouse's kitchen, and the bunnies were newly tasked with cooking a few other nights. It gave the guys several home-cooked meals a week, rather than fast food, since I don't think most of them cooked. Mom and I had jumped at the chance to help with it.

We were setting the table, when Tanner came racing in the door. He had a panicked look on his face. "Mom, Skye, Tyson is in trouble!"

"What do you mean, he's in trouble? Where is he? I thought he was playing video games with you and the prospects at the clubhouse," Mom asked in alarm.

"We were. Then they had to leave to go do something for the guys. So, we went outside, and we were throwing the football around. It went over the wall and out to the road. He went out to get it. Someone grabbed him and shoved him in a car. They took off!" he cried out. He shook in fear. My breath caught. Someone had taken

Tyson! God, please tell me I hadn't heard him right. But the fear on his face told me I had.

I picked up my phone that was on the coffee table and found Ex's number. As it rang, I was shaking and trying to get enough oxygen into my body. I felt a little light-headed. He answered on the second ring. He sounded distracted.

"What's up, baby? I'm almost done. I had to stop and shower really quick. Give me five minutes."

"Shower, why did you need to shower? Slade, I need you to come home now. We have—" I stopped talking when I heard   a rumble of a bunch of male voices. They seemed to all be talking and laughing. On top of that, I could clearly hear a female giggling. She had to be standing right next to Executioner for me to hear her so plainly.

I didn't bother to say anything else. I hung up. They'd obviously finished their business and were relaxing, and that relaxing didn't include him coming home. He'd gone to the clubhouse and didn't bother to at least tell me he was back or anything. I'd been here waiting on pins and needles to see if they found out anything. I didn't even want to think what had the bunny laughing. My gut told me it wasn't Ex, but then he hadn't come home to shower. Why not?

I grabbed my purse and my car keys. I headed for the door. As I opened it, I told Mom, "I'm going after them. Which way did they go, Tanner?"

"You can't go after them! Stay here and let Executioner go. What did he say?" Mom asked in a panic.

"He's busy. If they just left, I might be able to catch them, or at least see who it is and where they are taking him. Tanner, you can go tell the guys if you want, but I think they're busy having fun right now." I ran out the door and got in my car. I sped to the front and waited for the gate to open. I had the sensor on my car now that allowed me to open it. As I went to pull out, I saw Tanner and Mom entering the clubhouse. God, I hope they didn't see something they shouldn't. I shot out on the road and floored it. I had to find my little brother.

<|> <|> <|> <|>

Executioner:

I was looking at my phone trying to figure out what had happened. Skye had been there and then nothing. It showed that the signal was gone. I called her back. I was just about ready to go home. I'd showered off the blood and stopped for a second to tell Saint I'd meet them back here at ten thirty, so we could head over to that park and catch the other guy. He had Barbie standing next to him, rubbing his back.

Her phone rang but there was no answer. I clicked the end button. "I'm out of here. See you later. Skye just called. I need to go see what she needs." He nodded. As I started for the door, it flew open and in charged Tanner and Jackie. Both had panicked looks on their faces. I didn't see Skye. I ran over to them.

"What's wrong? Where's Skye?"

"She took off. Someone grabbed Tyson. She's trying to see if she can catch them or follow them," Jackie rambled out quickly. She was breathing fast.

"What the hell do you mean she went after them? Why in the hell was he outside the walls?" I shouted. Fear started to crawl up from my stomach to my throat.

"We'll explain later. Go after her! I tried to get her to send you, but she said you were busy having fun. I guess she was right," Jackie said in disgust as she looked around. I knew she was seeing the guys drinking, and a few had bunnies on their laps. They were blowing off steam after the interrogation and in preparation for our mission later tonight. Shit, I bet Skye heard that in the background and thought what the hell.

I gave a loud whistle that got everyone's attention. "Round 'em up. Tyson got grabbed and Skye went after them. Fuck!" I yelled. They all popped to their feet. I didn't wait around to see who was coming. I ran for my bike. Tanner ran after me.

"They headed toward town when they took him." I nodded and started my bike. I raced to the gate and got through as soon as I could squeeze through the opening. I heard other bikes firing up behind me. I swore. I didn't have a way to ride and call Skye at the same time. Shit! I hoped I would catch up to her soon. Why in the hell had she done something like this? She was fucking pregnant!

I fumed the whole time. The miles sped by and soon I had Sin and Saint right beside me. We were fast approaching town. As we came around the bend, I saw Skye's car sitting alongside the road with the door open. I put on my brakes and stopped beside it. A glance inside showed me it was empty. Her purse was on the seat and stuff was strewn all over the seat. I swore. All I could think is they caught her following them and they took her. My chest started to fucking hurt. I was about to take off again when my phone rang. I pulled it out of my rag and saw it was Skye's number. I quickly answered it. "Where the hell are you, Skye?"

"I'm in the fields right off of our main road. If you keep driving, you'll see my car. I'm off to the right. You'll see an old dried creek bed. They took Tyson that way. I barely saw the back end of the car before it disappeared down the wash. I'm about half a mile or so off the road." She was whispering like she didn't want to be heard.

"Skye, stay where you are and don't take another fucking step! We're at your car. I swear, I'm gonna smack that ass when I see you. You don't fucking take off after the bad guys! That's why you have me. Jesus Christ, you're pregnant, Skye!" I was ranting and I knew it. We were already starting down into the creek bed.

"Screw you, Executioner. I did call you, but you sounded like you were busy. So busy you had to take a shower! I thought you were still out interrogating the two bad guys. Guess I was wrong. I didn't have time to wait on you to get done with whatever you were doing. This is my little brother! And yes, I know I'm pregnant," she hissed and then I heard her phone go dead. She'd hung up on me! I growled and resisted the urge to throw my phone. Sin and Saint were beside me. I looked at them. "She's a half mile or so ahead of us in the dry bed. She says they took Tyson down it. No idea how far they went."

"Sounds like she's pissed at you. Couldn't hear the words but the tone said it all," Sin added.

"Yeah, it seems like me and my old lady will be having a talk. She's got shit twisted, but that'll have to wait. We need to get her and then get Tyson back. This has to be Pedro. He figured out already that those two were missing. It wouldn't be a big leap to figure we had them."

"Okay, let's go get your woman and Tyson. This'll save us waiting until later to get his ass," Saint said. He quickly told the others where we were going as we kept moving. I was constantly scanning for Skye. We'd gone what I'd estimated was close to a mile when up ahead I caught sight of her. It was getting darker but there was still enough light to see. She was crouched down right before a bend in the creek bed and there was some short scrub brush in front of her.

I signaled the guys to go low, and we crouched as we

sped over to her. She looked back when we were getting close. I saw she had a gun in her hand. What the fuck? I got to her first and tugged her to me after I made sure the gun was pointed away from me.

"What in the hell, Skye? Jesus, you're taking years off my damn life! Taking off like that and now I find you with a gun! You're going back with Boomer." I waved him forward. He could take her back in her car and then get one of the others to bring him to get his bike.

"Like hell. I'm staying right here until we get my brother back! They're around this bend about half a mile ahead. There's some old shack up there. That's where they stopped. I saw their car," she whispered.

"We'll get Tyson. You're going home. Be reasonable, Skye, you're pregnant. You could get hurt. I can't concentrate on getting Tyson if I have to worry about you."

"Fine, I'll go back to my car, but I'm not leaving, Ex. He might need me," she hissed. I saw the determined set of her jaw. I could have her carried out of here, but she'd fight, and there was no telling how hard she might fight if I tried it. I'd never do anything that might hurt her or the baby.

"Okay, Boomer will take you back to your car and wait with you. You listen to him. If I call and tell you to get the hell back home, you do it. They could move on us unexpectedly or something. I can't have them coming back and finding you. Got it?" She nodded. I couldn't resist. I gave her a hard kiss. "We'll talk later. Try not to shoot anyone who doesn't deserve it."

She wrinkled up her nose. "I don't see anyone yet who doesn't deserve it." She had a bite to her tone. Yeah, she thought something had happened at the clubhouse. Another thing I had to clear up. God, life sure had gotten complicated. Giving her one more kiss, I sent her off with my brother. I looked at the rest of my brothers. They were trying not to laugh.

"Wait, you fuckers. Sin knows. You'll do shit like this too when you get a woman. I can't wait to tell you I told you so. Let's go get my brother-in-law, so I can go home and straighten out this shit with my old lady." They quietly chuckled. A quick conference and we knew what each of us was doing. We split and would come up on the shack from behind it and from the side. Hopefully, it was just Pedro and he wasn't watching for us.

We double-timed it to our spots. It was like my days in the Marines. Each of us always carried a gun, so we were armed. It looked like Talon had been left behind with Sara, Jackie, Lyric, and Tanner. No way we'd leave them totally alone, even inside the walls. Not when there was any kind of threat. The prospects would be back soon from their trip to dispose of the bodies.

We broke up and creeped up on the shack. There was a faint light glowing from the windows. It was nothing more than what looked like an old fishing shack. One that someone had used when this creek bed had water, which was a long time ago. It was old and falling apart. There were big cracks between the boards. I peeked through a large one. Inside, I could see Tyson tied to a chair. A guy who matched Pedro's description was pacing around. He was on his cell phone.

"Listen, bitch, you have them bring my men to me, or I'm going to make sure you never see your little brother again. They have one hour to release them in town at the Haven apartments. Once they do and I have them, I'll tell them where to find your brother. Remember, one hour or he's dead." He hung up. He turned to Tyson and grinned. It wasn't a pleasant one.

"You're not going back to Mommy and your sister. I lied. They messed with my business too much. They need to be made an example of, so others won't get any ideas. I'm gonna make this better than Marcos ever imagined." He laughed as he said it. I'd heard enough. I rounded the front and kicked in the door. I knew I had brothers at the windows. They could take him out, but we needed to question him about who was backing him.

I came in low to the ground and immediately moved to the left. He whipped around when the door crashed open. This put the gun pointing in my direction and not Tyson's, thankfully. I took the shot. All my years in the military had taught me how to place my bullets where I wanted them. In most instances, it was a center body-mass shot or a shot to the head. This time, I went for the shoulder, in particular, the one to the arm holding the gun. He screamed in pain and dropped his gun. It was like a wave of leather and denim when my brothers came rushing inside. They were screaming at him to get on the ground and hold out his hands.

Rampage went over to untie a terrified Tyson. I hurried over to them. When he was free, he came right into my arms. I hugged him tight. He was shaking. "You're okay, buddy. We got you. No one's going to hurt you," I told him. He was crying softly. I let him get it out. I knew he'd be embarrassed if the guys saw him cry. Hell, who could blame him? He was fourteen fucking years old and was taken hostage and told he was going to be killed. I knew grown men who would have acted worse.

I watched as my brothers zip tied Pedro. He was swearing and crying about his arm. Sin was on his phone. We needed a way to get him back to the compound. We'd leave his car here. Let someone else find it and wonder. As soon as Tyson wasn't shaking anymore, I stepped back. "Let's get out of here. Your sister is waiting at the road for you."

"Why is Skye waiting?"

"Because she was the one to follow you and then told us where he'd turned off."

"Man, why'd she do that? She should have stayed at the compound where it's safe," he groused.

"I hear ya, but you know your sister. I'll have to talk to her about it."

He laughed. "Good luck. I'm glad she did, though. He was waiting outside. I think I startled him when I went to get the ball. He was in his car parked back in the trees across the road. I didn't see him at first. Not until after he came out of them and grabbed me. I tried to get away, but he had the gun and told me he'd shoot me if I didn't come with him. I'm sorry, Ex, I didn't know what to do."

"You did fine. You did what was necessary to save your life. Come on." We all exited the shack. Two of my brothers were dragging Pedro. We headed back toward the road. Boomer met us not too far down the creek bed. He had Skye's car. She was in the front seat. They stopped, and he got out and opened the trunk. Inside was an old blanket. Boomer unrolled it.

I hated the idea of Pedro in the car, but this way he wouldn't be inside with her and Tyson. They shoved his protesting ass into the trunk and slammed the lid shut. Skye was busy hugging the hell out of her brother. I gave them a minute then broke it up. "We need to get back. Tyson, ride with your sister. We'll be right behind you. Baby, when you get there, go to the clubhouse and wait for me. Boomer will take your car to the back of the compound. Don't go anywhere else, okay?"

She nodded. "Okay. Come on, Ty. Let's get you back to Mom." As he got into the back seat, I pulled her around and into my arms.

"I know you heard shit on the phone, but it's not what it sounded like. Let me get this settled and then I'll explain. We need to talk to this joker first. Just be patient." She stared at me and then slowly nodded. I gave her a kiss before I helped her into the car. Boomer got behind the wheel and took off.

The rest of us hiked back to the road and got our bikes. It took less time than going because we didn't need to be stealthy. I couldn't wait to get my hands on Pedro. He was going to be a pleasure to talk to.

Skye: Chapter 23

I paced nervously around the common room. It had been two hours since we'd gotten back to the compound and heard the guys come roaring in on their bikes. I was sitting here with Mom, the boys, Sara, and Lyric. Dash and Blake were inside with us. I think they had been told to make sure I didn't leave. They seemed to be keeping an eye on me at all times.

I knew Executioner was pissed I'd left and gone after my brother, but I would do it again. If I hadn't, we wouldn't have known he'd turned off onto a damn dry creek bed of all things. A part of me was still pissed that when I did try and get Ex's help, he'd been at the clubhouse in what sounded like a party. A party that involved the bunnies. He was supposed to be questioning those men. Was this what I had to look forward to? Him going off and me staying home thinking he was doing one thing while he went to the clubhouse and partied with his brothers and the bunnies? If so, this wasn't the place for me.

Mom stood up. "Honey, you need to stop pacing. You're wearing yourself out. They'll be here as soon as they can."

"That's not the only reason I'm pacing, Mom. I'm thinking."

"About what?"

"About what I heard when I called Executioner. He was here and they were laughing, and I heard one of those bunnies right next to him laughing. I thought he was questioning those men. He said he'd taken a shower. Why? I don't know. Maybe I made a mistake after all. I don't want to spend my life with a man I can't trust or one who does whatever the hell he wants, while I sit at home waiting for him. I'll be at home taking care of the baby by myself. I think I need to reconsider staying here with him."

She took my arm and tugged me over into a quiet corner away from everyone else. "Skye, don't do something you'll regret. Talk to him. Find out what was going on. I'm sure there's a good explanation. You have no idea what was going on."

"Maybe, but when I needed him, he was busy, and it wasn't with work. I want to come first. Not every second of the day, but when it's important. What if he can't give me that? Hell, look at us. He's claimed me as his old lady, I'm having his child. We're building a house and he says he loves me. But he hasn't asked me to marry him. Is that because he thinks this might not last? It's harder to get a divorce than to just split up."

"Skye, you're worried he doesn't want you? Why? Marriage doesn't guarantee anything. Look at me and your dad. I didn't even know you wanted to get married."

"I didn't either until now. I want to be tied to him in every way. I know bikers don't always get married, though Sin and Lyric are. But I want that. I want to share his last name. Maybe I'm expecting too much, but I want it and I think I might need it. What am I going to do? I don't want to tell him that and have him marry me just to make me happy. God." I sank down on the couch and held my head in my hands. My head was whirling and aching.

She sat down and rubbed my back. "I don't know

what to tell you, honey, other than you need to talk to him. Lay it all out. I have no doubt that he loves you. Please give him a chance." I sat and tried to let her rubbing soothe me, but it only made my stomach churn more. Suddenly, I bolted to my feet and ran for the bathroom off the common room. I hit the toilet just in time to empty my guts into it. It came in waves and I kept puking.

Next thing I knew, Executioner was standing beside me, holding onto me. I was dry heaving. "Baby Girl, what in the hell? Why're you puking like this?" I shook my head. I couldn't talk. I was afraid that if I did, I'd vomit again. I slowly stood up. When my stomach didn't seize, I shuffled over to the sink. He held onto me the whole way. I rinsed out my mouth, but it still tasted awful. I hung my head and took a few deep breaths to make sure I was settled enough to leave the bathroom.

I pushed on him to get him to move so I could leave the bathroom. He lifted me up and carried me out to the common room, but he didn't stop. He kept going. "We're going to the trailer," he announced. I closed my eyes. The day was catching up to me. I needed to lay down and sleep. In no time, he was carrying me inside and down the hall to the bedroom. When we got inside, I pointed to the bathroom. He took me there and sat me down gently on my feet. I grabbed my toothbrush and toothpaste. I had to get the awful taste out of my mouth. As I brushed, he started talking.

"What brought that on, Skye? You've been doing so good with not vomiting. I know I said we'd talk, but I think you need to rest. We'll talk tomorrow." I spit out the toothpaste and rinsed. Then I swung around to face him.

"I'm not waiting until tomorrow. We need to talk now. I need some answers, so I know what to do."

"What do you mean, so you know what to do?"

"I need to know if this relationship is what's best for me and my baby. I need to know if the man I love is really going to be here for us. I need to know that when I need you, I can rely on you. I need to know I can trust you. If any of those are a no, then we end this now and go our separate ways," I told him boldly. I wasn't going to mince words. This was too important. Mom said to talk to him. Well, here it was. I was laying it all out on the table.

He looked at me with a stunned look on his face. He seemed to be frozen. I tried to squeeze past him. That unfroze him. He grabbed my arm and swung me around. His arms came up around me and he pulled me to his chest. He was breathing hard.

"What the fuck are you talking about? You want to leave me? Over my dead fucking body are you leaving. What in the hell is happening here? Everything was fine a few hours ago when I left and then it all went crazy." He was half-yelling.

"What happened is I needed my man only to find out he wasn't where I thought he was, doing what I thought he was supposed to be doing. Instead, he was at the clubhouse with the sounds of a celebration in the background, telling me he had taken a shower and a woman's laughter was practically coming from what sounded like his lap! That's what happened. I've had a few hours since to think. I'm not willing to be second best or kept at home while you go do whatever you want. I need and deserve more!" I shouted back. His arms dropped and he stepped back. I walked over and sat down on the edge of the bed.

Before I knew it, he crossed the room and was down on his knees in front of me. He took my hands into his. He looked up at me and I saw pain, fear, and confusion in his eyes. Just what I was feeling. The idea of not being with him made me want to cry and crawl into a hole. But if I ignored this, I knew I'd regret it.

"God, Skye, you can't believe that I was cheating on you, surely? I swear it wasn't that at all. Yes, I was at the clubhouse. After we got done with those guys, I needed a shower. I went there and not here since I didn't want to have you see me like that. Jesus, I had to torture them to get the information. I had blood on me! When you called, I'd just finished showering and stopped to tell Saint I was coming home. I wasn't partying. Some of the guys were relaxing and having a drink. Yes, the bunnies had come in. One was standing right next to me because she was with Saint." I watched his face. He looked like he was being sincere. I let him continue.

"I never thought about telling you what I was doing. Baby, I'd never cheat on you. I fucking love you. You know that!"

"Do you? I mean, do you really? Or is this something you're not sure about and you're hedging your bets in case we don't work out? If so, tell me. I don't want to stay and then have you walk away later. It'll hurt like hell now, but it'll be worse if we wait. I can take care of this baby, Executioner. You don't have to stay with me because of this baby. And if you want to be in his or her life, I won't stop you, as long as you're never abusive to them."

He sat back on his ass and gaped at me. He ran his hands through his hair and tugged on it. "Am I dreaming? This can't be happening. Skye, I know how I feel about you. There's no uncertainty. I love you and I want to be with you for the rest of our lives. Do you love me? Is that it? You're not sure you love me?"

I sank to my knees in front of him. "No, I know I love you."

"Then what is it you need to know I love you. I'll do it. Just tell me." He sounded desperate. I didn't want to tell him I wanted him to marry me. I'd never know if he really wanted it or not.

"I can't. I'm sorry. If I do, then I'll never know for sure you meant it. I don't know what to do." I burst out crying. I cried so hard I shook with the sobs. He stood then picked me up and laid me down on the bed. He laid down behind me and curled around me. I sobbed into the pillow. I don't know how long I cried before I slipped off to sleep with him murmuring to me how much he loved me and begging me to stop crying.

◄II► ◄II► ◄II► ◄II►

Executioner:

My whole world was crumbling right in front of me. Skye was sobbing her heart out and I didn't know what to do to stop it. She needed something from me that I wasn't giving her. Something that she said would let her know I really did love her and wanted to live with her forever. God, what was I going to do if I couldn't figure this out? I would lose her and most likely my child.

All thoughts of what Pedro had told us went out the window. I couldn't care less about it. I had to save my fucking life from imploding. When she fell asleep, I reluctantly got up. I needed to talk to someone. I had to think. When I walked outside to get a breath of air, I saw Sin sitting out back. I wasn't sure where Lyric was. I went over to him. He was in a relationship, maybe he could help me figure this out. I sat down.

"What's got you looking like that, Ex? How's Skye? Is she feeling better?"

"Fuck no, she's not better. She's in there sleeping after she cried herself to sleep. Which was after she told me she needed to be sure I really loved her and wanted to be with her. She's threatening to leave me, Sin. I don't know what to do. She said she needs something, but she won't tell me what it is. Something about if she does then she'll never know if I really meant it. What the hell?" I shouted.

"Calm down. Let's think this through. Anyone can see you two love each other. Obviously, something has set her off and now she's having doubts." I quickly told him what she'd said about hearing me at the clubhouse. He sighed.

"Shit, okay, that's fucked up. But it got her thinking. What is it she could need that you haven't given her? You're having a kid. You've moved her in with you and brought her whole family here too. You're building not only a house for the two of you but for them. You're helping to support her efforts to become a full-time accountant. I'm assuming you're not keeping your hands off her in the sex department." He grinned when I growled at him. "You've just eliminated the threat to her family. Oh, and you've claimed her as your old lady. What else could a woman want? What else is a demonstration of your love and commitment?" he mused.

"Why haven't you asked her to marry you?" came a voice from behind us. We turned to look at Lyric in surprise. She was standing there with her hands on her hips and a pissed look on her face.

"What?" I asked dumbfounded.

"You say you love her and want to be with her forever, but you haven't asked her to marry you. To take your name. Why? Because if things don't work out, it's easier for you to walk away?"

"Fuck no! I'm never walking away. Why would you say that, Lyric?" I was starting to get pissed at her.

"Because I can guarantee you, that's what she's wondering. I knew Sin was all-in because he barely had his property rag on me before he was asking me to marry him. You've done everything but that. And you have a child coming. I can see where it might make her feel insecure."

"Why wouldn't she just tell me that, if that's what she wants?"

"Because then she would always wonder if you only

asked her to marry you, so she'd stay, not because you really wanted to marry her," she told me patiently and slowly like she was explaining it to a toddler.

I stood there stunned. Was she right? Was this all because I hadn't asked her to marry me yet? As I thought of what Lyric had said, I felt like a huge weight came off my chest. This I could fucking do and prove to her that I did want to marry her. I grabbed Lyric and gave her a kiss. "Thanks, Lyric." Sin growled as I ran back to my place. I was going to settle this right now. I ran down the hall and into the bedroom. She sat up groggily when she heard me.

"What's wrong?" she mumbled. I leaned down and kissed her. I took my time and made love to her mouth. When I was done, she was panting.

"Nothing. I have something for you." I went to my closet and got into the gun safe. She was watching me with a frown on her beautiful face. I could see the dried tears on her cheeks. It gutted me to see those. But I was going to wipe those away. I came back to the bed and kneeled beside it. "Skye Fulton, I love you so damn much it hurts. And every day, I love you just a little more. I want to be with you and raise our family and watch them grow. And when our time comes, I want to die with you in my arms and we'll continue on in the afterlife. I need you to marry me, Skye. Will you?" I held up the jewelry box I had in my hand.

She gasped and looked at me uncertainly. I opened it. Inside was my mother's engagement ring. It was the one my dad had given her. When he died and she later married Randall, she'd given it to me. She told me that one day I'd find a woman I would want to wear it. I'd rolled my eyes thinking she was crazy. But she had been right. I'd gotten it out of my safe and had it profession-ally cleaned and resized a few weeks ago. I'd just gotten it back and was trying to decide how to ask her to marry me.

I took it out and held it up. She slowly held up her hand so I could slide it on her finger. It was a perfect fit. It was a single solitaire set in gold and surrounded by small black onyx stones. My dad had saved for a long time to be able to buy it for my mom. "It's beautiful, Slade. Oh my God, when did you get this? How?"

"I didn't buy it. It was my mom's. Dad bought it for her. She gave it to me to one day give to the woman I loved and wanted to spend my life with. That's you, Skye. I had it cleaned and resized. I was just trying to decide how to ask you. God, baby, I had no idea you were doubting us because I hadn't asked. I want nothing more than for you to have my last name." She kissed me and it was a kiss that had my body catching on fire and my blood heating up. I knew exactly how we were going to celebrate our engagement.

I tore impatiently at her clothes, almost ripping them to shreds to get to her. She was tugging on my shirt and then the belt to my pants. I hated that I had to stop kiss-ing her to take off my boots and socks. As soon as I was naked, I crawled on the bed and started at her mouth and worked my way down. I kissed, licked, nibbled, and sucked all over her soft, beautiful skin. I left my mark in several places. I wanted an outward sign that she be-longed to me. We couldn't get a tattoo right now, so this would have to do.

I spent extra time on her gorgeous breasts, teasing those hard little beads. When I got to her pussy, I stopped for a moment to look at her. She was slick and her scent was heavy in the air. She was restlessly moving on the bed. I knew she'd be quick to get off once my mouth was on her there. I was going to get her to come at least once before my cock got inside heaven.

Spreading her pussy lips with my thumb and finger, I licked her up and down, fluttering my tongue from side to side and all over her clit. She jumped then moaned. She sank her hand into my hair and held me there. I smiled. As I worked to get her to come for me with my tongue, I also had my fingers in her pussy and her ass.

I was humming as her flavor slid down my throat. Feeling her tighten on my fingers just a little, I thrust faster and latched onto her clit, sucking then biting down. She pulled my hair and screamed as she came, coating my tongue in even more of her cream. She squeezed my fingers so hard they went numb. It took her a little while to come down all the way. I needed to be inside her, and I couldn't wait a second longer.

I laid down beside her. She looked at me groggily. I could see the bliss on her face. "Baby Girl, get on top and ride me. You control it and make me come," I whispered hoarsely. She smiled and then slowly sat up. She slunk over to me, taking her time, letting her hair tease my skin. I shivered. She kissed up my legs. "Fuck! Hurry," I cried out.

She finally took pity on me and straddled me. I held my cock so she could slide down my pole. As she did, the heat and tightness almost made me whimper. God, she felt so damn amazing. No one had ever come close to comparing to her. When she was flush against my groin, I groaned. Then she set out to make me lose my mind.

She put her hands on my chest and slowly lifted up

until only the tip remained inside of her. Then she swiveled her hips as she pushed back down. She repeated this I don't know how many times, but it was making me tremble. Her breathing came out in pants. She rode me until I was about to scream. Her breasts were bouncing up and down as she did. I kneaded them with my hands and tweaked her nipples over and over. Suddenly, she froze and cried out as she came. I bit my lip then grunted as my cum erupted. We both were crying out our pleasure as she milked me for everything I had.

When she relaxed and fell onto my chest, I was still slowly moving inside of her. Even after that fantastic orgasm, my cock was still hard. She sat back up and looked at me in surprise. "What can I say, you fucking turn me on," I told her with a grin. It looked like there was going to be some more orgasms before we were through.

She rolled off me. I tried to grab her. Where was she going? She went to my side table and opened it, taking something out. When she held it up, I saw it was the lube I used on her ass. I looked for the dildo or the beads. Maybe she wanted me to do that again. It had been hot the last time.

Not seeing either, I frowned. "Skye, where's the other stuff? I'll happily play with your ass. Just get back over here." I stroked down my drenched cock.

She got back on the bed and kissed me. When she stopped, she whispered to me, "It's time, Slade. I want to know what it's like for you to be in my ass, not your fingers or toys." I froze.

"Babe, are you sure? It's gonna hurt. I don't want to hurt you," I told her though my mind was screaming at me to shut up. I'd been dreaming of taking her ass. I wanted to feel how tight it would hug my cock.

"I'm sure. I know it'll hurt, but I want to try it. When you play with me there, it feels so good. I need you, Slade." She crawled over me and kissed my chest, nipping my nipples. Fuck it, if she wanted it, I'd give it to her. I just had to remember not to go too fast or hard. I took the lube out of her hand, opened it and put some on the head of my cock. I worked it down my length and then I held up my hand.

"Turn so I can lube your ass. We need you to be nice and slick." She turned around on all fours. I moaned as I worked one then two and finally three fingers in her tight-as-hell ass. She hissed a few times, but she kept pushing back on them. When I thought she was lubed up enough, I said. "Get back on top. You're gonna control this. You go as slow as you need. If at any time you want to stop, do it. This is supposed to bring you enjoyment, not pain." She nodded and got back over me. I held myself erect and helped her to place it at the opening of her ass. She took a deep breath and started to bear down. Slowly her ass opened. She hissed and stopped as the head slid inside. I waited to see what she would do.

She surprised me. She kept going. She went slow, which had my head ready to blow off, but she did it. There were some stops along the way, but eventually she had me buried in her ass. The sensation was so damn indescribably good. She sat recovering then slowly she lifted and then pushed back down. I wanted to howl, it felt so damn good. "That's it, baby, you're doing great. You feel so fucking amazing. God, that's it, ride me. Give me that beautiful ass," I growled.

That must have set her off, because she began to ride me faster. When she would come down on me, it was just a bit harder each time. I could feel the cum churning. I grasped her hips and thrust up as she was coming down on the next stroke. She sobbed and then she slammed down on me a few more times and came. Her ass was like a fist. I couldn't hold back. I erupted again, filling her ass with my cum. I shouted, "Fuck, Skye," as she rode me and screamed out her own release.

When we were done, I laid there feeling like I was floating. She was lying on my chest panting. I kissed her softly. "I love you, Skye Fulton, soon-to-be Ashton," I whispered.

"I love you, Slade Ashton. Let's just lie here and nap." I slowly pulled out of her. We were a mess, but right now, I couldn't walk.

"Okay, only until we can walk. You need to soak so you won't be too sore." She nodded and her eyes drifted closed. I wasn't far behind her.

Executioner: Chapter 24

I couldn't even describe what it was like last night when we'd made love all night. The connection between us was so strong and seemed to be getting stronger. Her asking me for anal sex had surprised the hell out of me. It had been amazing and all I wanted to do was stay in bed with her, but my brothers and I had some work to do. I slipped out of bed and scribbled a quick note for her in case she woke up. Then I got dressed and went to the clubhouse.

It was early, not even seven o'clock, but everyone seemed to be there already. We went into church and closed the door. I got to the point. "Did he say anything last night?" I asked Talon and Cuffs. They had been the ones to stay in the Gallows with Pedro. I'd worked him over good yesterday before the whole incident with Skye. I wanted to be sure he'd told us everything. Some time hanging there in pain would help jog his memory. They shook their heads no.

"He moaned and pleaded to be let down, but that was it. He's close to being done. I think. One more go at him and he's history," Cuffs told us.

"Then let's get this done. I need to get all the threats against my family eliminated as well as the threats to others."

"Is she better today?" Sin asked. He asked it quietly, but the others heard. I wondered if they had heard about our disagreement.

"She is." The others gave me curious looks. Fuck it, they were my brothers. "Skye had a meltdown yesterday. She thought I wasn't fully committed to her. She was debating whether she should leave." All of them sat up straighter and protested. "Lyric helped me to figure out why. I took care of it. I was planning to anyway. We need to get this shit settled, because after Pres here gets hitched, Skye and I will be getting married." I grinned as I said it. They all broke into smiles and shouted their congrats.

"Thanks. That's why I want this done and over today, if possible. Are Boss and his guys coming over?"

"I told him we'd be working on him again if they wanted. He said at least a few would be here at eight. That gives us time to talk over what he told us yesterday. What's your gut and Omen's saying to you? Pedro says that he doesn't know the identity of the guy who's giving the orders. He's never seen him or even talked to him. It's always a message sent to a burner phone that tells him what to do, when to do it, and where to make the money drops. Their cuts are also dictated by him. They take it out before making the drop."

I stood up and went to the window to stare outside. "My gut is telling me he's telling the truth. Though the one thing I don't know yet, is if he's lying about there being no others doing the same thing. We assumed it was just the four—Gene, Donnie, Pedro and Marcos. But what if we're wrong?"

"Maybe I can help with that," Phantom said. "Since we have their names, I was able to pull up their histories. I have their photos. We can show them to all the business owners and see if there was anyone else. It's the best I can think of to do. I'm searching their backgrounds, looking for known associates, but it takes a bit of time. Plus, I have the phone, in case whoever the boss is sends more messages. Can't trace them but maybe we can get an idea of who it is. Pedro deleted all the messages, but I can retrieve them."

"Great, thanks, Phantom. Anything else before we grab our coffee and then go calling on our guest?" Sin asked with a smirk on his face. We all chuckled and shook our heads no. Time to get to work.

We did get a chance to drink a cup of coffee and even had Boss, Chef, and Santa join us. When we were done, we went to the Gallows. Omen was standing outside. We kept a guard with Pedro even though he had no way to escape. As we filed inside, Sin told Omen, "Need you in here too, Omen. We want to use your gut again." Omen nodded and followed us in.

Pedro looked like hell. We'd left him strung up on the hooks used to hang animals when you're butchering them and draining their blood. He was covered in bruises, cuts and various other wounds I had made with several tools we had lying around just for this purpose. His face was so swollen and discolored, you could hardly recognize him. He moaned when he saw all of us.

"Good morning, Pedro. Hope you had a good rest because it's time to talk again. I feel well rested, so I can go all day. Yesterday I was tired, so I didn't go as hard on you." He groaned when I said that.

"Let me introduce our friends. This is Boss, Chef, and Santa. They are all members of the Time Served MC. In case you don't know him, Boss is the new chief of police here in Tenillo. He's really anxious to shut down this extortion ring. He's gonna talk to you as well." Boss stared at him coldly and cracked his knuckles.

"Please, I swear. I told you everything I know! The businesses, the guys helping me, the drop points, the pickup schedule. What else do you want?" he pleaded.

"We want to talk about your boss. See, I'm not so sure that you don't know who it is. I mean, who works for someone and doesn't even know their name?" I asked as I circled him. He tried to turn and follow me with his eyes, but he couldn't.

"I don't know. Marcos was the one who recruited me. He might have known who it was, but he never told any of us. He had the phone until he disappeared." He gave us an accusing look. Boss chuckled.

"Yeah, old Marcos was fun to play with. He didn't last as long as I wanted. Maybe it was because we cut off all his fingers and fed 'em to him. He seemed to lose the will to live after that. I hope you're made of stronger stuff. I want this to last." He had the evilest smile I'd ever seen on his face. Hell, I wanted to take a step back.

"Nooo! Don't. Please. I'll do anything. Just don't let him touch me!" Pedro shouted in horror. He kicked his feet like it would help him move away from Boss.

"You need to worry about all of us, not just Boss. Though I have to say, I think they hate lowlifes like you a tad more than us, and I thought that was impossible. Maybe it's because they had to put up with so many of you when they were in prison." He whimpered.

"Don't worry, you won't be going to prison. We have a special place for the likes of you. Now, let's get to work. Take us through everything from the first time Marcos contacted you until you took my brother-in-law." He spewed out all the details. He didn't tell us anything he hadn't already. I was busy watching his non-verbals and so was Sin and Omen. Sin had a way of sizing people up. When he was done talking, he hung there with his head resting on his chest. We walked to the small office to talk.

"I think he's telling the truth of not knowing of anyone else doing the extorting or who the boss is. He was just in it to make money without having to work for it. Intimidate and hurt people to get what you want," Sin said in disgust. I nodded.

"I think so too. What about you Omen? What's your gut saying?"

"Let me take a closer look. I want to say he's given us all he can, but I want to be sure. I don't want to miss someone, though it is likely whoever masterminded this, will be out there. Hopefully, they'll think twice before doing this again." He walked off to go stare at Pedro.

That damn stare freaked people out. He grabbed his hair and raised his head, so he had to look at him. "Look into my eyes. I want to see your soul," he said softly. Omen had eyes that went from bright blue, to green and then gray. When they were gray, he was pissed. Pedro shivered and stared helplessly at Omen.

"Ah, I see all the things you've done. Pedro has been a very bad boy. He's stolen, assaulted people, robbed, lied and wait... he's raped women as well." Pedro jerked in surprise. Shit, Omen was right. I hated a fucking rapist with a passion, along with pedophiles. The others all hissed their displeasure. Omen slapped him.

"Oh, you so deserve to die. Tell me, you did talk to the boss, didn't you? Just one time?"

Pedro's eyes darted around the room. Omen kept slapping him, so he'd look at him. Finally, Pedro broke. "Yeah, I talked to him one time. But it was only once. He called me after Marcos disappeared, wanting to know if I knew what happened to him. I told him I had no idea. I didn't know you'd gotten him. He said I was in charge and he'd be texting me from now on. He said not to fuck up."

"So, you lied to us. Tell me what his voice sounded like. Were there any background noises? Anything at all," Omen asked in a slow, almost hypnotic voice. Pedro hung there thinking for a couple of minutes.

"He was doing something to make his voice sound weird. It was muffled. I remember hearing a clock chiming like it does at the top of the hour. His voice was very... I don't know. Like he was higher class. You know how they talk snottily. That's all I remember." Omen looked at him for another minute then stepped back.

"He's done. That's all he has for us."

"You're sure?" Boss asked. Omen nodded. They looked at me. I nodded as well.

"Then end him, we have work to do. We'll check with the other business owners to be sure they didn't have anyone else picking up money. Boss, Phantom is digging into their pasts to see if he finds anything. I hope this will shut this ring down. We'll keep an eye out for it starting again. I wish like hell we could get the ringleader. Maybe we will one day," Sin added.

"Works for me. Let's get this over with. I have a lunch date later with my woman."

I went over to Pedro. He looked scared. I held up the big K-bar knife I always had on me. I'd used it to cut him several times yesterday. I showed it to him. "See this edge with all those teeth? It's meant to saw through things like trees. I think I'll see how it does on flesh and bone. I bet it'll go through it like butter." He sobbed.

"It does. It's great." Omen chuckled.

Pedro screamed as I slowly sawed off his left arm. Blood was pouring out of him. As he stared at me in horror, I grabbed his limp cock. "You raping bastard," I growled as I hacked it off. His screams made my ears hurt. He would bleed out in less than five minutes. I washed my hands and my knife as the others cut him down and rolled him in plastic. They'd dispose of the body. We'd found a while back an old chemical plant that had been shut down for years. It supposedly had been cleaned up, but inside there was one huge vat of some kind of acid. It was perfect for body disposal. They'd take him there. If we kept this up, we'd need to find others. We didn't want to have a pattern.

Omen, Dash, Santa, and Talon took the body. The rest of us headed back to the clubhouse. After a drink, Boss and Chef left. We needed to get on with our day. It was still a workday. I found Skye was up and getting ready to go to the shop. Her mom had opened it at eight. I took a quick shower and had her join me. One thing led to another, and I ended up taking her up against the shower wall. God, what a better way to start my day.

Just to be safe, I took her to work and worked in their office. I wanted to be sure the danger had passed. All I could think of now was when could I get her to the altar. Sin and Lyric's big day was just over five weeks away. I wanted to talk to Skye. I wanted us to do it soon. And I wanted my family to be there, if they could. I went out front. She was just ringing up a lady's purchase. I waited until she was done.

"Baby, come back to the office with me. I need to talk to you about something." She shot me a puzzled look but came with me. I smiled at Jackie. She'd been so happy this morning when she saw Skye's ring. She'd hugged me and gave me a kiss.

Skye sat down and I took the chair next to her. I

picked up her left hand and looked at the ring. "Baby Girl, I wanted to talk to you about the engagement."

"What about it? You're not having second thoughts, are you?" she asked fearfully.

I hurried to reassure her. "God, no, Skye, I want to marry you so damn bad. That's what I want to talk about. I want to set the date for our wedding. I don't want to have it be a long drawn-out one. How soon do you think you and your mom can get it together? You can have anything you want, as long as we do it before the baby comes."

She sat quietly for a minute as she processed what I'd just dropped on her. Then she lifted the hand holding hers and kissed my knuckles. "I'd love to marry you as soon as possible, Slade. As for what I want, I want you. I want my family and yours if they can be there. All your brothers and even the Time Served crowd. I have no idea of what it would look like, but it wouldn't be anything elaborate. I don't like the idea of being one of those brides all tied up in knots over a wedding that they spend way too much money on. For me, simple is fine. As long as you like it, then I'll be happy."

I gave her a tender kiss. "What do you think of us getting married in August? We can do it on a Saturday between your birthday on the fifteenth and mine on the thirtieth."

She eagerly nodded. "I love that. It gives us three months which surely will be enough. It's not going to be crazy. I can ask Lyric to help me find stuff, and I know Mom will love it. Yes, Slade, I'll marry you in August!" She moved over and sat on my lap so she could give me a passionate kiss. One that had me ready to lay her down on the desk and fuck her until we both screamed, but I had something else we had to do.

When we came up for air, I pulled out my phone. She frowned as I dialed. Her frown disappeared, and she smiled when my mom answered after a couple of rings. "Hello, son, what has you calling me in the middle of your day? Is something wrong?" she asked anxiously.

"No, Mom, nothing is wrong. Actually, everything is great. I wanted to ask what you're doing between the fifteenth and thirtieth of August?"

"Nothing why, are you finally coming for a visit?"

"No, I was hoping you would come for one. Skye and I would love it if you'd come here. Wouldn't we, baby?"

"We would, very much."

"Hello, Skye. Slade, next time tell me your fiancée is on the phone. It's bad manners. Forgive him, Skye, I did raise him better," she chided me. Skye laughed.

"Honey, I'd love to come and to be there around or on your birthday. That would be wonderful."

"Well, it's not just my birthday. Skye's is on the fifteenth and somewhere in between the two dates we're going to get married," I casually told her.

There was a pause then she yelled. "What? You're getting married! Oh my God, Slade, you should have said that first. Of course, we'll come. Oh, I can't believe my son is finally getting married. I thought it would never happen, then you met Skye and I've been praying you would."

"Hell yeah, I'm marrying her. I'm not stupid. I know the best thing in the world when I see it. She's it. We want to do it before the baby comes. Can you, Randall, Selena, and Shana get tickets and stuff? If you need money, I can help."

"Slade, you know we can afford the tickets. As soon

as we get off here, I'll tell the others. The girls are at the movies and Randall is at work, though he should be home soon. I'll start looking for tickets. What dates should we plan for?" I looked at Skye and shrugged.

She thought for a moment then answered, "How about we have the wedding on August twenty-ninth. You can come any time before that and stay however long you like. Hopefully, the house will be done by then and you can stay with us. It's a big one. I swear your son insisted on too many bedrooms. There's five of them, Mrs. Walker."

"Oh, honey, call me Sunny, or Mom. None of this Mrs. Walker. You're family. I can't wait to see the house and meet you in person. Slade, next time, we need to video chat so I can see her."

"Okay, we will, Mom. Listen, we have to go. I'll set up a video chat with you soon. Love you guys, and I'll send you the plans for the house."

"Sounds good, honey. I'll look at dates and let you know. Goodbye, love you. Welcome to the family, Skye."

"Thank you, I can't wait to meet all of you." After we hung up, Skye looked at me a little stunned.

"What's wrong?"

"Nothing. I just realized, I have so much to do and we need to tell my mom the wedding date. Are you okay with it being the day before your birthday?"

"Hell, yeah. Can you wrap up your work here and we'll go tell your mom and get started on planning? Maybe we can even get in a nap." I gave her a sexy smirk. She laughed.

"I don't know about a nap, but we could have some fun!"

We ended up telling Jackie, who as predicted was

thrilled and ready to start planning it immediately. I took Skye home and proceeded to make love to her for the next couple of hours. That evening, we announced to the club our wedding date. Everyone was thrilled for us and offered to help. I couldn't wait to have her name be Skye Ashton. Everything was falling into place. It had been a rocky start, but we were on the right path now and another step closer to finding out what all was going on in our town.

Skye: Epilogue- three months later

The last three months had flown by with all the wedding planning, the house, and the baby. Right after we'd set the wedding, the doctor had called with the test results. Everything looked good and he let us know we were going to have a son. Executioner was walking around, looking all proud and talking about all the things he'd teach him. On top of that, he was already talking about having a little girl. I told him to let me get the first one done. He'd laughed.

Lyric and Sin had gotten married on the Fourth of July. It had been a beautiful wedding and a fantastic reception. We'd gone until the early hours of morning. They took off and went on a honeymoon to Hawaii. Executioner and I were going to wait until after the baby came to take ours. We were going to go to Fiji. Mom already said she'd watch the baby and his mom volunteered to come from England and help.

Miracle of miracles, our house was finished in time. Executioner had paid for them to have two teams build it. It had gone up extremely fast. We'd gotten things moved in before his family came. That was another thing we'd done over the last few months, shopped for furniture and stuff. We'd taken a few things from Mom's house that had been mine, mainly my bedroom suite for one of the bedrooms.

I'd tried to convince him we didn't have to get every room done immediately. He wouldn't hear of it. The only room not done yet was the baby's we were working on together. Well, I supervised mainly since he didn't want me doing much. I loved it. The house was amazing and everything I could ever want. Only thing was he'd tricked me. When the house was done and I asked what the mortgage was, because I was going to help pay it, he'd told me that it had already been paid off. We'd argued about that. He wasn't a bit sorry he'd tricked me. In the end, we'd had make-up sex, which had been out-of-this-world amazing.

His mom, stepdad and sisters came on August twenty-second and were staying two weeks. They insisted when they got here that we go out to celebrate my birthday with Mom and the boys. It had been fun, and they had given me the most beautiful earrings and necklace set made with real stones that matched my engagement ring.

The only thing that had kind of put a damper on the last few months was Jonathan Bentley. He'd blown a fuse when he found out his brother had hired me to do the books. He said those were his job and he wasn't giving it up. Ben tried to reason with him, but he refused to budge. I was told the account was no longer mine. I hated to lose a client, but there was nothing I could do, though I did tell Ben about the properties and how they looked abandoned. He'd been so apologetic. I liked him, so we remained friendly. I didn't tell him I suspected something illegal might be happening on those properties. I had no proof. But I did tell Executioner and he'd told Boss. I think they were going to keep an eye on things.

Our wedding had been equally as amazing as Sin and Lyric's. We'd invited all the Time Served guys and their ladies, plus a few others like Sis, Kerrigan, and business owners I was working for. I was now only doing accounting. Mom had full-time help and the shop was doing well. We'd gone for a dusky blue-and-white color scheme with just a hint of pale mauve in the flowers, wedding cake and table settings. I had Lyric be my bridesmaid along with Executioner's sisters. Their dresses were long, flowy ones with an ombre effect to the fabric in white and dusky blue.

Executioner had Omen as his best man along with Boomer and Sin. They sacrificed wearing their rags during the ceremony. I'd gotten them all in khaki pants and dusky blue shirts. We held the reception at the compound like Lyric and Sin had. It was just the perfect amount of room, and no need to worry if you party late into the night.

There hadn't been any more trouble with anyone demanding money from business owners, thank God. Mom and the boys were doing well. They were getting ready to start back to school. Tanner would be a senior and Tyson a sophomore. It was hard to believe. Their house was being built and would be done in a few months. Now, all we had to do was wait for our little boy to arrive. I could barely stand it.

Executioner: Epilogue- three month later too

She was finally all mine! Some days it felt like it took forever to get here. Other days it seemed to be happening so quickly. As I watched my wife, I thanked God for sending her to me. She was what my soul had been searching for, even if I hadn't known it.

She was laughing with my sisters. Mom, the girls and Randall were in love with her. Mom had pulled me aside a few days ago and told me how wonderful Skye and her family was. Jackie and mom were getting along like they'd known each other for years. As I looked around, I took in our big extended family. How it had grown. And I hoped it would continue to grow. I wanted all my brothers to find someone to be their one and only.

As I glanced around, I saw Ben Bentley. He was talking to Sin's uncle Harvey. I paused. I liked Ben, but I was still a little pissed about how his brother had gone off and fired Skye. When she told me her fears, I'd listened and told Boss. Maybe we were wrong, but we couldn't afford to discount it. Not with the things still happening around Tenillo. Thankfully, no more extortion, even though we still didn't know who was behind it. Whoever it was, they were staying off the radar.

After perusing the crowd, I looked at my watch. It was time to take my bride and start our honeymoon. The one where we stayed here but celebrated it. Since Mom and them were staying at the house, I'd rented a suite at the best hotel in town, the Rosewood Resort. We were going to spend four nights there, then come home to spend more time with Mom and the family before they had to go back to Manchester.

I walked over and took Skye in my arms. My sisters smirked. God, they were growing up and turning into beautiful young women. I didn't envy Randall having to chase off the boys. "Hey, brats, I need to steal my wife away. We'll see you in a few days." They laughed and gave us both kisses. It took a little while to say our good-byes, then we were off to town. I was raring to get her alone.

Check-in was quick and I finally had her all to my-self. Her gown was a beautiful one that flowed around her and showed off her stomach. It was gauzy and cut to show her abundant cleavage. I'd been looking at that since she walked down the aisle to me. I dropped the luggage and swiftly took off my rag which I hung up and then my boots and socks. She stood there watching me with a tiny smile on her face.

I stalked over to her and took that mouth. I nibbled on her lips and our tongues mated. When I broke away, we were both panting. My cock was like a steel pipe in my pants. I wanted to go all slow and be romantic, but this first time, I didn't think I had enough control. The idea of her being my wife excited the hell out of me.

I began to undo the zipper on her dress. She wiggled and helped it fall to the floor. She stepped out of it and I laid it on a chair. She stood in her heels, panties, and a sexy silk bra. Her stomach was sticking out. The stom-ach that was protecting and growing my son. God, I was going to have a son! I growled and kneeled to kiss her stomach. I helped her step out of her heels and slid off those panties.

I could see she was wet. I swiped my tongue up and down her slit, causing her to moan and widen her legs.

I ate her pussy hungrily. Her taste was making me want more. In a matter of minutes, she came shaking and her legs trembling. I held onto her and stood up. I kissed her again and let her taste herself on my tongue. She eagerly took it. I undid her bra and let her glorious breasts show. I palmed them and gently squeezed as I rubbed my thumbs across her nipples. She moaned and then grabbed my hand.

"Slade, no more. I need you right now. If you don't make love to me this instant, I'm going to lose my mind," she pleaded.

"Your wish is my command, Baby Girl." I swung her up in my arms and took her to the bed where I laid her down. As she laid there all sprawled out for me to feast my eyes on, I stripped off my clothes. As soon as the last piece dropped, I got in my overnight bag and pulled out one of the playthings I'd brought.

I got on the bed and kissed her. I sat the dildo on the nightstand. I had plans for that. But first, I needed just my cock in her body. Later. I'd use it to pleasure her as if she had two cocks fucking her. I'd found that turned her on a lot.

"Skye, I need you on your hands and knees." She rolled over and got on them. I tucked pillows under her to take pressure off her stomach, then I pressed between her shoulder blades until her head was on the mattress. This put her ass at the perfect height. I spread her cheeks and looked at her ass and that beautiful pussy. I groaned.

"This is going to be hard and fast, Baby Girl. Tell me if it hurts. I'm barely hanging on here," I warned her. As she nodded, I notched the head of my cock to her entrance and powered into her. She muffled a scream of pleasure into the pillow. I gripped her hips and rode her. I rode her hard, fast, and deep. She was taking it and even thrusting her ass back to slam into me. My cock was in heaven and I was close to exploding. The pleasure was unbelievable.

"Come on, harder, wife. Your husband needs to come in his wife's pussy," I growled. Calling her wife had my balls drawing up. I was going to come. She moaned and squeezed her inner muscles around my cock. I moaned and sped up. The tingling was racing up my legs. Her breath was panting, and she was murmuring.

"I'm gonna come, I'm gonna come, husband." That did it. I slammed into her two more times. She clenched down on me and I blew. I shouted as my cum flowed out of me like lava. I filled her with it and watched as some of it ran out of her around my cock. I kept thrusting until we both stopped coming. We collapsed on the bed and I took her in my arms. I kissed her.

"Thank you, Baby Girl. Thank you for loving me and being my wife and soon the mother of my son. I'm so damn grateful I went to that bar in Fort Worth last February. Who knew my future was going to be there?"

"Slade, I can't imagine my life without you. I know what you mean about your future and I'm so damn happy I went there that night too. I love you, Slade Ashton."

"I love you, Skye Ashton. More than you can know. Now, let's have you take a short nap. I have lots of plans tonight." She giggled. I got up and got a cloth to clean both of us up. As I held her and she napped, I knew she would always keep me enthralled and in love with her. She was my baby girl. My happily ever after was now in full swing. November couldn't get here soon enough.

**AIMC Book 3: Pitbull's Enslavement
coming September 2021**